Mourning Dove

A Novel

By
Claire Fullerton

FIREFLY
SOUTHERN FICTION
LIGHTHOUSE PUBLISHING OF THE CAROLINAS

MOURNING DOVE BY CLAIRE FULLERTON
Published by Firefly Southern Fiction
an imprint of Lighthouse Publishing of the Carolinas
2333 Barton Oaks Dr., Raleigh, NC 27614

ISBN: 978-1-946016-52-2
Copyright © 2018 by Claire Fullerton
Cover design by Elaina Lee
Interior design by AtriTex Technologies P Ltd

Available in print from your local bookstore, online, or from the publisher at:
ShopLPC.com.

For more information on this book and the author visit: ClaireFullerton.com.

Brought to you by the creative team at Lighthouse Publishing of the Carolinas (LPCBooks.com): Eva Marie Everson, Christy Distler, Jennifer Leo, Lucie Winborne and Eddie Jones.

Library of Congress Cataloging-in-Publication Data
Fullerton, Claire
Mourning Dove / Claire Fullerton 1st ed.

Printed in the United States of America

PRAISE FOR *MOURNING DOVE*

Set against the backdrop of a complicated 1970s South – one both forward-looking and still in love with the past – and seen through the eyes of a Minnesota girl struggling to flourish in Memphis society, *Mourning Dove* is the story of two unforgettable siblings with a bond so strong even death can't break it. Claire Fullerton has given us a wise, relatable narrator in Millie. Like a trusted friend, she guides us through the confounding tale of her dazzling brother Finley, their beguiling mother Posey, and a town where shiny surfaces often belie reality. Like those surfaces, Fullerton's prose sparkles even as she leads us into dark places, posing profound questions without any easy answers.

~**Margaret Evans**
Editor, Lowcountry Weekly, Beaufort, SC
Former Editorial Assistant to Pat Conroy

Claire Fullerton knows how to get a voice going. I'm talking distinctive, authoritative, original as all get out. Narrator Millie Crossan will grab you by your hand and set you down in privileged Memphis with her family and not let you go.

~**Bren Mc Clain**
author of the award-winning novel
One Good Mama Bone

In *Mourning Dove*, Claire Fullerton deftly weaves the story of a Memphis family into a fine fabric laden with delicious intricacy and heart. A true Southern storyteller.

~**Laura Lane McNeal**
Bestselling author
Dollbaby

Every sentence tells a complete story in and of itself. A rare accomplishment by any writer! What an excellent novel—put it on your Must Read List for 2018! Millie Crossan tells the story of her brother Finley, life in the South, and the anguish and joy of growing up in an eclectic and ever-changing household with rare poetic prose. Such a wonderful book.

A wise and brilliantly evocative Southern tale enhanced by Claire Fullerton's inimitable wit. Indulge in this eloquent exploration of colorful and complex family dynamics.

Acknowledgments

Heartfelt gratitude to the beautiful souls who populated my coming of age in Memphis. If you think you can count yourself in this milieu, surely you should.

Thank you to artist Charles Inzer for your inimitable turn of a phrase and the gift of your stories. In my mind you're as fine as they come.

Thank you to Big Lila and Lucy. You may not have realized it, but when I was in your presence, I was taking notes.

Endless appreciation to my editor, Eva Marie Everson, for championing this book from the get-go. The story of how we came into alignment is too far-fetched to be anything less than an act of God.

To my agent, Julie Gwinn of The Seymour Literary Agency, thank you so much for your involvement in bringing this book to fruition.

To Roebuck, Biggin, and the memory of David Wren. You have left upon me an indelible impression.

And lastly, to my husband, Bill Feil. Thank you from the bottom of my heart for your endless support.

DEDICATION

For Haines
and
Miss Boo

1

I used to go home every Christmas to the house I grew up in, and Finley would be there—eventually, anyway. He'd come swaggering in, all blue-eyed, gray three-quarter coat swinging. In from Virginia. The educated man. All beaming, charismatic six-foot-two of him, setting the stage in that rambling Southern house, simply by virtue of his presence. It was that way every year because Finley was the kind of guy who could enter a room and take over completely.

My brother was that magnetic.

Finley was born eighteen months ahead of me, so I came into the world following his lead. Mom told me, in one of her rare confessional moments, that Finley was an accidental pregnancy, but that I had been planned. I remember furrowing my brow and thinking it odd. If anybody has a God-given, significant purpose for being on earth, it's Finley. Compared to him, everyone else is a random afterthought.

Including me.

Finley fascinated me. I used to study him—the way he walked, the way he talked, the way the air changed around him. He was absolutely something. But here's what bothers me—Finley's in heaven, and I don't know why.

When we were young, people thought Finley and I were twins. We were both delicately built, with that streaky red-blond hair genetically bestowed upon the Scots-Irish, and we both had huge, light-colored eyes that were disproportionate in scale to the size of our heads. Finley's eyes were a hypnotic blue, mine are a serious green. Beyond that, few people could tell us apart. When Mom moved us without warning from Minnesota to the Deep South—the summer she decided she'd had enough of my father's alcoholism and was going back home—I didn't mind because Finley was beside me. His presence was one part security blanket, one part safety net, and two parts old familiar coat conformed to fit my size after years of wear.

My love for Finley was complicated—a love devoid of envy, tied up in shared survival and my inability to see myself as anything more than the larger-than-life Finley's little sister. I'm thirty-six now and still feel this way.

Finley was easy to admire, for he excelled at everything he did, and the template of this pattern was evident from the time he was in kindergarten. His reading skills were fully realized, his teachers claimed he had a photographic memory, and the sum of the variables that made up the young Finley was such a quandary that his primary school teacher arrived at the exhaustive conclusion he should skip grades one and two altogether and enter the third.

After we moved down South, the issue of Finley's education continued to stymie everybody. For at the precarious age of twelve, Finley was in a scholastic league of his own. My mother's response to Finley's brilliance was feigned resignation. She'd wave her graceful hand and sigh. "Well, I just don't know where he came from," she'd say, as if she'd woken up one morning to the great surprise of Finley at the breakfast table in the stone-floored kitchen of the house she'd grown up in in midtown Memphis' Kensington Park and subsequently inherited.

By anybody's standards, 79 Kensington Park was not a kid-friendly house. Fashioned in the style of a stucco French chateau, it was sprawling, it was formal, and most everything in it was breakable. It was the antithesis of the bucolic comfort we'd left behind in Minnesota, and being dropped into its clutching embrace felt like being jolted from a dream into disparate circumstances. But my genteel mother was back where she belonged. It was only Finley and me who had to get used to the idea of being displaced Yankee children deposited into a culture whose history and social mores don't take kindly to outsiders. We were suspects from the very start. We had Minnesota accents, we were white as the driven snow, and we both had a painfully difficult time deciphering the Southern dialect, which operates at lightning speed and doesn't feel the need for enunciation. Instead, it trips along the lines of implication.

Although I wasn't aware of it at the time, my mother's plan was pin-point specific. She simply picked up in Memphis where she'd left off before marrying my father, as if she'd changed her mind over which cocktail dress to wear to a party. The dress would look good on her, she'd make sure of it, and it'd show off her curves and float lightly above her delicate knees with airborne fragility from every step of her enviable narrow, size-seven feet.

My mother didn't walk into a room, she sashayed, borne from the swivel of her twenty-four-inch waist. Her name was Posey, and although there was a lot more to her than she ever let on, by all appearances, the name suited her perfectly.

At the end of the summer of 1970, when my mother reconciled herself to the idea of divorcing my father, she needed to devise a long-range plan. She wanted to keep up appearances, my father had lost all our money, which left her with four years until she could access the money her father left her in trust. After uncharacteristically humbling herself for financial assistance from my father's wealthy relatives, she packed Finley and me in the car and drove with steel determination to Memphis. She'd left my father standing drunk and hopeless in the driveway, watching his family evaporate in the distance, wondering how his life had come to this.

Her mother, senile and incapacitated in Memphis' Rosewood Nursing Home, barely clung to life. Although the house at 79 Kensington Park was in Gaga's name, my mother had power of attorney. So, first things first, my mother moved her mother from Rosewood to the guest house in Kensington Park and solicited the services of one Rosa Mae Jones to tend to her needs. After moving all of us into the big house, Mom set about the business of doing the two most important things: invigorating her social standing in Memphis and finding an escort, preferably a rich one looking for marriage. She set those wheels in motion after she tackled the problem of where to send Finley and me to school.

According to the dictum of Memphis society, there was only one acceptable answer to the question of where to educate a girl—the private Miss Hutchison School for Girls, and it had been that way since 1902. My mother told me she'd made no leeway from calling the school's administrator, so without skipping a beat, she slid on her stockings, zipped up her Lilly Pulitzer dress, stepped into her Pappagallo shoes, and—because a lady never steps a toe in public without it—smoothed on her pale-pink lipstick, and drove to East Memphis, where Hutchison sat regal and tree-lined, overlooking a serene lake. She marched the two of us unannounced and entitled into the ground-floor office of the school's headmistress, and seated herself cross-legged upon an upholstered chair while I found a seat on a chintz-covered sofa and wondered what to do with my hands.

When Miss Millicent Mycroft appeared, my mother stood and welcomed her into her own office, disarming her with her cultured charm and spilling forth from her cup of Southern gentility.

"Miss Mycroft, I hope you don't mind our dropping in like this," Mom lilted, "it's just so wonderful to see the school grounds. You know, when I went to Miss Hutchison, back when it was on Union Avenue, it was never as grand as all this. I'm Posey Crossan." She offered her slender hand. "I'm a good friend of Mrs. Winston Phillips and Mrs. John Turner. We all went to Hutchison together. I believe you have both of their girls here now."

"Yes, I have both girls," Miss Mycroft answered.

Miss Mycroft, practiced at the art of quick discernment, sat behind her desk and studied my mother, arriving at the accurate conclusion that she was society-born and wanted something from her. "Please sit down. What can I do for you, Mrs. Crossan?" she asked.

Mom perched lightly and launched her campaign. "I just don't know how I could have missed the enrollment deadline for my daughter, who'll be going into the fifth grade this year. I can't tell you how much I apologize for this, but you see, there simply is no other school I would consider sending her to. I'm hoping you'll make an exception and let her attend?"

"Mrs. Crossan, not only have you missed the deadline, the first trimester began last week," Miss Mycroft remonstrated, giving me a slight glance. "We've already been through orientation."

"Miss Mycroft, now I realize school has started, but what's a week to a fifth grader? My daughter, Camille, is bright. She belongs in the same school I attended. I want her in an environment that'll give her advantages, and would hate to see her compromised because of my bad timing. But you see, none of it could be helped, so here we are. Since I won't change my mind, what can I do to persuade you to make an exception?"

After achieving her objective, my mother and I got back in her car and drove two miles to the neighboring campus of Memphis University School, where she waged a similar performance on Finley's behalf, tailor-made to accommodate the fact that her audience was now a man. With iron conviction, she first stepped—heels clicking through the white marble foyer—and entered the boys' lounge, where a handful of students draped languidly in overstuffed chairs, waiting for their next class to begin.

Uncertain of the way to the headmaster's office, my mother leaned down to a conservatively dressed boy and asked for directions. With the facts in hand, she crossed the lounge and made it all the way to the hallway, before a thought came to her that wheeled her around and nearly into me. Retracing her steps, she marched into the middle of the lounge and raised her voice to a pitch accessible to all. "Boys, a lady has just entered this room," she announced. "Where are your manners? I expect every one of you to leap to your feet." My mother was a woman who knew the game rules of life, and she wielded them to expert proportion.

The Memphis Finley and I landed in was my mother's Memphis. It was magnolia-lined and manicured, black-tailed and bow-tied. It glittered in illusory gold and tinkled in sing-song voices. It was cloistered, segregated, and well-appointed, the kind of place where everyone monogrammed their initials on everything from hand towels to silver because nothing mattered more than one's family and to whom they were connected by lineage that traced through the fertile fields of the Mississippi Delta.

My mother's friends had known each other from birth and coexisted like threads in a fabric. They started families together, sent their children to the same schools they attended, and set up their cloisonné lives in congruent patterns of neat inclusivity. They threw dinner parties in stately homes, on tables set with inherited Francis I, polished to a shine by the help. In my mother's Memphis, the conversation stayed pleasant and light over lingering cocktails, until dinner was served by a staff that dropped their own lives in deference to their employers.

At an age where many women have seen their crescendo, my mother had only started to come into her beauty. She had the kind of looks that waited in arrested development during her youth, then pounced like a cat around the time she turned forty. With the passage of time followed by motherhood, her long limbs, flat chest, and slightly recessive chin filled out to capacity. Her face displayed sharp cheekbones that balanced her chin to a perfect heart-shape, and earned her a self-confidence she wore with sparkling alacrity. But a woman in possession of unique beauty and charm was in a precarious predicament in 1970s Memphis. There was always the dilemma of where to seat her at a dinner party, and without an escort to take the edge off of feminine rivalry, she was easily held in contempt.

No, that position was not for her, and my mother—as a master of networking—knew exactly what to do. She acclimated herself to the women in town, joined the Garden Club and the Junior League, lunched at the Memphis Country Club, played bridge, and hosted sip-n-sees. It wasn't long before the dates started rolling in, though she should have issued a red-flag warning that read: Ladies, hide your husbands. Posey's back in town.

2

There are gray areas in the dating world, especially when one is trying to find an escort. The signals of availability one has to transmit are sometimes picked up by men who are already tethered. It was a confusing year while Mom tried to find an escort. A handful of her women friends became casualties, but Finley and I passed no judgment, for we had no moral compass in our formative years. The way we saw it, it wasn't Mom's fault men fell prey to her blue-eyed, golden glory.

Finley and I were bewitched too.

Moments after the cathedral front doors banged open, I heard a commotion downstairs followed by the clatter of hard heels tapping across the black-and-white tiled entrance hall, until they fell cat-like to a muted padding across the parlor and ended with a clatter in the adjoining card room. I crept down the serpentine front stairs to see Finley pushing through the beveled glass doors that partitioned the entrance hall from the back hallway.

Finley and I had an uncanny, almost telepathic way of pursuing the same moment. We looked at each other wordlessly, listening to the cawing of Stella Richmond from the big Tudor house across the street, who'd come to fetch her husband home. It was ten o'clock on a Tuesday night. Earlier Danny Richmond had taken it upon himself to walk across the street and chivalrously offer his assistance to the unmarried Posey for whatever she may need, right in the middle of the cocktail hour. Hours transpired, the sun had set, dinner had been forgotten, and there the two sat, drinking and chatting as if they had all the time in the world.

"Danny Richmond, how dare you? And how dare you, Posey?" Stella raged, glaring at her husband. "You get yourself home right now, and I'm not speaking to either of you any time soon after what you've put me through."

Stella Richmond was not the kind of woman who ever meant "maybe," and her sphere of not speaking came to include Finley and me. Many months passed before she looked either of us in the eyes without suggesting our guilt by association, and for a while I innocently assumed word of that episode had ricocheted among the twenty-six homes in Kensington Park, which I thought explained others' cold glances. I had no way of knowing similar episodes had transpired, with wandering husbands in search of my mother. She probably should have discouraged the attention instead of soaking it in. If she had, she might not have lost her childhood best friend, Shuggs, whose only contribution to the rift was telling her husband that Posey was looking for a new car.

The ways of the South, I was to learn, were such that upon hearing word of a single woman in need, the only gentlemanly thing to do was offer assistance, which is exactly what Virgil did, to his wife's tufted pride. For the first week, Shuggs was magnanimous and happy her husband could help. She yielded agreeably when he went to Kensington Park after work instead of coming straight home. Shuggs reported the arrangement to all her friends, and basked in the recognition she received for the security she enjoyed in her foolproof marriage.

But as time stretched on, her goodwill became tested. She avoided the clock and battened down her emotional hatches as the weeks multiplied, and tried to talk herself into justifying the cocktails Virgil stayed for after making the dealership rounds. This worked until the schedule became a habit and her benevolence wore thin. By the fourth week, Shuggs had lost compassion. By the fifth week, she had none at all.

I knew Virgil had succumbed to my mother's charm, when I rounded the back driveway looking for Finley. It hit me like an incestuous crime against nature. There was something salacious and shameful about finding my mother chest-pressed in Virgil's arms as they leaned against the blue Gran Torino they'd just driven home. A movement above broke my astonishment, and I looked up to see Finley undetected, a voyeuristic bird in an aerie of an oak tree, looking down at the improper scene. From that day onward, Finley and I quit calling Virgil our "uncle." Not long after, Shuggs and Virgil did the unthinkable by moving from Memphis to their vacation home in Florida. We never heard from the pair again, even though Shuggs was my godmother who gifted me with a single pearl every birthday since my birth.

Two things happened on the night of my mother's first date with the colonel— William Porter fell off the wall, and the card room caught on fire. It was a school night in early September, and Finley and I were alone in the house with our two Scottish terriers.

16

I didn't like being in the house without Mom at night. The chasmal manse gave me the heebie-jeebies, especially downstairs, where the ceilings towered and the vast room in the middle we called the parlor was lit by interspersed table lamps, whose dim coronas left too many possibilities lurking in the contrasting shadows. The light from Kensington Park's street lamps crept in burnt-gold through the wrought-iron latticework over the six cathedral glass doors along the front of the house—eerie from the grass on the park's median, and everywhere inside, ringing wall-to-wall silence that waited for someone to spring out and scream "boo."

Everything in 79 Kensington Park had been hand-selected by my mother's mother, who had a lifelong passion for collecting antiques. Every piece of furniture, every chandelier, every Oriental rug, and every fragile porcelain piece had either been passed down to her, or acquired at auction. Many of the walls were adorned with full-sized oil portraits of one forebear or another. Finley and I stood like gallery spectators as Mom gave us the abbreviated histories of how the subjects were connected to us. Looking up from the entrance hall at the portraits of her parents, I'd think they may as well belong to somebody across the street for all the affinity I felt. Doctor Joe—my mother's father—died before my birth. He hung in colors of charcoal, beige, and black beside Gaga, the original Camille whom I'd been named for … because it would have been unthinkable for Mom to name me outside of family lines.

I'd stand and narrow my eyes to search for similarities between myself and the portraits, since I had no history with either of them. All I knew was Gaga was lying out back in the guest house, withered and mindless, lovingly stroking and folding aluminum foil in her hospital bed because it shines so prettily when the sun catches it just so. I thought the foil must have triggered something archival in her memory, connecting her with a time before Alzheimer's arrived. Rosa Mae cracked the guest house door open when she saw me staring in from the driveway. She'd speak in hushed tones and say, "Shhh, Miss Millie. Miz Hawthorne, she sleepin' right now," and the pent-up, antiseptic air would escape noxious and deathly through the door.

But in her oil portrait Gaga was beautiful. Regal and high-cheekboned, dark-haired and elegant. She wore a long-sleeved black dress and a diamond baguette on her manicured left hand. She stared across the entrance hall to the serpentine stairs, where a portrait of her grandfather, William Porter, glowered back.

In his day, William Porter was a revered judge in Philadelphia. In the portrait, he wore the magisterial black robe and chestnut curled wig to attest to his regional importance. Disturbingly supercilious, the painting had eyes that followed me no matter where I stood in the hall. Finley and I tested his eyes from every angle, walking backward and forward, up and down the stairs, daring him to look elsewhere.

But Judge Porter remained supervisory and threatening from every angle.

One evening while our mother was out with the colonel, Finley and I were in the card room trying to ferret out the good FM radio stations. Since Finley was a self-taught musician who'd picked up a guitar when he was eight years old and had hardly ever put it down, he left me alone in the card room and went upstairs to retrieve his instrument, saying he just felt better with it in his hands. I kneeled on the Wedgwood-blue rug to test the radio dial on the upright radio, more often than not tripping through static. Just as I decided to wait for Finley to figure the radio out, audio clarity sprang crystal clear as an announcer reported a prison break somewhere in Shelby County. When I heard the name William Porter included in the escapees, I took off in an airborne flight of terror, out of the card room, through the parlor, across the entrance hall, and halfway up the front stairs. "Finley," I screamed, but he had already heard me coming and started his descent. We could have reached out and touched hands when it happened—we were that close when the portrait of Judge Porter fell off its mount and landed with a thud on the stairs. We both froze for a petrified second until Finley bent down and picked up the portrait. He had to stretch his arms as wide as they'd reach to put the portrait back on the wall, then he stepped back and steadied the rectangular spotlight above to examine it for damage.

I found enough breath to exclaim, "I just heard Judge Porter on the radio."

"What are you talking about?" Finley furrowed his brow. "What do you mean? Just now?"

"Yeah, they're looking for a guy named William Porter who escaped from prison. I just heard it on the radio." I thought for sure Finley would register the news and be just as shaken as me.

"That's not the same as the judge, but I get what you're saying." We stood on the stairs looking at each other. "That's weird," Finley finally added.

"Should we tell Mom it fell?"

"Not tonight," Finley answered. "We have no idea when she's coming back. Let's not get her date all involved, 'cause we don't know if we're ever going to see the guy again."

"But you'll tell her in the morning?" I pressed.

"I don't know. Let me think about it. It's not like she could do anything about it. Why don't you go on to bed? It's getting late."

"That was weird," I said, climbing the stairs. I turned to look back at him. "Do you think this house is haunted?"

"Oh, yeah. There's definitely a presence around here. I always feel it upstairs."

"And you're just now telling me this?" I always looked to Finley to tell me what was going on, and I felt slighted.

"Millie, you don't have to be so dramatic. Nothing can hurt you. Ghosts don't go around killing people like you see in the movies. They don't even have bodies, so you don't have to get all worked up over this. Just go on to bed. Nothing's going to hurt you."

Immediately appeased, I continued up the stairs to my room.

"At least not tonight," Finley called out, and I turned to tell him to cut it out, but changed my mind when I saw his teasing smile, the one that made me laugh every time.

Later that night, the card room caught on fire.

By the time the fire ignited from the smolder of the colonel's poorly extinguished cigarette, it was well past midnight, and Lt. Colonel Commander of the United States Air Force Charles Devlin Henry had chastely kissed my mother good-night and gone on home to his horse ranch in Collierville. My mother closed the door behind him and climbed the back stairs to her bedroom, where she wasted no time in locating the Memphis Country Club's registry to see if the colonel was listed.

When the fire erupted at one o'clock in the morning, it sprang us careening from our beds in terror, interrupted our lives, and damaged everything in the card room with noxious smoke that lingered and assailed for weeks. Finley said later that if we had been on our toes, we would have seen it as a sign.

My mother was in the habit of holding court in the card room. In late spring, she'd have Murl Winfrey, the black groundskeeper since she was a girl, roll up the Wedgwood-blue rug to expose the gray granite twelve-by-twelve-inch tiles in preparation for the sweltering summer. She'd throw open the cathedral doors to coax the air in through the screens, and as summer progressed, she'd open the north-facing door to the adjacent gazebo to circulate the stifling humidity. Beneath a ten-foot ceiling, the card room was fashioned Southern-style, with multicolored patterns arranged just short of clashing, yet cleverly synergistic from a secondary color scheme. The room was handsomely understated, with overstuffed upholstered furniture arranged in a seating style before the carved marble mantel above the fireplace. No surface was without decorative art— sterling silver pheasants, hand-painted porcelain bowls, Chinese Foo dogs, Wedgwood urns, lead crystal ashtrays, and paired antique plates on stands everywhere you turned. Ida Ella Morgan, who came to cook and clean three times a week, paid more attention to the card room than any other room in the house because decades of working for white people taught her every grand house has its center. In that room, at the afternoon's end, when the grandfather clock in the entrance hall struck five, my mother could be found taking up residency over cocktails, just as her mother had done before her.

During the cocktail hour, my mother typically had an audience. Kensington Park is centrally located in the antebellum part of midtown, adjacent to Memphis' three hundred and forty-two acres of verdant crowning glory called Overton Park, and many in my mother's circle lived close by. Her friends often dropped by during the cocktail hour—a time Finley and I were not invited to participate in—so when Mom called Finley and me into the card room at five o' clock on a Tuesday, one month after the fire, it came as something unusual and out of step. She leaned back in her favorite coral and light-blue slipcovered chair, with one elegant leg tucked beneath her and the other crossed and dangling over her knee. Nobody occupied a chair quite like my mother. There was an effortless femininity to the way she arranged herself in a chair, just as there was to her every gesture. Finley sat in the matching chair across from her, and I pushed the ottoman out of the way to sit Indian-style on the floor between them.

"I've heard from your father," Mom began, and my heart flipped over and landed in my stomach. I looked up at Finley, trying to detect what he was thinking, but he didn't flinch.

"He's going to move down here to be near y'all," she continued, her chin lifting as my blood ran cold.

Try as I may in the moment, I couldn't picture my father living down South. In my mind's eye, he still stood in the driveway in Minnesota as we'd left him.

But no amount of creative imagination could codify the fragments he'd scattered with the wrecking ball he sent through our lives.

3

Before I was saddened and ashamed of my father, I loved him without reservation. But I learned the hard way some things can alter love's form, and disillusionment is one of them. My mother said, in the beginning, Sean Crossan was larger than life and predictable. A massive six-foot-three Irish-American, whom many would define as a man's man, in that he exemplified all things commanding and virile. Solid and imposing, a product of Minnesota's timbered sky-blue waters, he was never more at home than when he was outdoors.

He met my mother in 1950 while crossing the Atlantic aboard the Queen Mary as he traveled to school at the Sorbonne in Paris. He'd been peripherally aware of my mother's debutante friends, who were on board as a group, en route to tour Europe. My mother said everyone in the group had been all atwitter over the mysterious Yankee on board, who solitarily walked the ship's bow at night smoking a pipe. My mother was competitive for an eighteen-year-old girl. She assessed the competition quickly and strategically devised a plan. She waited patiently for her peers to spin a web around Sean Crossan. Then, when the timing was right, she elbowed them all out and moved in for the kill.

After they married, my father knew he had done what was expected of him. He'd completed his education and settled down with a wife in the affluent suburb of Wayzata, not far from his parents' home, near Lake of the Isles in Minneapolis. His friends were exceedingly well-to-do, the scions of families at the helm of such flourishing companies as Cargill, Pillsbury, and General Mills. He was charismatic, able, and self-assured, yet it didn't encourage his father to acknowledge his worth. George Crossan, my grandfather, was a twisted and bitter man, consumed with jealousy by his only son's virility.

A first-generation Irish-American, George Crossan had followed in his father's footsteps and taken up the presidency of the Crossan Lumber Yard in Minneapolis. Four years into his tenure, a freak accident changed his outlook on life when he was deprived the use of his right leg and rendered an amputee. In time, he took to drinking Irish whisky, and sat in his wheelchair deep in the throes of his shades-drawn den, feeding a manic depression that relegated his three children to tiptoe warily past, lest they trigger the rage he nurtured every night. His long-suffering wife Helen was devoutly Catholic, and interfered for her children until she could do it no more. The taxing years of living with George grew untenable, and the leukemia that resulted sent her to an early grave, the very year I was born.

Left alone in the big house after Helen died, George's alcoholism festered. He rejected all conciliatory gestures from my mother with fevered rebuke, which my father took personally. Although my mother continued to dig deep from her resources of etiquette and compassion, George Crossan remained unresponsive. He wanted nothing to do with any of us, so Finley and I followed our mother's lead by pretending it didn't matter, and my father soldiered on as if it didn't cut him to his core.

Everything about our lives in Wayzata seemed ordained for the explicit purposes of constructing a childhood paradise. We lived in a four-bedroom house with a screened porch at its end, on a sparsely populated, unpaved street named Lindawood. The converted basement had a bar made of solid oak, with high stools in front of it and a regulation-sized captain's wheel mounted on the wall behind it because Dad's Irish blood charged him with an affinity for the sea. On Sunday nights, he grilled hamburgers in the basement's fireplace, while we watched *The Ed Sullivan Show* followed by *Bonanza*, but only if Finley and I promised to go to bed immediately afterward, in preparation for school the next day.

In the dense woods surrounding our house, we built tree houses and horse corrals, just like the Cartwrights in *Bonanza*. We cleared the earthen floor with brooms made from twigs, and lined the boundaries with rocks we rolled heavily in to set the stage for cowboys and Indians because Finley liked creating imaginary worlds, and I never cared what we did as long as I was with him.

When we felt adventurous, we'd wade through the woods at the top of our street and skid down the unstable dirt mounds bordering the east side of the railroad tracks, then pick our way beam by beam to the part of the bridge suspended over the ravine. We'd jump off the tracks and run the full mile through the wheat fields that led to Woodhill Country Club, where we swam on the swim team during the summer and skated on the pond during winter.

But most of the time, Dad drove us to Woodhill when we wanted to go, because there was nothing he wouldn't do for Finley and me. He was our ring-leader, our pied-piper, and his powers of creativity knew no limits when it came to our entertainment. To hear Finley tell it, nothing worthwhile ever happened until Dad walked in the room.

Every morning, Dad called us to action whistling a bird call that began at the end of the hallway and grew louder with his imminent approach. He'd pick me up and carry me safely against his broad chest to the living room, while Finley followed at his heels, clinging to his shirt tail. We'd look expectantly through the bay window to the front yard, waiting in quivering anticipation for Dad to spin his magic in a liturgy we never outgrew.

"Good morning, sun," Dad's melodic baritone prompted.

"Good morning, sun," Finley and I chimed, squinting our eyes.

"Good morning, yard," Dad continued, and we repeated, matching his inflection note for note in our childish rhyme.

"Good morning, birds. Good morning, squirrels. Good morning, chipmunks," Dad intoned, and we repeated until he covered everything he saw outdoors.

Every day, Finley and I were lit by the fire of his presence, of beginning each day with this wizard of magic, this caster of spells, this weaver of delight. Every morning of my early childhood, I watched my father throw his soul out the window and commune with God's wonder. Without any other semblance of religious influence in our lives, he taught Finley and me by the power of example to do the same. Our father saw the layers beneath the surface; his spirit was intuitive of dimensions the five senses cannot detect. And although he was not a denominationally religious observer, he was the most naturally pious man I've ever met.

When Dad took Finley to The Gunflint Lodge, he brought me back a fairy-stick. At one fruitless juncture, he suggested we all go to the Northeastern Minnesota gaming resort, but Mom had vetoed the idea with one perfectly timed raised eyebrow. She was a woman who thought ahead, who'd redirected a nurse from inflicting an inoculation shot on my infant left shoulder to the area tucked beneath my left shoulder blade, so I'd look good in a strapless evening gown. She had plans for my path through life that didn't include making a tomboy of me.

Dad, hyper-sensitive to my emotions, saw my pout coming. He took me for a walk and held my hand all the way down the Old Long Lake Road in Wayzata, where he promised I was headed for a big surprise.

"Millie, do you know why we can't take you with us this weekend?" Dad queried.

I looked up at him with innocent eyes and uttered, "Uh-uh."

"It's because you're a girl, so you're special. You wouldn't want to sleep in a tent and cook over a fire. It'll be cold up there, and you don't like being cold."

"Yes, I do. I can be cold. I won't mind, I promise." I had never been separated from Dad and Finley before, and the desperation I felt consumed me.

"Finley and I are going to be doing boy things like fishing and canoeing. Your mother wants you to stay here with her," he explained.

"I can do anything Finley can do," I lobbied.

"Of course you can, but it'll be rough where we're going, and I want you to stay safe."

"But I'll be safe with you and Finley," I persisted.

Then Dad looked to the left and said, "Ah, this is it."

A dirt road scattered past a hand-painted sign that read "Firebrand Scottish Terrier Kennels." We walked into the office, then around back to the kennels. Though Dad had been there twice before, he never mentioned his plan until this very moment.

"You see the smallest one there?" He pointed to a large wire cage with six mewling puppies, all obsidian black with stub noses and squinting eyes. "She'll be ours in another two weeks. Your mother had one just like her when she was six, just as you are now. The puppy's too young to take home right now, but we'll come back and get her. We'll surprise your mother, so promise you won't tell," he said, which accomplished exactly what he'd set out to do.

I forgot all about the trip to The Gunflint Lodge, until the day before he and Finley left, when they loaded up the car with provisions, which, for Dad, meant a list of essentials, but for Finley, meant his guitar.

Eight days later, Dad pulled in our driveway and walked straight to my room. I heard Finley clatter up the stairs behind him, and turned to see him standing in the doorway, smiling Cheshire cat-like because he knew something I did not. Seven days in the woods with Dad, and Finley was an eight-year-old initiate, indoctrinated into the mysteries of manhood by the man who hung the moon. It was clear Finley decided to be smug about it, but I didn't rise to the bait because in that moment Dad beamed his light over me. He held something long and slender wrapped in burlap. He handed it to me, saying he'd acquired it from a fairy in the woods, who'd told him to give it to me. I unfurled the wrapping and didn't understand. It looked like a stick the color of buttermilk, with its bark shaved off to a pointed end.

"It's a magic wand," Dad whispered. "It has special powers. If you hold it and make a wish, it'll come true." I looked up at Dad only half-believing. Mom never suggested anything like this, and I thought about running to ask her. After all, she'd been the one to tell me the truth about the magic rings. Had my mother not volunteered the facts, I would have spent the rest of my life thinking Dad was magic, that the plastic, gem-colored rings he pulled from behind my ears really were manifest from his sleight of hand, instead of the five-and-dime around the corner. Although I was torn by which parent to believe, there were so many reasons to side with Dad. He was guileless, wondrous, and fantastic. An unrestricted dreamer preferring to stand outside of society because he wasn't interested in the company.

He preferred Finley and me instead.

In my father's den were many mansions. Every object within its dimly lit walls was either an expression of his interior life, or a symbolic clue to his past. The den was off the beaten path from the rest of the house and was his sequestered sanctuary, rich in earth-tone fabrics and hues of cherry wood. His personal haven was appointed with everything that ever meant anything to him: his pipe collection, his antique maps of the world, his duck calls, his German beer steins, his framed Parisian sketches, and his Crossan coat of arms with its Latin motto scrolled across the top. According to the motto, our last name has something to do with birds, which never surprised me, and I didn't need Finley to spell it out. I already knew Dad had a weird thing with birds.

When my father attended the Sorbonne, he kept a flat on the Left Bank, where the highlight of his Parisian experience arrived not scholastically, but airborne, on the wings of an owl that crashed into his balcony window and damaged its wing. Seeing the owl stunned and injured, Dad cranked open the window and coaxed it inside. He kept the owl as a pet for months—feeding it, tending to it, and monitoring its recuperation until he deemed it fully recovered, at which point he cranked open the window and set it free.

Feeling a vacancy from the owl's departure, he filled the void by acquiring a blue-front Amazon parrot he named Coco, which he took with him everywhere and taught how to talk. Four times, Dad crossed the Atlantic with Coco, but ship regulations meant housing the parrot below deck with the crew, where Coco learned to swear like a sailor. When the story of Coco reached Finley's ears, he got all wound up and prepared to launch an eight-year-old's pleading attack on why he had to have a bird for himself. But Finley needn't have bothered. Dad already had a plan.

In order to throw Mom off the scent of the puppy trail, my father decided to buy a myna bird and slip it inside when her head was turned. He reasoned once she'd gone a few rounds with her protestations, she'd get over the shock and think that would do him for a while, because Mom had experience with the way Dad liked to surprise her. She didn't always like it, but she couldn't say his impulsiveness didn't keep the whole house on its toes.

Finley and I were beside ourselves with excitement. We were looking out the living room window when Dad pulled in the driveway with the bird. We liked that he was being sneaky. We could just imagine Mom's surprise when she returned home from her weekly appointment at the beauty parlor. Dad reached into the back seat and lifted the unwieldy cage, while I stood nose glued to the window and Finley rushed to the front door.

"Where we gonna put it, Dad?" Finley bounced out to the yard. "Can I keep it in my room?"

"We'll keep it downstairs," Dad said. "Remember when I told you it was a myna bird? Myna birds are social. They like to be around company, so we'll keep her in the den where she'll be out of the way but can still hear our voices."

Dad walked through the dining room and into the den, where he placed the cage on a table in indirect sunlight. He lifted the blue cotton cover to reveal the glossy black bird, which hopped on its knobby, yellow-clawed feet.

"Dad?" Finley gushed, his words running together, "I know all about myna birds. I read everything in the *Encyclopedia Britannica*."

"Is that so?" A smile sprang to my father's face, lighting his cornflower-blue eyes, which always animated Finley.

"Yeah," Finley said, ramping up.

"Let's hear it, Finley," Dad encouraged.

If I hadn't been looking straight at Finley, I would have thought he was actually reading from the *Encyclopedia Britannica*, so succinct was his coverage of the facts. No eight-year-old talked like this, but I was used to it. He had a way of using big words like *passerine*, *plumage*, and *invasive* in such a way that tripped along so nicely, it didn't bother me that I didn't know their meaning. I counted on the common DNA that ran in our blood as being a psychic link that connected us telepathically. I didn't have to know everything; it was enough for me that Finley knew.

The cage was the Cadillac of all bird cages. It had shelves and a mirror, bells and a bathing dish, toys and a water bottle arranged above a newspaper-lined tray. Finley reported birds like to perch on natural branches, so Dad took us outside to look around in the woods. We gathered sticks while Dad reached high and broke branches, which we measured against the drawing Finley had made of the cage's dimensions.

Dad and Finley played "name that bird," like they always did whenever we walked in the woods. They identified sparrows and wrens, blackbirds and finches, wood warblers and blue jays, then Dad cupped his hands and whistled a lonesome hollow sound, imitating the loon—the Minnesota state bird. Try as I might, I couldn't mimic the sound, but neither could Finley, although he had an innate musical ear. But Finley could cry out in perfect imitation of the mourning dove. Every morning of our young lives, we'd hear a measured coo-ah-coo-coo-coo somewhere off in the distance, and Finley could match it note for note.

My mother's reaction to the bird in the den wasn't as dramatic as we anticipated because she didn't consider Dad's den her domain. It was as if a psychic forcefield blocked the door, and the truth is she wasn't interested in anything beyond it. I'd seen my mother in my father's den maybe twice in my life. She looked incongruous in it, ironically positioned, like Scarlett O'Hara holding the radish she'd just pulled from the earth. It was unspoken between them, but my parents were fully aware there wasn't a wide enough berth in my father's den for the enormity of my mother's petticoat. She preferred to remain a stranger in self-imposed exile, which suited both of my parents just fine.

But the puppy was different, and it came joyous and wagging into the center of our lives: a squirming black Scottish terrier my mother named Inky, identical to the one she'd had as a child. How my mother carried on over that female puppy. When Inky grew to maturity, she was such a fine-looking dog Mom decided to have her bred. Inky waddled low to the ground, fat with pregnancy. When her time was near, Finley and I helped Dad prepare her whelping box by wadding up sheets and towels and covering them with layers of shredded newspaper. Finley and I took Inky and showed her, repeatedly saying, "Here, Inky, this is where you're going to have your puppies."

We walked the high wire of anticipation for weeks, until Inky's time came. Then we followed Dad's lead while Inky gave birth to five replicas of herself. For the next eight weeks, Finley and I were personally involved as the puppies grew. As we came and went from the house, the puppies were the first things we'd rush home to and the last things we'd see. We were emotionally attached with a proprietary love for the first time in our lives, and although Dad rightfully warned us the day would come when we'd have to give the puppies away, as the time neared I grew despondent.

I'd never had a broken heart and didn't understand the difference between what you feel and what you have to do. I considered the pending removal of Inky's puppies an insufferable loss, and Mom and Dad couldn't talk me into reason, but neither of them had a way with words like Finley. He simply walked into my room and threw his arm around my shoulders while saying, "Come on, let's go get the puppies." We went down to their basement bed and carried them, one by one, to the multicolored hand-woven rug before the fireplace.

Watching them navigate within the scrum of each other, Finley looked at me sidelong. "You have to understand that things don't stay the same way forever, or at least not the way you think they're going to. You have to be okay with change, and anyway, these are Inky's puppies, not ours. Inky can't take care of all five for the rest of her life, but maybe we should ask Dad if we can keep one. I bet he'll say yes."

Finley was right, and we only had to ask Dad once. We kept the smallest of the puppies, which Mom named Ike, for two reasons: it had a nice ring in tandem with Inky, and she loved America's 34th president.

4

In winter, Finley tried out for the Woodhill Country Club hockey team because Dad, in his day, had played a regionally lauded center. One good look at the eight-year-old Finley, and anybody would have said he didn't have the stature for a contact sport. But Dad took Finley seriously and shepherded us to the rink, where he coached Finley into membership while I skated figure-eight into arabesque. Mom had no interest in skating but she loved standing on the ice socializing in her fabulous full-length beaver coat, deeply engaged in gossiping, which was the only contact sport that ever truly held her attention.

Chuck Dudley was part of the parents' crowd that stood on the ice unshielded in Minnesota's ungodly winter temperatures. The grown-ups huddled in a cluster, drinking Schnapps from plastic glasses after smearing Vaseline on their children's faces to abate the whipping wind. I didn't like Chuck Dudley from the first moment I saw him. There was something smarmy about him, something slick, wormy, lax-muscled, and weak-shouldered, but my mother sure liked him. I couldn't tell why. He had a mousy wife he ignored and a nine-year-old son named Derrick, who was just as unsavory as he.

The attention Chuck Dudley slathered on my mother made me uneasy, yet for some reason it made her shine. She became animated in his presence, laughing and charming and fluid, as if Chuck were the most captivating person in the world. Every time we went to Woodhill, Chuck was there laughing and grinning with his big white teeth and blond receding hairline. The women at Woodhill vied for his attention because they subliminally subscribed to his self-image, which he cast about like a net designed to ensnare. Chuck Dudley got my mother's competitive nature riled, and it was clear he had his sights set on her now that his three-year affair with Sandra Hardwicke had ended. He'd preen and strut under my mother's encouragement, and they flattered each other's vanity like pleasure-seekers in need of a high.

I didn't know if Finley intended it or not. I didn't know if he presciently intuited disruption brewing and wanted to rail against it, or if Derrick Dudley was just a pansy in the wrong place at the wrong time. I leaned down to tie my skate laces. When I looked up, I saw Derrick on his back, crying and bleeding from his forehead, with Finley at a T-stop standing over him wearing a scowl. Even though they were on the same team, Finley had managed to head-butt

Derrick with an impact that started on the ice, landed in the hospital, and wove its way into the fabric of our lives.

From that moment on, Mom said we had to be nice to Derrick, and we were savvy enough to interpret we were paying for Finley's crime. When his parents started coming around for cocktails, we stood side by side with faithless smiles. Then they'd all go out to dinner and leave Derrick behind. It morphed into a pattern that included a babysitter, but no amount of contact encouraged us to like Derrick any better. We'd be antsy for Mom and Dad to return, even though we knew they'd be loud and tipsy and all the more ingratiated into the fold of the Dudleys. Finley and I would watch the clock until their arrival because then we could be shed of Derrick until the next time.

And there was *always* a next time. It suddenly seemed the Dudleys were foursquare in the middle of our lives. They came to Mom and Dad's parties, joined us for Christmas Eve dinner, and every time we went to Woodhill, the Dudleys were underfoot. But I could tell Dad wasn't a fan of Chuck Dudley. That there was more to it than their being two different breeds of cat. Unlike Chuck, Dad wasn't the social kind. When it came to people, Dad could take them or leave them, which irritated Mom no end.

"Let's have Sam-and-Betty-Whomever for dinner Saturday night," Mom would suggest, or perhaps, with great enthusiasm exclaim, "Bitsy-and-What's-His-Name-Thompson invited us to a party next Friday," to which Dad would reply in all seriousness, "How will I know if I'll be in the mood Friday night?"

Along the tributary of my parents' attraction, clashing temperaments coexisted like the metaphoric coordinates of Minneapolis and Memphis on the mighty Mississippi: disparate in nature, yet vitally occupying the same stream. They were distinct opposites going through the motions of co-creating a life, but the gossamer veneer of their marriage started to shred the day my father impulsively quit his job as vice president of a bank in Minneapolis. One hundred thousand dollars from a deceased aunt I'd never heard of must have seemed like a lifetime cushion to my father, but when he shared the news with my mother, Finley and I heard the ballistic reverberation in every room of the house.

My mother, Posey Hawthorne, was not cut out for discord. She had no frame of reference, having been born to a life of privilege as the only child of Dr. Joseph Finley Hawthorne and the stately Camille Garret, who hailed from

Philadelphia. After seven miscarriages, Gaga—as we called our grandmother—was so thrilled when Mom came along that she ceased looking the gift horse of fate in the mouth and took up residency down the hall in one of 79 Kensington Park's five bedrooms, never again to digress to her husband's bed. She named her daughter Posey, after her fortunate older sister, who had successfully married a diplomat and lived in a mansion that later became the Russian Embassy in Washington D.C.

My mother enjoyed a cushioned upbringing, of which the singular aspiration was a center position in Memphis society. Her innate intelligence was not squandered academically, but applied to attributes such as charm and feminine wiles. In first grade, she entered Miss Hutchison's School for Girls, where she began lifelong alliances with girls named Lila, Eugenia, and Adare, all with gentrified surnames. Each weekday, she was chauffeured to school in a town-car by a black man named Herbert, who lived on the opposite side of the lake from his cousin, Murl Winfrey, on the expansive, wooded property Gaga and Dr. Joe owned out in East Memphis. After school, she took her Shetland pony from the backyard stables and rode it along East Parkway's oak-canopied median to Overton Park's vast acreage of public grounds.

After six years at Hutchison, Gaga put Mom on a train and sent her to Ethyl Walker's Boarding School in Simsbury, Connecticut, where she—confronted for the first time with cultured East Coast girls—inexplicably decided to reinvent herself. She introduced herself as Sherry Hawthorne, and taped the tip of her Scottish nose with masking tape each night, thinking she'd magically arise one morning with an upturned nose, the standard of cuteness among debutante of her day. She tried out for field hockey, though she wasn't athletic, and auditioned for glee club, though she was completely tone deaf. She was young, impressionable, and casting about for her identity, when Margaret Mitchell's *Gone with the Wind* was published, which serendipitously proffered a role model in its main character, and set my mother's fledgling personality on course.

She got along famously at Ethyl Walker's, for she had an implacable, sunny disposition and a wicked sense of humor, which she carried out of boarding school and into her one-year tenure at Hollins College, in Roanoke, Virginia. During the first summer break, her chaperoned tour of Europe aboard the *Queen Mary* provided the chance encounter with Sean Crossan and laid down the parameters for the rest of her life.

After a year of handwritten correspondence, it took another six months to convince her mother to send her by train to New York's Barbizon Hotel, where she waited for Dad's ship to bring him back to America. They spent a solid week—young and vibrant and splendid—together, dressed to impress over nightly cocktails at Twenty-One, then whiling away the next day so they could do it all over again. Another six months of letters gave way to further intimacy, and in July of 1951, Dad came down to Memphis, where a party was thrown at 79 Kensington Park announcing their engagement. Dr. Joe was wary. He took Sean Crossan's measure and proclaimed him antisocial, for he mistook my father's self-possession as arrogance, and feared him a nonconformist. He couldn't fathom how this Yankee would mesh with his gregarious daughter. In the midst of the party, he pulled his daughter aside.

"Posey, are you sure this is what you want?" he queried, the harmony of doubt and concern unmistakable in his tone.

"Yes, Daddy, my sights are set. I realize he may seem like something untamed, but I believe he is malleable."

"He tells me one day he'll want to move you to Minnesota. Do you think you could live that far from home?"

"Oh, Daddy, he only thinks that way *now*," she dismissed. "After we move into the house you bought us around the corner, he'll change his mind."

But four years after they married, Mom found herself a transplanted Southerner, a predicament she used to her full advantage, for there is nothing that will more firmly ensconce a Southerner in their own Southerness quite like moving to a disparate land. All cultural contrasts were heightened in Minnesota, and once Mom became aware of her show-stopping allure, she wielded it to exaggerated proportions. It never occurred to her to try to fit into a culture already firmly in play; it was far easier for her to sway the uninitiated to her gravitational pull. There are some people who do this effortlessly—natural-born stars in the center of an orbit that emanates from the influential power of their internal glow, and because my mother had danced through her youth entitled, it was her assumption she'd always maintain status quo.

"How *could you* quit your job?" The tone of Mom's voice was remonstrative, desperate, and uncharacteristic of my singing, self-possessed mother, who never bowed to the coarse display of histrionics in any variation.

I started to run down the hallway toward her raised voice, but Finley reached out a hand and pulled me into his room. "Don't go in there now, this isn't about us. Mom's mad at Dad, so leave them alone," he warned. We both pressed our ears to the door, trying to listen to the beginning sounds of our life changing course.

It was a slow, steady bleeding out, years in the letting, rife with one bad investment after another, while the tension between our parents grew thicker and Dad's nightly drinking escalated. In time, it was clear he had gambled and lost. Without the daily ritual of an office to go to, he was cut off from the outside world, adrift in the mistake of a shameful, self-created hell. He grew disappointed and angry with himself, unable to see through his disillusionment with a world that did not shape itself to his fanciful expectations.

Beaten, he no longer waited for Mom and the civility of the five o'clock hour, for his pain had no schedule and time had no relevance. He became unconcerned with what he drank, as long as the white-lightning anesthesia saturated his blood and kept the wolves of delirium tremens at bay. He drank well before the sun set, shut away in the sanctuary of his den. There were the rare nights when he attempted the pretense of normalcy by staggering into dinner, but eventually he quit trying, and the house sighed with relief when he stumbled upstairs to bed.

Finley and I were only intuitively aware of the serious trouble, for it was not our mother's way to divulge to her children. Instead, she kept up appearances. She shared only enough to appease our questions, while the three-year attrition of Dad's alcoholism accrued in fits and starts, turning him into a man we didn't recognize anymore. There were long, unexplained absences we blindly accepted as "business trips," even though the reality was they were trial separations instigated by Mom, who tried to do battle with a beast she was unqualified to confront. In her desperation, she begged, made threats, bargained, and manipulated. All Finley and I knew was that our father was no longer consistently around.

The interior of the treatment facility for alcoholism in Center City, Minnesota, was desperate. It was sterile, antiseptic, linoleum-floored, and shoddily furnished. Finley and I sat in "the pit" watching our parents across the way standing like strangers. Dad looked bloated and confined, disproportionately large in the space that incarcerated him. The air was fraught with unassigned shame. I had no idea to whom it belonged. I looked at Finley, who sat staring at the new tennis shoes Mom had bought him on the ride over, before we learned we were coming here instead of enjoying an afternoon of shopping.

We watched Dad turn away from Mom and walk down the four steps to where Finley and I sat. He told us he was going to stay for a while, that when he came home we were going to move into a wonderful new house right on Lake Minnetonka. Finley and I were so excited, we completely forgot we were guilty of putting Dad in this place and leaving him for ninety days. Mom kept telling us we had something to look forward to, so the connection we made was that Dad's self-sacrifice was for our benefit. Three months later, when Chuck Dudley rolled up in our driveway and deposited a freshly sober Dad, I was uncertain of what to say and Finley paced around, waiting for instruction. But no instruction came, and within the hour of Dad's awkward re-entry, we all got in his car and headed for the lake.

The house was smaller than the one on Lindawood, but it had features and character appropriate for a lake house. It was painted blue-gray with white trim on its wooden A-frame exterior, with a circular gravel driveway in front and a back yard thick with spongy green grass ambling down to the lake. Finley and I couldn't believe our luck. We took off running the second we got out of the car and couldn't cover our new territory fast enough.

"First dibs on the room over the garage," Finley called to me, which sent me into a dramatic tizzy Dad had to referee.

"Fair is fair," Dad said, and pulling a coin from his pocket, he looked at me saying, "Call it."

"Tails," I demanded, but of course Finley won the toss, which didn't even surprise me. I'd already decided Finley deserved the room much more than I.

The second time we visited the house, Mom walked around with a measuring tape and spent the day inside doing boring things, while Dad took Finley and me down to the water's edge. We dove and did flying cannonballs off the dock until we were exhausted and begged Dad to let us take Inky and Ike swimming, though he never acquiesced.

"Don't worry about it," Finley said, trying to staunch the pout spreading under my lip. "We'll take the dogs swimming after we move. Dad just wants them to get used to their new home first, that's all."

But the day never came. Came the day instead when a representative from the Wayzata Children's Shop came to take Inky and Ike as collateral against a year of unpaid bills.

5

Clay Cliff sat grandly at the end of a mile-long, oak-lined driveway, on a precipice above Lake Minnetonka, in an area named Navarre, twenty-five miles from Wayzata. The first time I saw the seven-bedroom estate sprawled upon its springy lawn with its red-painted front door centered and balanced in the saltbox design, my imagination took flight from the backseat of Mom's car. As we inched up the gravel driveway, the dock over the little lake to the right shimmered in the June afternoon sunlight, eliciting visions of Finley and me standing at the water's edge, holding slender fishing rods in the promise of a new life.

I was sure we'd come to know the house and grounds in a proprietorial manner. We'd evolve into people of purpose and belonging, and stake our claim and make forts in the woods behind our new home, overlooking the north shore of Lake Minnetonka. There'd be worlds to create and secrets to discover. We'd compose our own language to delineate this indescribable, enchanted place from the harshness of the outside world.

I was sure of it.

The back of Mom's neck stiffened as she gripped the steering wheel to guide the station wagon in an arc to the back of the house, where a caretaker's cottage stood plainly at the driveway's end. Stopping the car, she turned to Finley in the passenger seat and sighed with such resignation, I thought her whole body would deflate. "Well, here we are," she said, her hands releasing the wheel and falling heavily to her lap. Her blue eyes caught mine in the rearview mirror, then I looked at Finley's profile and waited for him to speak.

"Should we get out of the car?" Finley asked, and simultaneously, he and Mom opened their doors.

I sat stunned and immobile until Finley rapped on my window. His lips moved as if in warning, so I picked up my crestfallen heart and got out of the car.

The summer we put our worldly belongings in storage and moved into the caretaker's cottage of the vacation home of a wealthy family from Birmingham, Alabama, James Taylor dominated the airwaves with "Sweet Baby James," and Dad went on another extended business trip. To hear Mom sell the move as she directed Finley and me in packing our rooms, you would have thought we were upwardly mobile. She made no mention of our family losing everything, she never mentioned the words *bankruptcy*, *foreclosure*, or indicated that anything was amiss.

When Dad appeared at Clay Cliff with the reclaimed Inky and Ike, our terror overshadowed our joy before anything even happened.

Finley cupped his hands and pressed his forehead to the window, looking at the backseat of Dad's car. "Dad's dry-out didn't take," he said. "There's a six-pack of beer on the floor."

My blood ran gun-metal cold. I knew very well what this meant: we were in for a ride.

"Should we tell Mom?" I looked through the window at the red, white, and blue contraband menacingly positioned on the floor.

"Definitely not. We're going to Woodhill tonight for the swim team awards. Whatever you do, Millie, don't say anything, it'll just stir everything up," Finley warned.

Woodhill Country Club was festooned in green-and-white pageantry everywhere I looked. Beneath the massive striped marquee at the edge of the golf course, the club's WCC logo was embossed importantly on matchbooks, cocktail napkins, and placemats, while twined green-and-white streamers cascaded from the lectern at the end of the tent. We knew everyone there that night: the kids on the swim team, their parents, the three coaches. Even the employees of the pool's snack bar came out for Woodhill's biggest night of the year.

Derrick Dudley sat flanked by his parents, too close for my comfort. But Mom had overseen seating, so there'd be no reassignment. Finley was ecstatic. He'd be awarded the year's most improved swimmer, and wasn't even jealous I'd be awarded a trophy for highest team points in the girls' ten and under. I figured since he'd already been given every scholastic award known to man, he didn't begrudge me my moment, but then Finley had a magnanimous love for me devoid of competition.

White-coated waiters moved through the banquet aisles as Coach Nichols took the lectern, clearing his throat and tapping the microphone. I'd never seen Coach Nichols when he wasn't striding along poolside like a panther on the prowl, his tanned chiseled body long and lean in his green-and-white Speedo. The ringing of knives upon crystal silenced the voices under the tent.

"Thank you all for coming out tonight," Coach began, loosening his necktie as if to gain breath. His gleaming smile flashed proudly as he went down the list of award winners to enthusiastic applause.

The first thing I noticed was the color of Finley's eyes after his name was called, the very second he turned to strut back to the banquet table carrying his trophy. It was the strangest thing, but Finley's eyes had a way of changing color according to his mood. They deepened from baby-blue to gray at the slightest provocation, as if different levels of intensity lay within him like color filters on a slide projector. I pivoted in the direction of Finley's gaze to see blood trickling down Dad's forehead. In that moment, Dad tried to rise to his knees, the blood pulsing from where he'd hit his head on the table's edge, on his stumbling way flat to the ground. A pair of men angled beneath his arms to try and haul him to his feet, but Dad pressed them off in a drunkard's attempt at self-sufficiency.

Mom didn't waste a second herding Finley and me to the car. She took off in a disgraced flight of panic, keys from her purse already in hand. When the struggle began in the parking lot, Mom fought physically with feral abandon, but it wasn't enough to keep Dad from twisting her arm behind her back, until the keys fell from her gripped palm. Behind the wheel, Dad weaved in and out of the yellow highway lines, with all of us screaming in ungoverned terror, until the car careened into a tree and buckled like a decompressing accordion. Mom sprang out, rounded the back of the car, yanked open the driver's door, and dragged Dad to the earth by his massive shoulders. She angled behind the wheel, turned to Finley, and shouted, "Lock the doors," and pressing the gas pedal to the floor, she backed out in a screeching fishtail that propelled us like a bullet straight into the night.

Two policemen found Dad the next morning on Woodhill Country Club's golf course. They took him delirious and hungover to jail, where he stayed caged for twenty-four hours. Late the following afternoon, he walked unsteadily up Clay Cliff's driveway to find us packing the car, with Mom not in the mood for discussion. She was beyond talking, and had called her friend, Katherine, to come over and help. Dad walked straight to the kitchen of Clay Cliff's cottage and poured himself a stiff one, while Finley put Inky and Ike in the back seat with me.

Katherine reported much later that Dad had taken a deep drink of his Bushmills, then turned to her for sympathy. "Jesus Christ himself would drink over this," he had said as they stood watching the car sail away.

I crossed then uncrossed my Indian-style legs on the card room floor between Mom and Finley. I couldn't get comfortable. I kept slipping a covert eye at

Mom, who'd just dropped the news like an atom blast that Dad would be moving down South. She wasn't asking for our opinion. She was delivering the facts. I wanted to say something to challenge the inevitable, but I was a prisoner to my inarticulate emotions, and it was all I could do to sit there petting Inky and Ike.

"Where's he gonna stay?" Finley asked, the color of his eyes darkening.

"I found him an apartment on Poplar," Mom said. "He'll be here in three weeks."

Three weeks later, Mom dropped us off at Dad's apartment and said she'd be back around four. Finley and I stood under flickering fluorescent lights in the worn, unembellished lobby, waiting for the elevator to come and lift us to the sixth floor. I had the same sick feeling I had at the treatment center in Minnesota and started to tell Finley, but he seemed so withdrawn that I kept my mouth shut. I followed him straight to apartment 624 and stood quietly behind him as he knocked on the door.

When it opened, Dad was backlit by a beam of dancing dust motes that split through the shady room from the little balcony over Poplar. Traffic swelled through the plastic venetian blinds that needed replacing. The apartment was a one-room efficiency, with cottage-cheese walls and an eight-by-six-foot kitchenette. I didn't know enough then to know the accommodation was depressing. I was only aware that we all looked awkward and out of place standing in it. That none of us knew where to look.

After I gave Dad an obligatory hug with my head turned sideways, I couldn't decide if I should sit somewhere. Finley spied a catcher's mitt lying at the top of an opened moving box. He picked it up and looked around until he found a baseball. It seemed the air had vacated the cramped, inhospitable space. Dad seemed nervous. His eyes darted around the room as if assessing it through our eyes. He seemed eager to entertain us, so we filed to the elevator in discordant steps and rode down to the parking lot, where Dad threw the ball repeatedly to Finley.

I leaned all sixty-eight pounds of myself against a wall as if it had become my idea of fun.

"Millie, do you want to try?" Dad had a false ring in his voice like he really hoped I'd say no, so I shook my head.

"Are you hungry?" he prodded.

I started to shake my head again until Finley shot me an arresting glance and—even though Ella had given us cereal right before we got in the car—interjected, "I am, Dad."

We walked down Poplar Avenue—the gritty, obscure part of the Memphis artery that can only be described as that part nobody notices while on their way somewhere else. I studied the sidewalk, making sure not to step on the cracks (so I wouldn't break my mother's back) while Dad held my hand nice and tight. Habit held hard. I remembered to walk on the inside of the sidewalk when I was with Dad, in case a car veered off course—he taught me this the day we walked down the old Long Lake Road in Minnesota to see Inky, and I remembered, oh, I remembered, so I kept walking even though I knew I'd been dropped into a parallel universe.

We bought popcorn in a 7-Eleven where derelicts loitered and winos panhandled outside. I turned my head as if I'd never seen an alcoholic and clenched my mouth into a hard line, thinking that if Mom were there that's just what she'd do.

"What time is it?" I asked Dad.

"Why? Do you have a date?" he returned like he always did whenever he wanted to tease me.

Ashamed, I realized I'd just given myself away. Dad knew I didn't want to be there. Finley was looking at me with one of his shut-up-now looks as we walked the other side of Poplar back to Dad's apartment, where Dad said he had a present waiting for me.

The present wasn't wrapped well and its paper was slightly tattered, but it smelled like crushed gardenias. I tore the paper off and held the bar of soap in my hand, then turned it over and brought it to my nose as its floral fragrance overwhelmed me.

"It's Faberge, like the French girls use," Dad said, and I was blushingly taken aback. It may have been a bar of soap, but, to me, it meant that Dad acknowledged I was a girl.

I looked at Finley, wanting to deflect the moment, then said, "Thanks, Dad."

Later, as we followed Mom down the hall to the elevator, I could tell Finley didn't hold the present against me. That nothing between us had changed. Mom kept her back to us when she pressed the elevator button, so she didn't see Finley reach out and squeeze my hand.

Even though my bedroom in Kensington Park was connected to Finley's by the white marble bathroom we shared, it was so beautiful that I felt disconnected, like a transient who knows they don't belong in a place for the long haul, so they'd best not get comfortable. I couldn't look around the room without seeing myself reflected in the three folding mirrors atop the blue taffeta-skirted vanity table, where Gaga's twelve-piece monogrammed toiletry set lay evenly on the table's mirrored top.

Sometimes, I'd screw the silver top off the crystal powder jar and twirl its matching brush inside, then lean back against the pillows of the upholstered chaise lounge. I'd hold the silver hand mirror in front of my face while I dusted the fading freckles on the bridge of my nose. From this position, I could look in the mirror hanging over the mahogany chest of drawers, where its brass handles hung like jewelry on the other side of the room. I'd lie there gazing around, looking through the double windows to the magnolia tree shading the swimming pool, thinking of that picture over the back stairs where a young Posey sat with three perfectly coiffed girls in their pearls and sleekly parted collar-length hair. I wondered if the photograph had been staged, or if the girls had been caught candidly in a moment that captured their inalienable beauty. It was the kind of question I wanted to ask Mom in the throes of my ineffable, adolescent discomfort, but never could bring myself to do. I didn't know how the business of becoming a woman evolved … if one day my mother would reveal the secret, or if I'd arise one morning fully realized and captivating.

Like her.

Mom and Finley and I kept our bedroom doors open to the hall at night so we could call to each other if we needed to, or at least that's what Mom and Finley pretended with me. They knew I grew afraid at night because the rooms were so spacious and the air so deathly still that my creeping imagination got the better of me. I developed the habit of tiptoeing into Mom's room and standing over her bed until she rose and settled me onto the daybed with a peach silk blanket in the glassed-in sleeping porch adjoining her room. I liked the sleeping porch because it felt safe next to Mom and because it had an interesting history.

It had been Dr. Joe's office while Mom was growing up, and the masculine room gave me a sense of the grandfather I'd never known, who had meant the world to my mother, and who had died unexpectedly of a stomach aneurysm at age sixty-one. The sleeping porch was sophisticated and purposeful in its orderliness. Its ceiling sloped down at an angle above a glass wall where two oak trees cast shade in the daytime, which gave it the feel of a treehouse. Mom never minded when Finley and I camped out on the porch. She was generous with her space and could clearly see the attraction.

6

When Finley found Bizzarro, Mom let him keep it in a cage in Dr. Joe's sleeping porch.

Finley had gone to the horror movie *Willard* at the Malco Theater in East Memphis, after learning the plot involved a misfit boy who had a secret relationship with a rat. Something within Finley identified with the premise. In the middle of the film, someone released a white mouse, which zig-zagged in a frantic maze-like pattern, aisle to aisle, through the audience. When it ran over Finley's sneakers, he bent down and put the mouse in his blue-jean jacket's pocket. He bought a wire cage outfitted with a wheel, and a glass water bottle at the pet store around the corner. Back home in Kensington Park, Finley walked straight to the sleeping porch and settled the cage on the mantel over the fireplace and Mom never once complained.

The view through the portal window on the sleeping porch was level with a flourishing magnolia tree, halfway down the sloping front yard. I'd never seen anything like its blue-green, massive majesty in Minnesota. Its twenty-five-foot height and vigorous twenty-foot wingspan was weighted with flowering blossoms like giant, hovering lily pads silken to the touch. In my twelve-year-old comprehension, the tree was emblematic of Memphis's essence. In its imperial sentry, there seemed an enigmatic aestheticism a hairsbreadth beyond my reach. But if I stood on my tiptoes and stretched high enough, I could grasp the base of its lowest branch and leverage my feet on its trunk to shimmy up a couple of feet. If I tugged down hard enough on the branch, I could release one hand for a moment and snap off a candlelight blossom, then float it in water to scent my room in a celestial fragrance that lasted a week.

On a Saturday morning, Finley stood looking toward the magnolia tree through the sleeping porch's portal window. "Dad's here," he said in an emotionless tone.

Although conditions with Dad had changed, I was still capable of responding from the momentum of habit. I rushed to the window and said, "Move over, I want to see." Then, seeing him, I asked, "Do you think we can bring him up here to meet Bizzarro?"

"I don't see why not," Finley said. We both knew Dad would get a kick out of the mouse.

I bolted out the side door and ran across the front yard toward my father. "Dad, Finley got a mouse," I exhaled.

"Of course he did," Dad returned with encouragement.

I tugged at his hand, impatient for him to come meet Bizzarro. Some things just weren't as exciting without his involvement.

Dad dwarfed the sleeping porch by the sheer volume of his frame. There was no overlooking how out of place he seemed as he stood uneasy and awkward, an interloper desecrating the inner sanctum of my grandfather's sacred space. Still struggling with sustained sobriety, the AA program was teaching Dad how to reconcile his guilt and shame with the profound sense of pride that comes from a commitment to recovery. He had admitted his powerlessness over alcohol and had turned his will and his life over to a higher power. Apart from a few setbacks, he had found his way to a better way of living, yet no amount of amends could reverse the damage he'd done. Something unspoken freighted the air.

Mom entered the sleeping porch as we stood admiring Bizzarro. She wore a fitted sundress and white sandals on her feminine feet and a thick gold-mesh bracelet on her left wrist, which I saw Dad glance at before turning away. Finley, who never missed anything, gave me a steely look. I drew my brows together and mouthed "What?" but he just shook his head.

Later, Mom and Dad sat side by side in lounge chairs by the swimming pool, as if there'd never been a disruption. As if there'd never been estrangement. As if the fact that we were all in Memphis was just a temporary misunderstanding. I stood over Dr. Joe's desk and watched them through the window, deflated by a sinking mixture of sorrow and nostalgia. To my eyes, Mom and Dad belonged together—like characters in a novel dependent on each other to give meaning to the story. They looked like two halves of a whole, and I narrowed my eyes to the space between them, thinking, *There's my comfort zone.* Maybe everything that had happened wasn't so bad. Maybe everything would right itself so we could all go back to Minnesota.

I turned from the window and started to say something about it to Finley, but my tongue had other plans. "Why are you always telling me to shut up?" I demanded.

"Because you were getting ready to say something you shouldn't, that's why," Finley said in that matter of fact way of his that usually settled the score. But I felt put out this time, and continued to press.

"How do you know?" I challenged.

"Because everything you think is written all over your face. You were going to ask Mom about her gold bracelet. I could tell."

"No, I wasn't," I protested.

"Yes, you were," he said because he was right. "You saw Dad looking at it."

"Well, so what? What's wrong with that?"

"Chuck Dudley gave her the bracelet," he said.

"How do *you* know?"

"I just do, Millie. That bracelet's going to be the last we ever hear from Chuck Dudley. I'm pretty sure Dad knows that too, so he's going to drop it."

"All right, so everybody knows everything, but nobody's talking," I interpreted.

"Exactly," Finley said in a tone that was final.

That night, as the wind scratched the branches of the oak against my window, I pulled the covers over my head in fright, until I decided to get up and risk making my way through the dark hallway to Mom's room. Standing over her bed, I whispered, "Mom, can I move in?"

Without saying a word, she got up and settled me onto the daybed. I had no way of knowing it then, but it was the last time I would sleep on Dr. Joe's porch.

Ida Ella Morgan let herself in through the back door every Monday, Wednesday, and Friday. She'd leave her purse and then change out of her street shoes in the walk-in cupboard off the butler's pantry. She'd be well into her day before any of us got up. She adhered to a schedule that was a mystery to me, but I knew I could find her in the kitchen first thing in the morning and last thing in the afternoon before she'd take the key to Kensington Park's back gate and stand out on Poplar, where the four o'clock bus took her home to the shanty side of Memphis.

A black woman in her early sixties who hailed from Tunica, Mississippi, Ella was strong-boned and square-faced, with penetrating brown eyes and an imperious nature. She commandeered our house and anchored it with a dignity so implacable she never resorted to superfluous words. Solid, proud, and streetwise, Ella compensated for her illiteracy by being the best cook in town. When she wasn't engaged in the finer points of running the house, she could be found assembling her infamous lemon meringue pie, oftentimes at the request of one of Mom's friends.

I walked into the kitchen and found Ella grating lemon. "Who's that for?" I said by way of good morning.

"Miz Wilbourn mother done passed," Ella said. "Miz Posey gone carry it over there this afternoon, then she'll come back directly. She having a dinner party tonight."

I rifled through the refrigerator looking for butter, then pulled open the drawer directly in front of Ella to find a knife before I put bread in the toaster. I was in the habit of sparring with Ella, and moved my elbow to her side in jest. "You're in my way," I said.

Without taking a breath, Ella stood back and eyed me tip to toe. "Skinny ol' you, you ain't got no way," she dismissed.

Just then, my mother entered the kitchen.

Ella turned and met her eyes. "You fixin' to go?"

"I'm off to the beauty parlor. I'll be back around one for the pie. Thank you, Ella." Mom snapped the purse that matched her yellow sundress and turned toward the door. "Anything I need to pick up while I'm out?"

"No, ma'am, we gots it all here," Ella said.

"Millie, if you and Finley could clean up your records in the card room, it'd be a big help."

"Okay," I said.

"And be sure to take Inky and Ike out," she continued.

"I will, I promise."

"All right, I'll see y'all later," Mom said, turning to go.

Whenever I didn't have much to do, I'd hang around and watch Ella. I followed her back to the butler's pantry and sat on the counter beneath the window that housed the double porcelain sinks, watching her polish silver as she did every Friday. It was a big job, and I helped her bring the sterling silver in from the dining room, then watched her scrub it down with Wright's polish and a toothbrush, before she submerged it in sudsy water shot through with lemon and ammonia.

"Run, fetch me the silver service on the sideboard." Ella nodded, her rough wrinkled arms elbow deep in the metallic-gray water. "Bring it to me piece by piece. Miz Posey having twelve tonight," she said as Rosa Mae came through the back porch door from the guest house.

I don't know why, but Ella and Rosa Mae didn't cotton to each other. I know because Ella never once called Rosa Mae by her proper name, even though they worked in tandem every time anything of significance happened at 79 Kensington Park. They shared duties each time Mom threw a dinner party, while Rosa Mae's sixteen-year-old daughter sat out back in the guest house and tended to the dwindling Gaga—something that didn't take much beyond sitting there.

Rose Mae and Ella rarely exchanged words beyond a harrumph, and they set about their individual tasks in a competitive king-of-the-heap game. Should anything have been called into question by my mother, Ella would purse her lips with disdain and confide, "Rosemary done did it."

I couldn't figure out what there wasn't to like about Rosa Mae. She never said anything unless she was spoken to, and when spoken to, she didn't do anything but laugh. It made everyone feel like they'd said something exceedingly clever, but Ella only stood there frowning, wielding her superiority around what she considered her exclusive domain.

I've never seen two women take up a kitchen quite like Rosa Mae and Ella when unwittingly thrown together. I could have sliced the air between their attitudes … if I had the right kind of knife. There's never been a kitchen in the world big enough to accommodate the pair when they were jockeying for position in their identical white uniforms and orthopedic white shoes. Where Ella was imposing and stately, Rosa Mae was short and round, and every quadrant in the kitchen gasped for breath when the two of them were in it together.

When Finley stepped barefoot across the russet tiled floor and sat at the round marble table, all activity in the room came to a halt because he was a male. The way Rosa Mae and Ella were programmed, males didn't fend for themselves in the kitchen.

"He hungry," Ella directed to the air, but Rosa Mae got the picture and snapped into action, bending low to pull out a skillet from the cabinet under the counter.

"What's going on?" Finley asked, looking from Rosa Mae to Ella. He knew they were never together unless something big was about to happen.

"Miz Posey having a dinner party," Ella said, and Finley looked over at me as Rosa Mae pulled out a carton of Double-A eggs from the refrigerator.

"Is the colonel coming?"

"How would I know?" I shrugged.

"I bet he is. They've already had five dates," Finley said. I hated to hear it because Finley was usually right.

7

Whenever Mom threw a dinner party, a rote system of protocol ensued that began with over-the-top air kisses in the entrance hall and landed in the card room, where an ivory marble-topped French console, veined in swirling earth tones, displayed a Sheffield serving tray the size of the great outdoors. In pride of place, various types of liquor gleamed in cut crystal decanters, with brass generic tags hanging like jewelry—the better to relieve the hostess from the burden of her guests' opinion. Scotch, bourbon, vodka, gin, and vermouth sat alongside soda water, tonic, green olives, pearl onions, lemon twists, highballs and lowballs, all arranged so prominently that the hors d'oeuvres on the coffee table played second fiddle.

Never was there a more scintillating cast of players than those discovered at one of my mother's parties. They were ebullient, expansive. They were chic. Individual. Fun. The Austrian crystal chandelier in the card room twinkled like a spotlight on their haute couture, and their voices carried all the way upstairs, to where Finley and I kept out of the way. But we knew what was expected of us, and we were better off doing it early, before the night turned to full swing because it was anybody's guess what this crowd would do. Finley and I would slink down the front stairs to smile and shake hands, knowing full well we were on display as a reflection of our mother.

I shook the colonel's hand that night, and registered the curt nod he gave when Mom twittered, "You remember Colonel Henry?" She had a look on her face that brimmed with follow-my-lead encouragement, all raised eyebrows and prodding, quivering smile. I hadn't seen the colonel since the night the card room caught on fire. For a second, I wondered if he'd make mention to give us something to talk about, but he never did. He stood tall, erect, phlegmatic, his steel-blue eyes unblinking, the slash of his noncommittal smile balancing his square jaw as he leaned down and placed his vodka-ice square in the middle of a coaster, as if aiming for a bulls-eye. He extended his hand and froze me in place with his disquieting stare.

"Hello, Mr. Henry," I said, giving him a hot potato handshake. "Or should I call you 'Colonel'?"

Mom chimed in immediately. "He's *earned* the title Colonel." Call him that, she said, her voice ringing from the freedom of a tall Scotch and soda, which always unleashed her charms.

"You can call me either," he said, glancing from my eyes to Mom's, then back again.

"Oh, no, everybody calls you 'Colonel,'" Mom flirted. "Finley, come over here," she called over my shoulder.

"Colonel is fine," he said before turning to Finley, who stepped forward in a one-two and offered his hand.

It crossed my mind that the colonel was being treated deferentially, but I couldn't fathom why. He seemed the antithesis of my mother's type, not that I knew exactly what that was. I'd been so used to comparing every man to my father that any of her dates, after their divorce, only looked like ad hoc stand-ins. As long as my father was living down Poplar, their separation seemed negligible and ambiguous, as if any day things could reverse themselves. If only my father would pull himself up by his bootstraps.

"You're at MUS now, are you? What is it, tenth grade?" the colonel grilled Finley.

"Yes, sir," Finley said, now that he'd grown used to the formalities of the South.

"Are you involved in civic duties outside of school?"

"No, sir, I just play the guitar," Finley returned.

The colonel nodded, and every internal mechanism within me battened down its hatches as I watched the exchange, noting how the colonel's brow tightened upon hearing the word *guitar*. I couldn't shake the feeling he wasn't engaging in idle banter. It felt more to me like a forced inquisition.

"Are you interested in colleges yet?" the colonel continued.

"Not yet," Finley answered.

In my feeble attempt at cracking a joke, I said, "Finley's so smart, he ought to apply to college faculties," but the colonel didn't change his expression, and my words fell flat on the floor until Mom intercepted.

"Millie, be a dear and run ask Rosa Mae in here, will you?" She put a guiding hand on my shoulder.

I walked through the parlor, through the dining room, through the butler's pantry, and into the kitchen. "Mom wants you," I said to Rosa Mae.

I looked at Ella, who was filling one decanter with red wine and another with white.

"What she want?" Ella said, a steel look of concern on her face.

"I don't know, she didn't tell me."

Presently, Rosa Mae returned. "Miz Posey say we got a half hour," she said to Ella. I took this to mean it was crunch time, so I cleared out of their way.

Once up the back stairs, I saw Finley at the end of the hall. "I've got a feeling we're in it now," he said.

Had everything been the way Mom wanted it to look, Finley and I would have liked the colonel just fine, and he would have felt the same for us. But we were never given the chance to warm up to each other before he married my mother, six months later, in the middle of 79 Kensington Park's parlor.

I hated my dress, a dark-rose chiffon number that brought out the pink in my skin and clashed with the red in my hair. Although it may have been pretty on someone else, on me at thirteen, awkward in my long-legged, budding adolescence, it looked like a costume. Mom had selected it the day she took me to Minor Francis Dress Shop in midtown because its shade was two complementary tones darker than the dress she'd chosen to wear. She'd looked at me appraisingly and held the dress beneath my chin from its satin hanger, then stepped back to take in the effect.

"One day, you'll have bosoms to recommend you, but no matter, this will be perfect with my wedding dress. You know, it's tacky to wear white to a second wedding. Some poor fools don't know that, but I'm not one of them. Believe me, I'm not going to pretend to be a spring bride," she said to the delicate attendant who flitted around my mother and seemed to know the details of her pending nuptials.

I wasn't surprised by the attendant. People always acted this way around my mother. She had a charming, nonthreatening way of transcending social strata that was so intimate and inclusive, it turned anyone into her willing accomplice. And she was upbeat and funny. The combination of her intelligence and ready wit made her quick on the trigger of a snappy comeback or sarcastic remark that typically reeked with cutting truth.

"Mom, I hate this dress," I said. "It doesn't look good on me."

"Nonsense, Millie. Anyone young is cute," she dismissed. "As Gaga used to say, you're older a lot longer than you're young. I say enjoy your youth and let's get the dress."

Reverend McAlister of Independent Presbyterian Church in East Memphis arrived at four o'clock as scheduled. In his buzz-cut gray hair and floor-length black robe, his pious eminence overshadowed the parlor, and the beam from his sober blue eyes made me self-conscious. We hadn't been to church enough for me to feel anything but landlocked in his presence. We'd only gone on the odd, indiscriminate Sunday, which made me uneasy seeing him in our house. I knew it had taken Mom everything she had to cajole him into officiating at her wedding. Not only was she a divorcée, the colonel had buried his wife after she'd concluded a long run with cancer only ten months before, which set up all kinds of crimes against etiquette and fully explained why the colonel's eighty-year-old mother harbored a grudge that didn't acknowledge any of us for the first year of their marriage.

"The woman is always to blame," Mom confessed, and because she knew the rules of society as though someone had given her a rulebook, she cared not one iota. In her mind, it was only a question of time before she won the matriarch over. My mother was a single-minded, long-term player who possessed the convenient juxtaposition of a dog with a bone and sage serenity when it came to achieving her goals.

Although it was not an auspicious marital beginning, my mother was so gifted with placating everybody, she made the entire affair look like a holy arrangement ordained by God. Fifty-eight of her friends bustled to the understated ceremony, which carried a general tenor of solemnity and discretion, as the colonel stood impressively at attention, holding my mother's hands, staring into her eyes. The gravity of the moment was serious and anchoring, a pivotal moment in my life I didn't recognize for its full import.

Two full bars with white-coated waiters from the Memphis Country Club flanked either end of the entrance hall for the reception, which flew into full swing as if someone had flipped a switch after the ceremony. Ella and Rosa Mae weaved around with bacon-wrapped water chestnuts and pigs in a blanket, and the liquor flowed freely, lubricating a revelry that swept to the rafters.

A friend of Mom's named Daphne sidled over in her taffeta dress and three-stranded pearls to pinch my cheek. "Why, Millie, I bet you're excited," she gushed, in that sanguine manner characteristic of my mother's friends.

"Yes," I said, although I didn't know why I should be.

"You're going to have a stepfather. He's a wonderful man and your mother is so happy," she sang.

"I guess so," I nodded.

"You *guess* so?" She arched an eyebrow, laughing. "You're so cute, I hope you're having a good time." She looked around. "Where's your handsome brother?"

I spotted Finley standing in the parlor in his navy suit and thought there was something handsome about him, inexplicably eye-catching. He'd recently gone through a growth spurt but had yet to fill out, which rendered his coltish movements graceful and compelling. "He's over there." I pointed into the parlor.

Daphne teetered over to Finley on her strappy high heels. I saw him rear back like a cat as she leaned in to kiss him. I couldn't help but wonder if the alcohol fumes from her breath preceded the wet kiss she slobbered on his cheek. Finley turned his head and looked straight at me as if to say, "Why'd you send her over here?"

I shrugged my shoulders and pointed upstairs.

Up in the sitting room, Finley loosened his necktie and sat with an audible exhale on the loveseat facing the fireplace. He looked up at me as I stood in the doorway. "Well, you might as well sit down. Nobody's going anywhere for a while," he said.

"How long do you think they'll stay?" I asked.

Finley looked at his wristwatch. "Forever," he said. "It's only six. This crowd doesn't have dinner when a full bar's involved."

"Nice of your friends to come," I said. "I didn't know who to invite besides Cissy and Lucy. I don't really know anyone else."

"Don't worry about that. We'll both make as many friends as we had in Minnesota. It's going to take a little more time. The point is Mom wanted us to invite *any* of our friends."

"I don't know why. It's *her* wedding."

"Because everything's done in a pack down here. Mom wants us to get in the habit of tapping ourselves in. This kind of thing's important to her. It's the importance of connections." He looked at me, eyeing me in that way of his. "She's not as superficial as you make her out to be. She has her reasons. You just want her to over-explain everything to you."

I grinned. "But you love me anyway."

"Yeah, I do, in spite of yourself." He laughed. "Sit down, Millie, you're making me nervous."

I glanced out the window over the front yard and saw Murl Winfrey walking up the driveway wearing a gray suit and wide-brimmed hat. "Murl's here," I said. "I'm going to go say hi." I landed in the back hall at the exact moment Murl let himself in the through the back door.

"Well, there you is, Miss Millie," he said, taking his hat off and giving me a nod.

"Murl, you missed the ceremony," I said. "I wish you would have been here."

"Oh, I knows that," he said just as Ella came out into the hall, looking at Murl. The pair gave each other no hint of salutation. It seemed to me they never did. It was as if they existed in the cycle of my mother's ongoing universe as supporting players, floating in and out of the scene with nameless prompting while accommodating the roulette of each other's presence without surprise.

"You here to carry people tah-home?" Ella asked.

"Yes, ma'am. Miz Posey got me here in case people ain't fit to drive." He gave a firm nod. "She a woman who look ahead, Miz Posey is."

When Mom and the colonel returned from their honeymoon in New Orleans, the colonel moved into our home bringing his clothes, his dog, and his hostility, which changed the energy in the house and ushered in a living, breathing subtext that seeped into the walls and created subliminal warring factions, all in competition for my mother's love. But Finley found a way around it—we spoke to the colonel when we were spoken to, volunteered nothing.

And we went about the business of growing up covertly through the hard-won years of our maturity.

The colonel moved in a stray dog that hated Ella. It was a shepherd-collie mix that showed up one rainy night on a country road out in Collierville. Anyone would have thought the dog was rabid, for all its bedside manner. I never knew if the dog was male or female, even though it lived in our house for ten years. The colonel never allowed Finley and me to get near it. He kept the dog shut up in the bedroom and pulled it by the collar from room to room ahead of Ella's cleaning on Mondays, Wednesdays, and Fridays. We all tiptoed around as if it were perfectly normal to have a dog that bared its teeth and frothed at the mouth as the colonel marched it military style from corner to quadrant. Ella never said a word as she went about her duties. She just knocked for admittance to come in and clean.

Now that the colonel was among us, my mother's bedroom door was always locked. Something told me it wasn't just about the dog.

Ella maintained the rhythm of habit after the colonel moved in, and although I wasn't standing there the first time they met, I was lurking in the background at the exact moment the indelible die of their relationship was cast. Ella had just finished vacuuming the bedroom and had gone out to the sleeping porch with a feather duster in hand. She had started to wield it over Dr. Joe's desk when the colonel bellowed, "Ella, don't move any of the papers on this desk. Don't clean it. Don't move anything around. Don't touch anything on my desk."

His tone curdled my blood.

Ella bristled but recovered quickly. She stood at her full height, adjusted herself, and—with more dignity than I'd ever seen displayed in my life—looked the colonel straight in the eyes and said, "Thank you."

This was the moment I learned that dignity is the best defense.

8

It took Finley and me a while to put two and two together, but eventually we realized the colonel had an obsession with the lights in the house. We figured that the key to avoiding the colonel was turning off the lights when we left a room, which seemed petty to us, but Finley said there's no arguing with anyone's fixation, and if we did, we wouldn't have to keep having the same conversation. Beyond this, the colonel didn't pay much attention to us except when we committed the egregious error of disrupting his routine. From reveille to taps, every minute of the colonel's day had a corresponding movement you could have set your watch by. He rose at first light and shattered the silence in the upstairs hall when he turned the bedroom door key with an echoing click-crackle-click then took his dog outside for its fifteen minutes of supervised business. I'd lie in bed listening to the mourning dove that lived in the oak outside my window and think of Minnesota, until I heard the clatter of dried kibble hitting the aluminum dog bowl out back on the kitchen porch. I'd wait until I heard the bedroom door lock again, knowing I had forty-five minutes to move about the house freely before the colonel reemerged wearing a suit. He'd leave for his job, as head administrator of the black community college in South Memphis, at the exact same time every weekday, which Finley said was poetic because the colonel didn't like blacks.

But I knew it was far more than a simple case of dislike. The colonel thought blacks were inferior. I surmised this the night he received a nine o'clock phone call from the security guard down at the college. He'd disrupted the whole house with his put-upon exit from the bedroom to his car. Mom stood in the hallway outside my bedroom door when he returned, and I heard her ask if everything was all right.

"The niggers tried to break into the chemistry lab," he'd said with a note of pure disdain, as if the episode or its variation were predictable and came to him as no surprise. But it lit my blood and set my soul sideways. I'd never heard this hurtful talk in Minnesota, and knew something about it was wrong.

Finley and I would be long back from school when the colonel returned from work. We intentionally stayed upstairs until he marched his dog out and then returned to settle in for drinks with Mom in the card room at five.

Neither Finley nor I bothered pretending the colonel was in our life in any paternal capacity. He'd already raised two children who had children of their own, and he was well aware that Dad lived around the corner down Poplar. But we went through the motions of a family routine every night because gestures of civility mattered to Mom. We assembled in the kitchen at a quarter till seven and fidgeted through dinner while Mom chattered on as if we were all together by choice. But Inky and Ike decided they had a choice, and they proved it by finding a new home, which Finley said did the talking for everybody.

Anybody who knew us rang the one-note doorbell under the portico. So when the front doorbell rang with its ubiquitous, eight-note chime, Finley and I sprang to attention. I stood on the front stairs when Finley pulled open the cathedral doors to find Mrs. Saunders from the neighborhood behind Kensington Park standing there. It was the fourth time she'd appeared with both Inky and Ike in tow and the first time she asked to speak to "our mother."

I ran up the stairs to get Mom, who said she'd be right down after she got off the phone. I returned to deliver the news, but stopped short when I saw Finley's eyes turning a stormy blue.

"We've had them for about six years," Finley said. "Why do you ask?"

"Is that all?" Mrs. Saunders' voice rang with disbelief. "I would have thought they were much older than that. This one seems a bit senile." She pointed at Inky, who lay prostrate on the black-and-white tile floor. "And this one has gray in his coat, so I just assumed they were old."

"That's not gray. Ike's brindle," Finley clarified.

"Well, they sure have made themselves at home at my house. If they're not lost, then I think they like being with me better than here. They keep showing up at my door, so I just let them in and feed them."

"Well, if you're over there feeding them, that's why they keep showing up," Finley said.

I turned and saw Mom coming down the front stairs just as the colonel walked through the back door.

"Let's go back in the card room," Mom said graciously. "Would you care for a drink?"

And that's the night the colonel gave Inky and Ike away. It was also the beginning of how I learned that bad things happen in threes.

A year later, as I walked up the driveway after school, the sight of an idling ambulance jolted me sideways. Mom and Rosa Mae stood before the guest house as two paramedics wheeled a gurney inside.

"Mom?"

"Gaga died," she said without preamble.

Rosa Mae stood beside my mother, her eyes cast to the ground and her hands folded piously together. I looked at Mom, waiting for a bigger reaction, in part because I wanted instruction on how I should feel. Whether I should consider it a blessing or not since Gaga had dwindled so long. I would have gladly shared in my mother's emotions, if only I knew what they were, but she was not one to reveal her layers. I never saw her admit to the complete gamut of emotions inherent in all of mankind, and I thought it was because not all of them played well on her stage. I often wondered if she even possessed unattractive emotions, or if they'd shriveled up and died from lack of use.

Whatever it was she felt over her mother's death, she kept to herself, and because I sought to emulate her unwavering composure, I became an unskilled laborer in the construction of my own emotional life, uncertain of what I did and did not have a right to feel about anything. But in following my mother's lead, I knew the logistics for any occasion. I knew the details of acceptable behavior under any circumstance, and I thought that counted for something.

Dad didn't go to Gaga's funeral. Finley told me that now that the colonel was in the picture, there was etiquette rule at play. So the gathering at Independent Presbyterian Church consisted of Mom's friends, who came out in full force for Reverend McAlister's service. Afterward, they followed in caravan behind the limousine Finley and I rode in with Mom and the colonel to Elmwood Cemetery. We gathered beneath a cloudless sky in the rolling historic churchyard, with its boxwood hedges and limestone crosses in varying stages of decay.

Back in Kensington Park, my mother's friends carried on as if it were a party. Finley and I hid halfway up the back stairs in our funeral attire, balancing chicken salad sandwiches and potato salad on russet-and-white Herend plates. Although it was just high noon, Murl was down from the country in his white coat and tie serving drinks, while Ella and Rosa Mae weighted the dining room table with enough food to keep everyone a week. I kept thinking how sickening it was to watch everybody stuff their faces while Gaga lay dead to the world in Elmwood Cemetery.

I looked down at the sandwich on my plate, contemplating how food sustains life up until the moment the body just quits and you're lying in a graveyard. I thought about Gaga's last bedridden days, when she lay out back smoothing aluminum foil just to put her hands on something that shined. It made me think people value things arbitrarily so that, at the end of it all, a sheet of aluminum foil is just as prized as sterling silver, which made me question the true value of anything. I hoped these thoughts would flit through my head and then dissipate like most of the thoughts in my undisciplined mind. I set my plate on the stairs beside me and moved in closer to the touchstone of Finley, so that I could feel anchored to something real. I started to ask what he thought about death, but the click of Mom's heels on the back hall stopped me.

"There you are," she said, looking up at us. "Y'all shouldn't disappear. Get up and come say hello."

Finley and I got up and moved through the crowd with the obligatory manners that placated our mother, not knowing we were in the midst of a dress rehearsal for what was to come.

I opened my eyes to the early morning light filtering through the gossamer treatment of my bedroom window. I stretched languidly, then got up and padded through the bathroom to Finley's room. I started to knock but paused at the sound of five notes climbing from the strings of his guitar. It seemed Finley was working something out, repeatedly practicing the bending of a note from something staccato into something that curved. When I knocked, I entered to find Finley sitting Indian-style on his bed, sliding his long, artistic fingers along the frets of his guitar. I sat on the floor and watched him for a while, then asked if he'd called Dad.

"Not yet," he answered. "Why don't you call him now?"

"I will in a minute. Is Mom gonna let you take the car?" I asked. Since Finley had recently acquired his driver's license, to me his driving was a big deal.

"Yeah, she knows we're going over there. She's going out with the colonel to his daughter's farm in Olive Branch. She's not going to need the car."

I pulled my knees against my chest and heard the colonel unlock the bedroom door at the end of the hall.

"You'll call in a minute." Finley winked, and the implied understanding of avoiding the colonel hung code-like and humorous through the predictable sounds of his movements throughout the house. When I heard the bedroom door lock again, I crept down the back stairs to the telephone perched on the back hall's console beside a solitary high-back chair. Being that this was a Saturday morning, I knew Dad expected our call. I let his phone ring until it became unreasonable, then hung up and tried again. Perplexed, I returned to Finley's room to report there'd been no answer.

He looked up without missing a note and said, "He's probably outside or something. Just call back in a little while."

I figured we wouldn't be going to Dad's until later, so I went down to the kitchen and pulled out the smallest skillet we had to make Finley an omelet, the only thing I knew how to cook. Ella had taught me the fine art of egg whisking when she saw me mishandling the task. "Gotta put some wrist into it, beat 'em like the devil's on your heels," she'd said.

All I had to do to get it right was think of the colonel. Mom walked into the kitchen reeking of perfume and wearing what she considered appropriate country attire. Her purple cropped jacket was three shades too loud and her gold costume necklace would chase off the horses, but I knew that wouldn't matter to her. She wasn't the equestrian sort. It was enough for her to look splendid sitting out there on the porch. "What time will y'all leave?" she asked as Finley came into the room.

"We haven't gotten in touch with Dad yet, so I don't know."

I saw the flash of worry flit across Mom's brow, and although she said nothing further, I knew what she was thinking. Any variation in what was expected of Dad made us all think the worst—he was on a bender. His last relapse had not been discussed, but I had overheard Mom's end of the telephone conversation as it happened.

On that particular morning, Dad had called from Orlando, Florida. He'd reached out in frightened desperation to tell Mom he was drunk in a hotel room and couldn't stop drinking.

"Well, there goes the job I begged my friend to give you," Mom said. "Your days as a traveling salesman are over. You can't even handle that. What is it you think I can do from here?" she emoted before she slammed down the phone.

I poured the eggs in the skillet, set the lid on tight, cut the burner down low, and looked at Finley. "Do you think we should just drive over to Dad's place?" I asked.

"Yeah, probably," he said. "But let me call again first."

I got in the passenger seat of Mom's Gran Torino as Finley took the wheel. As we drove through Kensington Park, the oak trees towered brittle and ominous on the grassy knoll of the median, throwing burnt-orange on the ground from leaves curled at the edges the size of a catcher's mitt. Seeing any activity in Kensington Park was rare. There were never children tumbling on the neat lawns, or dogs in the yards of the regal homes set back from the street. The atmosphere was stolid and subdued, but there was something reliable about its exact constancy that made the whole of the park feel like hushed, hallowed ground.

Heading toward the river down Poplar, Finley took a detour through the ancient third-growth forest of Overton Park for no good reason that I could see, but I was used to the capricious way his mind worked. I never expected an explanation. As we drove past the modern College of Art building, geese sailed the ripples of Overton Park's lake. We got out of the car to walk its circumference, buttoning up our coats and picking up pebbles to skip from the water's edge.

"Look, Millie," Finley began. He spoke haltingly, as if he were testing the waters. "If we get to Dad's and something's not right, just let me do the talking, all right?" He raked his slender fingers through his long red-blonde hair, and I saw a worried look he didn't bother to hide.

"Okay," I said, "but what do you mean by 'not right'?"

Finley tucked his hands in his coat pockets and looked at me levelly. "You know exactly what I mean."

"You mean in case he's drunk," I interpreted.

"Obviously," he said.

"Okay," I said even though it wouldn't be okay with me. Drunk meant anything could happen in Dad's helpless confusion, which I couldn't help but take personally. I thought for sure his drinking was his way of saying he was better off not being fully present with me. It tap-danced on my self-esteem to think he preferred to create a psychological divide. I didn't know if Finley felt the same, or what it was he planned on saying if we found Dad drunk when we got there, but I did know Finley always had a plan.

We rode the elevator to Dad's door, and took turns knocking to no avail. We went down the outside stairs to the parking lot and circled around, searching. We walked to the 7-Eleven down Poplar like sleuths on a mission, then fruitlessly returned to the sixth floor one last time.

Finley's way wasn't to be easily defeated, but once he'd made up his mind, he was quick to move. "Come on," he said. "He's not here. Let's go."

9

Your heart breaks only once in a lifetime. Every offense in its wake is only a variation of the original laceration. Only once can you say you have no frame of reference. Only once are you knocked to your knees by an intractable powerlessness, where the only option is surrender in listless defeat. Subsequent infractions are damaging in their own right, but they're only a visitation of the original wound, which remains half-healed forever, with scar tissue that defines you for the rest of your life.

Built into the wall at either end of the Kensington Park stairs were two discreet servant's buttons, which Finley and I found fascinating, mostly for their antiquated symbolism. We'd invented a game of call and recall, letting each other know we were coming. The intrusive sound of the strident buzz split the air in the house with an urgency that catapulted us to immediate action, wherever we were in the house.

I was at the top of the back hall stairs when the news of Dad made its way to me in slow motion. I'd pressed the servant's button and stood waiting for Finley to answer. I pressed it again, then held it insistently the third time. Irritated, I walked down the hall to Finley's room and looked through his door, then trudged down the front stairs to the foyer. Two Queen Anne chairs sat decoratively in the entrance hall. Like many things in the house, they occupied space for effect, so Finley sitting in one of them seemed unusual.

"What are you doing?" I stood over his bowed head.

"Mom wants to see you," he said without raising his blue eyes.

"Where is she?"

"Up in her room," he said in a tone that made me think he wanted to get rid of me.

I retraced the front stairs and knocked on Mom's door. "Mom?" I called.

She opened the door in her flimsy peach-colored dressing gown, then turned her back slowly, crossing the length of the bedroom to her vanity table in a walk that appeared tentative. Lowering herself gently, she pivoted to face me. "Something very bad has happened," she said flatly.

"Where?" I asked. I thought it couldn't be here. If anything bad had happened beneath this roof, I would have known about it. For some reason, a picture of a car accident flashed in my mind because I had an indelibly etched frame of reference from back when we lived in Minnesota, when there'd been a catastrophic car crash in Wayzata, and Dad had saved a man's life.

I heard it, yet didn't know what it was until later. I was up our neighborhood street in Wayzata, at the Loosens' house, playing outside with their youngest daughter, when a jolting sound came rolling and echoing up the street like the reverberation of a bomb. I took off in barefoot flight down the unpaved street, only to be intercepted by Finley, who ran full throttle from our driveway toward the sound. We reached the car crash together, and froze in horrified shock at the splattered carnage. The cab of a semi-truck had careened into the opposing lane, hitting a family of five packed into a Chrysler, instantly killing all but the driver.

"Go get Dad," Finley ordered, but he changed his mind immediately and ran up the street because he knew he'd be faster.

Dad must have been sitting on ready because he came from behind me in what seemed like seconds, and dove into the mangled wreckage without hesitation, pulling the surviving passenger from the Chrysler onto the highway, where both blocked lanes emitted travelers springing to emergency assistance. I stood aghast at the juncture where our street met the highway, watching Dad delegate over his shoulder, crouching over the man who'd been driving the car. He pressed his balled fist into the man's stomach, staunching the cascading blood that sought to escape as the man fought for consciousness.

"Get Millie out of here," Dad barked at Finley. Around us, the scream of sirens rushed to the fatal scene from the phone call Mom had instantly made.

"Go back home," Finley yelled, but I stood dumbstruck. Not just from the starkness of the accident, but from the knowledge that something so macabre and altering could happen in this world. I looked over my shoulder to see Mom walking toward me. She held out her hand and turned me back toward home, where she took me up to my room and put me in bed.

That Sunday night, the prospect of putting ketchup on the hamburger Dad grilled in the basement fireplace was something I just couldn't bring myself to do. I was shell-shocked and inarticulate, traumatized with the day's grisly events, and ketchup looked too much like blood.

I watched Dad perform the same ritual I'd seen him perform every Sunday night, but this time I watched with new eyes a man who had more gravity than I'd previously realized, even though I already thought he was Hercules. He was so big and solidly built that his physical presence cornered the universe. Being near him meant everything in the cosmos was in its place, and all was right with the world. He leaned into the fire, stoking its flames by pushing newspaper beneath the grate with his bare hands, and I knew without doubt he wouldn't be burned because nothing on earth could touch him. He was beyond the reach of laws applicable to mortal men. In my eyes, he was the master of the universe, the Alpha and Omega, the man who could conquer all. Amen.

"It's Dad," Mom continued, and I could tell she'd been crying. I'd never seen my mother cry, not even when Gaga died, but here she was now, fighting for composure.

I stood bewildered, waiting.

"Millie, Dad's dead," she said. As soon as I heard the words, everything else came through a tunnel. "He died four days ago. I had the superintendent go into his apartment. He was found sitting in a chair. He'd had a heart attack."

My mind blocked out my devastation and turned to my repeated phone calls the Saturday before. I was ashamed to think of what Finley and I didn't know as we stood at Dad's door knocking. He'd been on the other side of the door, dead, while we'd assumed he'd forgotten us. Or worse.

Maybe his passage into death began as Finley and I stood there knocking. Maybe he'd called out to us, yet we couldn't hear him. I stared at my mother in my devastation, trying to fit a list of regrets into a line of alternative scenarios, as if understanding the right combination would alter the immutable result. I wanted to know what Dad had gone through, how badly it had hurt, and if he'd been scared. I had no idea of what happens during a fatal heart attack, or how long it lasts. I wondered if Dad knew it was death as it happened, if the white light of clarity had shone through to put his life in perspective and made him realize he should have lived differently. It suddenly hit me Dad had died alone and undiscovered for days, the sorrowful testimony to what his life had become.

The ways of my mother's Memphis were such that people carried on gracefully in the face of awkward circumstances. The dictums of manner and form were a rote safety net that gave shape to ritual with a sigh of relief. In my mother's Memphis, people knew what to do for every occasion, and the small detail of Mom no longer being married to Dad was a technicality everyone agreed to overlook. Linen tablecloths were laid, food flooded in, cocktails were served, and Mom's friends streamed into 79 Kensington Park for the rites of a three-day mourning.

News of Sean Crossan's death meant that Memphis society dressed up and appeared in the parlor. They stayed until the sun set, gave appropriate berth overnight, then reappeared the next day in a circuitous display that lasted until the night of the funeral. My mother's friends took over Kensington Park like central command of a beehive. From all quadrants of the house, phone calls were made to the nearest florist, Canale Funeral Home, and Independent Presbyterian Church. Ella and Rosa Mae didn't have to be told what to do, so fleet of foot were they in the ways of white people's tragedy. They conducted themselves with discretion, and Mom never lifted a finger, while the colonel lurked uneasily on the periphery of a scene that only touched him by marital association.

Finley and I were bit-players to our mother's starring role. We kept out of the way with hollow eyes, aimlessly adrift in the pall of our youth. We stayed in the upstairs sitting room drinking Coca-Colas and pretending to watch television, while muffled voices wafted upstairs as if it were any other party Mom had thrown in the house. Because Finley and I didn't know what to do with ourselves, we sat in self-imposed confinement until Finley decided it was wearing thin.

"You coming?" he asked as he pulled his coat over the wingspan of his slender, broad shoulders and headed to the back stairs.

I didn't care where we were going, I just put on my coat and followed.

Down in the stone-floored kitchen, Ella tied the back of her apron and gave me her all-knowing look. "You gonna wear them shoes?" she said, looking at my feet. She turned to look at Finley and said, "Take your good tie off and leave it be, before y'all goes out who knows where."

Through the back porch we sidestepped over coiled garden hoses, rusted-out dog bowls, and discarded bric-a-brac, making a stealth maneuver to freedom undetected. We rounded the back of the house, crossed to the backyard's edge, climbed a stone wall, and landed in the back driveway of a house whose front faced East Parkway. We crossed the northbound lanes and climbed to the grassy knoll of the median where Mom used to ride her Shetland pony. Autumn leaves cushioned the median's path as we walked to its bitter end, then crossed the parkway's southbound lanes and started down Court Street. I knew where Finley was leading. I wanted to see it too.

I was nostalgic for a place that was never my home, but it once was Finley's. The house on the corner of Washington and Court in midtown Memphis was iconic, a haven that housed my family in better times, and it was just dumb luck that I'd been born after the move to Minnesota while Finley had been born here. The house was ivory stucco and A-framed, with a manicured lawn and magenta azaleas along the front. A house so achingly pretty that I felt gypped I'd never lived in it.

I stood on the sidewalk beside Finley, looking through the living room's bay window, thinking this was supposed to be my house. Everything looked so perfect outside. I was sure everything within was equally ideal, just like my life would have been if only I'd lived here. I could see Dad out front raking leaves on the lawn so Finley and I could jump in and play war. When sunset came, we'd set fire to the leaves and soak in the earthy, burnt aroma. Mom would be inside talking on the phone in one of her flowered tea-length dresses, and she'd wait for us to come inside so we could all have dinner together in the dining room. The house was so charming, I imagined every waking moment under its roof a safety zone in which a child could grow up under the watchful eyes of two adoring parents. I bet if we all lived here, my room would be across the hall from Finley's and we'd be able to hear Inky and Ike clicking their nails down the hardwood floor separating our rooms.

Instead, I stood looking in the window, feeling displaced from a life that was never mine but definitely should have been. Inside was a best-case scenario. A life I should have belonged to with the three people I loved most in the world.

Finley sat on the curb in front of the house. "You know Dad's going to be buried in Minnesota," he said.

I dropped to the curb beside him and looked up to meet his eyes. "Are we going home?" I asked. It didn't occur to me otherwise.

Finley looked at me as if I should know better. "No," he said.

"Why not?"

"Because we live here now. Mom's just going to send him up there. He'll be in the same cemetery with George and Gaga Helen."

"Mom's going to send him up there alone? But he moved down here to be near us. Who's going to bury him?"

"I don't know. I didn't ask. The colonel was standing there."

I looked at Finley, then back to the street before me. In the imagination of my wounded heart, I pictured Dad's coffin flying through the air and landing between the graves of his parents, where a carved stone marker would finalize his life. I'd never seen the graves of my grandparents, but the vision I held in mind was cold, distant, something to which I'd never have access.

"Dad didn't even like his father. Why's he going up there to be with them? Shouldn't he be near us? I want to put flowers on his grave like they do in the movies."

"This isn't a movie, Millie."

Finley picked up a twig and started scratching circles in the dusty street as a future scene played out before me: I stood beneath a gray Minnesota sky, the bare winter trees eerie and rustling from the cold splatter of rain. Solemn in my black wool coat, I stood before an upright gray granite marker that blended with everything around me, where SEAN CROSSAN in bold block letters was carved indelibly beneath the straight edge of its top. I stood alone with a bouquet in my hand in this desolate black-and-white vision. Looking down, I tried to discern how much of the ground held the inanimate body of my father, who lay enshrined just as I remembered him—big chest, long legs, broad nose, regal as a statue with blue Irish eyes. I looked at Finley, noting the similarities, knowing he was well on his way to growing into an exact replica.

Finley stood and took a pensive last look at the house before I joined him and we walked through the well-tended neighborhood where the privileged lived in tasteful homes behind paint-by-number lawns, way back from the street. On our way to the record store down Madison, we walked through that part of midtown where an inviolate exclusivity kept it sacrosanct from the outside world. Only the old guard lived in the part of midtown between Poplar and Madison. We walked the streets, recognizing the homes of Mom's friends, until the neighborhood ended abruptly on Madison at the east side of Overton Square, where the record store Finley loved lay between a musty old bookstore and T.G.I. Friday's.

Finley sailed into the record store as if he were walking into his element. The man at the register rounded the counter to shake his hand, man-to-man style, while I basked in the importance of being Finley's sister. At seventeen, Finley was already a minor celebrity in Memphis' musical underground, for word had traveled fast that there was a prodigious guitar player in town.

The man before us was also the bass player in a band Finley had met at a gritty little club down Madison called The Well. The way he firmly clasped

Finley's hand made me look at my brother in a new light. He was tall for his age, and fluidly built. The dusky red-blond of his hair waved gently, in a manner mine never could manage. There was something hypnotic about the blue beam of his eyes as they focused from the long-angled planes of his face. He stood soldier straight and balanced, exuding an enviable self-assurance in his burgeoning manhood. There was something captivating about Finley, something compelling and electrifying, although few people would call him handsome. But Finley was unique. The kind of guy people turned their heads to watch because something about him was so magnetic.

"I know what you're looking for." The man released Finley's hand. "We just got it in." He made his way through rows of albums displayed upright in alphabetical order. I stood like a third wheel behind Finley as the man handed over *There's the Rub* by Wishbone Ash. On the cover, a pair of men's ochre pleated pants stood, feet apart, and with a hand holding a red ball. I didn't get it, but neither did I comprehend when Finley brought David Bowie's *The Rise and Fall of Ziggy Stardust* and *The Spiders from Mars* home two years earlier. Finley always had his finger on the pulse of what was happening musically, well before anyone else knew.

"You're coming Friday night, right?" The man looked at Finley expectantly.

"I don't know. There's been a death in my family," Finley said without elaborating. "I'll see." His nonchalance collapsed the floor beneath me. I wondered how Finley could carry on so effortlessly after what had happened to us. Studying him, a lesson in comportment was upon me, the rules of civility gamely in play, and I was struck by the feeling that life is an oxymoron, that your entire life could be shattered, leaving you victim to an outside force you never asked for. Apparently, you were supposed to pretend that wasn't the case. If this was maturity, then I wasn't ready. I wanted the whole world to stop so I could cry. Had I not worshiped my brother, I would have resented this casual art of deception. I took his calm, cool collection personally, as if he were withholding something from me when he knew very well I looked to him for guidance.

"Your brother is a hell of a guitar player." The man turned to me with convincing eyes.

"How do you know he's my brother?" The words flew from my mouth before I thought them through. "I could be anybody," I insisted.

The man looked at me, laughing. "Yeah, but you're not. You're the female version of him." He reached out a hand and mussed my hair.

I shut my smart mouth and stood a little taller from the perfunctory pride that sprang from the validation of my association with Finley.

Out on the street, Finley reached into his bag and handed me Carole King's *Tapestry* without saying a word. It was typical of his personality to produce through sleight of hand and keep walking. Finley wasn't the kind of guy who waited for a reaction he already knew was coming. He was too smart to waste his time on redundancies. "We should head back," he said, although he didn't walk like he was in a hurry. His long athletic stride was rhythmic, steady, purposeful, yet it took its time moving through space, as if he were experiencing the atmosphere as opposed to moving through it.

I looked down at the album I carried. Carole King on the cover in curly hair and blue jeans, a gray cat staring drolly toward the camera in front of her. Finley knew I liked the song "So Far Away" because it painted pictures with words, or at least that's what he told me.

Finley knew how to put things into words better than I.

Although I felt everything deeply, I lacked the ability to articulate my unwieldy emotional weight. But Finley was just the opposite. He wore the entire English language on the surface of his skin and could command it with one arm tied behind his back.

Kensington Park had a wrought-iron sign at its entrance that stood stately and weathered on top of a pike announcing, "Private, Residents Only." We walked beneath tree limbs stripped bare in the November air, along a sidewalk cracked uneven from being laid over tree roots. Now more than a hundred years old, the sidewalk pitched and rolled and rose up unexpectedly to trip the surest of foot.

Mom had staked an indelible claim to the sidewalk in her youth by co-conspiring with one childhood friend against another, spitefully scratching "Mary Jane is grumpy" in the summer's melting tar with a stick. Each time I walked over the spot I thought, *Poor Mary Jane*, and noticed how time had ravaged much of the message. But the words reminded me that this walkway was initially claimed by my mother, which left me with the impression that Finley and I were just passing through.

Or, at least, I was.

Up the front yard past the cars parked nose to end, we sidled the periphery of the house, where Ella and Rosa Mae had the porch door propped open with a mop. The thick, mingled aroma of shallots and roasting fowl drifted fog-like from the kitchen whose round center table ached with the weight of silver serving trays laden with biscuits and gravy, turkey slices and greens, potato salad, and condiments.

"You back?" Ella said.

"You tell Mom we were gone?" Finley asked her.

"Y'all ain't been missed," Ella stated, drawing her thin black lips to a clamped righteous puss.

Dad's funeral was depressing. Three days of Mom's friends carrying on at the house made me assume they were all coming to the service, but I was completely wrong. Instead, it was just the four of us: Mom, Finley, the colonel, and me. I couldn't fathom why the colonel was there all stiff and suited up. The good Lord knew he wasn't there for Finley and me, but he had gotten in the habit of standing guard over Mom. It was like any other time we were thrown together with the colonel—he stood sentry while Finley and I stood in detention. On the best of days, it was an uneasy alliance striving for détente for the purposes of placating Mom.

Sometimes a parent can surprise you. Just when you've reconciled they're hopelessly out of vogue, just when you've conceded their generation renders them bereft of popular culture, they turn around and do something like Mom did at Dad's funeral. Heaven knows whom she talked to, but James Taylor's "Fire and Rain" played over hidden speakers as we walked into Canale Funeral Home's visitation room, and Judy Collins' "Send in the Clowns" played as we walked out.

In between, I sat stoically next to Finley. Neither of us shed a tear while Reverend McAlister droned on from the Bible, dressed in his funeral robe looking like overkill in an anticlimactic setting. His sermon was short, general, and impersonal. It bore no relationship to the spirit of Dad, but then again, Dad wasn't the churchgoing type. My father found God out of doors. He felt Him viscerally in nature, His mysteries descended upon him as intuitive inner-knowing. My father's universe was lit up in symbols and talismans that guided him onward through the fog of life's riddled path. He must have known he'd fallen short in God's cosmic test, but it wasn't for lack of trying. There are some men too gentle to live among wolves, and the dichotomy of who he was versus who he tried to be got him in the end.

So, there we all sat in the cold visitation room like we were observing the funeral of a stranger. I determined that I wasn't going to cry for my father in this sterile place. I looked over at Finley and could tell he wouldn't either. He sat catatonic, staring straight ahead, looking at the obtrusive casket at the top of the center aisle. The coffin stood ugly and claustrophobic—a big, rectangular box that screamed death, and it scared the life out of me. Not that anybody asked, but would I have had my druthers, I would have never seen it sitting there. I could have gone the rest of my life without the vision of Dad in a box infiltrating my psyche, and been better off for it.

But humanity requires us to fit into society, and being civilized implies we observe ceremony when someone dies, in the interest of closure, as if marching through a labyrinth of rites will quell the tangled and broken spirit within. At Dad's pathetic, stripped-down service, I learned that forced ritual only makes me debilitatingly self-conscious. The entire affair was like playing Twister without a mind-body connection. I didn't like one millisecond of any of it, and wished to God Mom didn't always have to adhere so perfectly to appearances.

I thought, if this were a movie, it would have been better if the scene depicting the worst moment of my life ended in Mom's bedroom with her succinctly saying, "The life of your father is over. He is gone. He is no more."

10

All that winter, Finley existed in the prime of his golden-boy youth. By the first semester of tenth grade at Memphis University School, the seventeen-year-old Finley had finally morphed from a Yankee outsider into a member in good standing among the privileged boys at the prestigious school dedicated to higher learning. It hadn't been easy. When Finley arrived at MUS two years before, the boys didn't know what to make of him. I knew this as a certainty because my friend from Hutchison, Jenny, had a brother who went to MUS, and he'd told me in that cruel, uncensored way, typical of boys in the throes of their swaggering youth.

"Your brother is weird," he'd said one day when I'd gone home with Jenny after school. "We all think he's a little light in the loafers."

I didn't have a comeback for this, but if the roles were reversed and it were me being disparaged, Finley would have thrown wide and decked him.

But I knew why Jenny's brother passed judgment. On Finley's first day at MUS, he'd committed the unpardonable sin of wearing the wrong clothes. Mom, in her distraction, neglected to mention the tacit uniform at MUS was an Oxford-cloth shirt, khaki pants, and brown loafers. Finley had walked into the prep-school classroom, tall and gracefully thin, with collar-length hair and seventies bellbottoms, looking like a degenerate from an Isaac Hayes film. But it wasn't his fault. His fashion sense had been influenced by the bad luck of timing.

Because our first year in Memphis began in the month of August, Finley's September enrollment into MUS was deferred for one year. In the interim, Mom entered Finley in a public school called East High, which was the first school in Memphis to experience racial integration through busing. Finley was thrown in with coeds who lived on the other side of Mom's tracks, and spent the whole year as if he were attending a carnival instead of a school. He achieved immediate A-student status, with all the applied effort of one arm tied behind his back, and ingratiated himself into a pack of irreverent, edgy youths he would have otherwise never met.

While Finley waited for the hallowed grounds of MUS to begin molding him into a model citizen, he picked up with a devilishly good-looking boy from the wrong side of town named Eddie Dean. Blond, strutting, and smirking,

Eddie took to Finley like a house on fire. They aided and abetted each other's delinquency and filled in each other's gaps. Where Finley was cerebral and quick-witted, Eddie was charming to the point where even Mom forgave him his rough edges. She told me, on the afternoon Eddie broke Finley's nose as they wrestled in the back hall, that Eddie didn't come from much. She'd gathered this from telephoning his mother after the wrestling episode. Upon registering her lack of parental alarm, Mom declared the poor woman didn't know how to do, which was about as low as people could go in her book.

I typically learned about Finley and Eddie's antics on the back end because I was cloistered away at Hutchison during the week, and only privy to their creativity on a need-to-know basis, which was fine by me. I stayed involved in my own streamlined world comprised of school, keeping out of the colonel's way, and listening to music with Finley at night.

On the weekends, Finley and I were like every other coming-of-age kid, in quieter times under little supervision. We tested our wings and formed new friendships as we navigated our standing in Southern culture.

Unbeknownst to me, WHBQ radio in Memphis held the citywide "Pinball Wizard" contest, spawned from The Who's 1969 groundbreaking album of the same name. On a Saturday morning, Finley and Eddie went down to the station and stood in line with more than a thousand entrants who waited to play relentless hours of pinball in the hope of winning a pinball machine as the grand prize.

Of course, I learned all this at the exact same moment I heard that Finley had won.

You could have knocked Mom over with a feather. And you couldn't have irritated the colonel more had you left every light on in the house and tried to make friends with his dog. The pinball machine was so unwieldy, there was nowhere to put it in the museum-like elegance of 79 Kensington Park, so it sat in the middle of the entrance hall for weeks, until Finley saw the chance to create his own private universe.

There was a nondescript door incidentally positioned, not far from the back hall stairs. Most people didn't even notice the door. Out of the three possible channels into the dining room, this particular stretch of the back hall was the least frequented because it was inconvenient from the kitchen and didn't have as impressive an entrance as the parlor. An unsightly metal key with two raised teeth protruded from the keyhole. With a twist, the door opened, leading to fifteen steps descending to the basement. The wooden stairs creaked, the walls were moist plaster, there were no windows to speak of, and the outdoor concrete stairs in the back funneled in water every time it rained. Nobody ever went down to the basement except for Murl, who kept rakes and yard implements hidden from view in the dank creepy cellar, where a discreet toilet was partitioned by six feet of warped plywood. But Finley never saw the basement's inhospitality. All he saw was a chance to create his own private universe.

Finley and Eddie hauled the pinball machine down to the second room and put it next to the couch from Minnesota, which Mom didn't think was nice enough to put elsewhere. They spent a month fixing the two rooms up. They painted the walls, tacked up posters from "The Jimi Hendrix Experience," Pink Floyd's "Wish You Were Here," and Yes's "Close to the Edge." Eddie donated the pool table he'd won with a winning hand of five-card draw against a guy in his neighborhood, and they angled it alongside Finley's Marantz stereo, Panasonic cassette deck, and ever-expanding record collection. With a lot of work, the basement became Finley's happy hunting ground. There he played his guitars and turned his amplifier up to his sole discretion without it disturbing the rest of the house.

Whenever Eddie came around, he'd swing in unannounced through the back porch off the kitchen. He'd present himself to Ella to ascertain the climate of the house, for in some deep-seated, unnamable way, Eddie and Ella understood each other. They were equally tentative and circumspect, vigilant in that wary, streetwise way that intuits danger and knows how to avoid it. They'd lock eyes wordlessly then Ella would dart her eyes in the general direction of the colonel, and Eddie would stand informed.

I was sitting unnoticed at the top of the basement stairs listening to Finley play his Les Paul Jr. through a Fender amp, marveling at the way he played along lick for lick with Dickie Betts in the Allman Brothers song "Blue Sky." It seemed to me Finley came to the guitar the way he came to most everything—naturally, second-naturedly, as if he recognized something he could master with very little effort. It probably never occurred to Finley he couldn't. His mind was so fierce, any type of challenge was almost a relief, for it gave his weighty intelligence an outlet, and he was never more at home than when involved in the pursuit of perfection. When Finley played guitar, he aligned with a dimension of his inner sanctum wherein there was no past nor future, only the present moment, and it was perfect.

I was so absorbed in listening to Finley that I didn't hear Eddie sneak up behind me.

"Hey there, Millie-Tilly-Filly." Eddie put a hand on my shoulder and sat beside me. "You know what time Percy and Allen are coming?"

"They're on their way. Allen called about a half hour ago."

"Good," Eddie said, making no attempt to walk farther down the stairs.

Suddenly, the basement door opened, and Ella loomed large. "Mr. Henry done ask is that your car," she said to Eddie.

Eddie sprang up. "He knows it is. What's he want?"

"He say you blocking his car."

Eddie gave me an exasperated look, then went out to reposition his car.

The second Eddie closed the door, Finley walked to the bottom of the stairs and looked up at me. "What's going on?" he asked.

"Eddie's here and the colonel wants him to move his car. I thought Mom told me they're not going anywhere until tonight."

"They're not," Finley said.

"So what's the big deal about Eddie's car?"

"He's correcting the assumption that anyone can take up space in his personal jurisdiction without asking. It's the principle of the matter. He's just leveraging his authority."

Finley's trigger-ready habit of simplifying the colonel's pettiness always highlighted the comedy and lessened the sting. In that automatic way we had of wordless communication, I rolled my eyes, then Finley raised his eyebrows and walked back to his guitar.

When Eddie reappeared, Percy and Allen walked behind him. The three clattered around me down the stairs as if they were the best of friends now that Finley was their rallying point. Were it not for Finley, Percy and Allen would have never crossed paths with the likes of Eddie Dean, but now they met as equals on that desegregated playing field, where young boys align when they have the world by the tail of its unlimited potential.

Percy stopped as I rose to leave. "I'm sorry to hear about your dad," he said with measured sincerity.

Allen nodded. "Yeah, me too."

"Thanks," I said, feeling caught out and arrested. I felt the heat of embarrassment light my face, and wanted to immediately deflect. I was crushingly ashamed, even though I didn't know how much they knew. I hoped

Finley had kept his guard up and had only told Percy and Allen the highlighted facts, that our parents had divorced, then our father had died. I hoped he hadn't divulged the gritty minutiae, then realized it wouldn't have been Finley's way at all. He was perfectly fine with being unreadable, and all I wanted was for Finley and me to fit into this place, as opposed to seeming like tragic figures with an aberrant past.

"Are you and Finley okay? Anything I can do?" Percy asked.

"We're fine," I assured him, although I wondered what anybody thought they could do. I'd been asked that question many times before, and it was always delivered in the same tone of voice they'd use if they were to ask if you wanted a Coke. I knew there was a perfunctory response floating around somewhere. "Oh no, I'm fine, thank you," or some such, then I could release the petitioner and send them on their way after everyone fulfilled formal courtesy.

But I was starting to realize everyone walks around with their personal subtext, and the only question I had was how much should you let show? From what I'd observed by watching Mom, the process of personal grief involved never letting on, never confessing. "You know, people don't really want to hear about your problems," she'd said one time, which for me sealed the deal with a Band-Aid forever.

I reached for the door.

"Millie, wait," Finley called. "We need a fifth person. Come back down."

"For what?" I returned.

"We're playing pool."

"You know I can't play pool," I said.

"You don't have to play, you just have to watch. Keep Eddie from cheating," Finley said to his friends' delight.

The boys had been in the same room for all of thirty seconds and already they were in full tilt. Together they were like a kennel of puppies, all lean knees, sharp elbows, and crooked angles in constant motion. I blushed to think they liked having me around. I walked down the stairs and sat on the sofa by the pinball machine. (When we were in Minnesota, we called it a couch, but in this house that same piece of furniture turned into a sofa. I had no idea why.)

"Rack 'em and break 'em," Allen directed.

"Stand back and watch how this is done." Finley leaned low with laser focus.

79

"Finley's over there like Minnesota Fats," Eddie said over the rat-a-tat-tat of balls cracking in the air. The Beatles' "Good Day Sunshine" played on the stereo, and all four boys were singing.

"No, you take Lennon, I'll take McCartney," Percy said to Finley.

"Which is exactly why I won't," Finley said. "You have to take the part that doesn't come easily to you."

"None of it comes easy to Percy," Allen jibed.

"Shut up, Allen. I have more of a musical ear than you ever will. What do you know beyond playing drums?" Percy lobbied.

"You ever try playing drums?" Allen shot back.

"No," Percy answered.

"Then you shut up," Allen said, taking the stick from Finley and hovering over the table.

"Millie, you got your eye on Eddie?"

"I'm on the case, Finley," I said.

"Good, don't let him shark my game," Finley instructed.

"What do you mean shark?" I asked. "What am I looking for?"

"Deception," Finley declared.

"My inning," Eddie said. He elbowed Allen, who backed away from the table.

"Yeah, Finley, like you're not a bigger deceiver than everyone in the room put together," Allen said, ramping up to share more.

"Maybe when it's convenient, but never at pool," Finley said.

"You should have seen Finley in Mr. Hatchett's 'Three Critics' English class last Friday," Allen said to Eddie. "It was the funniest thing you've ever seen in your life. Absolutely priceless."

"What?" Eddie stood up, squinting at Allen. "What's three critics?"

"No, the question is, who are the three critics," Allen said. "Steinbeck, Sinclair Lewis, and Wolfe. We're reading *Look Homeward, Angel.* Hatchett unexpectedly called upon Finley, so Finley stood up and gave a long-winded recitation on the book's theme. It was unbelievable. He droned on for about twenty minutes, then wrapped it up with, 'All that, and I didn't even read the book.' He had the whole class going. Hatchett was so blindsided he couldn't even get mad. All the man could say was, 'Gentlemen, there's nothing funnier than an intellectual sense of humor.'"

"That wasn't all he said," Finley teased.

"What else did he say?" Percy looked at Finley.

"That's for me to know and you to never find out," Finley returned with mystery.

I wanted to rise to the level of worthiness of being included in this mix of boys. As it was, I was only an enthralled observer. In it, but not of it. I figured that was because I was a girl. The boys exuded the collective energy of male free-falling youth, where erudite sarcasm was the binding glue. I thought it must be something they learned at MUS, while Hutchison was busy hammering me into one of the women expected to follow boys such as these. They were being groomed and made ready, instilled with a superior sense of themselves as entitled heirs to the Southern gentry. When MUS finished with its recruits, the boys would stand taller than those around them. The world would recognize them for their refined cultured breeding, after Ivy League doors swung wide and paved the way to their eventual takeover of their family's business.

As I watched Finley set down his cue stick and reach for his guitar, I couldn't help but wonder where in the world he'd fit in.

11

Even though the subject of Dad was the white elephant everyone tiptoed around, I would have liked to have talked about him. I wanted to march into Mom's room and announce I was soul-sick, but there was no separating her from the colonel, and she wasn't the type to take me aside to ask how I felt. Instead, she gave me a ring.

Made of gold vermeil with three jade ovals in its wide center, the ring was decidedly too old for me and looked like something Mom would wear. Even to my untrained eye, I could tell it was nothing fine, but she had come into my room that first Christmas Eve after Dad's death and handed it to me. "Your father would want you to have this," she said, presenting me with the ring.

For a split second, I wondered how in the world she divined this. She sounded as though Dad had sent her a telepathic message from heaven. I examined the ring, put it on my middle finger, and watched the heavy stones swing the band upside down. I looked at Mom and started to say it was too big, but she read my mind.

"You'll grow into it," she said, turning to go, and I glanced back at the ring and accepted it as my mother's idea of complete and intimate discourse.

I walked through the bathroom and stuck my head through the crack in Finley's door. "You getting ready?" I asked, and he nodded without breaking his guitar rhythm. He was wearing his blue Christmas Eve blazer and khaki pants, which looked perfectly appropriate until I scrolled down to his black Converse high-tops. I couldn't think of how to say what I'd come to say, so I ended up extending my left hand.

"You too?" he asked flatly. He stopped playing his guitar and set it down. Walking into his closet, he reached overhead to the dangling string, switching on the naked light bulb. He emerged with an empty twelve-gauge Benelli shotgun whose weight he balanced on the butt of the gun. I met his eyes for a second, looked back at the gun, and asked, "You taking up hunting?"

"What I'm going to do with it isn't the point. Mom's giving me something of Dad's for sentimental value. She went out and bought you that ring so you'd have something to remember him by too."

I looked down at the ring on my finger and felt my heart drop down into no man's land, knowing, as I did, that the ring would never remind me of the living Dad, only of the Christmas Eve when Mom gave me this emblem of his having died.

The front doorbell chimed in its eight vacillating notes, alerting us to the arrival of the colonel's daughter and son-in-law for Christmas Eve dinner. With her highlighted pageboy hair and petite perky nose, my stepfather's daughter looked like she'd just walked off the campus of an East Coast boarding school where she'd met her pedigreed husband at a sorority mixer aimed at pairing Anglo-Saxon socio-economic equivalents. They arrived with their two-point-five kids (one boy, one girl, one on the way), who were dressed in the latest of J. Crew. The colonel's daughter didn't know to use the side door under the portico—she'd been too busy employing the etiquette of resentment over her father marrying my mother before he'd mourned a proper year, and therefore hadn't been around. Finley said in some rule book she cared about, it's written in stone that society's rules trump happiness, and if she wanted to compare notes on the damaging repercussions of our parents' marriage, he and I had her outranked.

Rather than acknowledge the thick air of hostility over her hasty marriage to the colonel, Mom had invited the players in the colonel's former life to dinner, thinking this time she'd win them over. The fact that his first wife's sister, Miss Mycroft, was the headmistress of the school I went to was almost too much for me, but Mom had been giddy over Miss Mycroft condescending to come. It'd taken Ella and Rosa Mae days to get the house in order. The day before, they'd stood side by side at the double porcelain sink in the butler's pantry, elbow deep in sudsy water, polishing every piece of silver in the house. It was such a to-do that Tito, Rosa Mae's daughter, put on a white button-down uniform and came out to help. Watching Tito navigate the kitchen bothered me more than I could say because we were so close in age. I wanted to take her aside and whisper that all that glitters is not gold. That things were nowhere near what they seemed. And that I hoped she wasn't fooled by appearances.

The colonel's octogenarian mother arrived with cacophonous fanfare in her stiff Aqua Net hair and filigree brooch, clinging to the arm of her liveried chauffer for support, lest she teeter off her rubber-soled shoes. I'd never seen such an overt display of genuflecting sycophancy as Mom and the colonel's daughter fell over themselves vying for position. For someone so diminutive, Belle, as she was called, stood imperious, clearly expectant of the fawning attention as the colonel offered his arm and padded her across the coral-colored Oriental rug in the parlor and straight to the card room where we all pretended to be happy. We fidgeted over cocktails and hors d'oeuvres, searching for something to talk about while we waited for Uncle Wick to arrive and complete the group.

Uncle Wick wasn't really our uncle, but Finley and I understood that when someone is given that moniker in the South, what they really are is part of the "in crowd." Uncle Wick arrived fashionably late—and by fashionably, I mean in full Highland dress, complete with kilt, sporran, sgian dubh, and ghillies, which complemented his blue eyes and white tousled hair. He'd parked his pickup truck at the bottom of the driveway, and kept looking through the card room's cathedral doors to where his border collie napped in the front seat, which thrilled me. Since nobody could touch the stray dog the colonel moved into our house, the thought of having a dog on the property I could pet made me think maybe the entire night wouldn't be so bad after all.

Even though Uncle Wick indulged in his cups, nobody minded because he could always be counted on for entertainment. He extended his weathered hand to my face and cuffed me under my chin, tilting it up to study me. "Child after me own heart," he said, affecting a Scottish burr. "You look like a wee lassie and a lot like your father, God bless his memory." I was so glad Uncle Wick mentioned Dad's name. I hoped everybody in the room had heard it and been reminded that the colonel was in our house like a second fiddle.

The colonel's daughter sized me up with dagger eyes, as if there were a territorial war at play. But I didn't care because Finley stood beside me, and the way I saw it, she was in our house by default.

12

The nine-drawer mahogany sideboard in the dining room was laid buffet style, with a twenty-pound turkey on a silver server beside a stack of Royal Crown Derby china and folded green linens beneath sterling Melrose cutlery. Green beans with slivered almonds, corn pudding, squash casserole, sliced cranberry, cornbread, and Ella's incomparable gravy were arranged to the point that nobody knew where to start. We all stood awkwardly, deferring to each other, saying, "You start. No, you start. No, please, go ahead. I'll go after you," until it became dizzying.

Because Miss Mycroft was too feeble to do for herself, Mom took the initiative by assembling her plate, calling over her shoulder, "Now, Helen, what will you have?" The colonel had lowered Miss Mycroft onto one of the petit-point high-backed chairs, where she sat cocking her head like a bird on a wire, trying to hide her embarrassment over being the center of attention. Beneath the tear-dropped Austrian crystal chandelier—bigger and heavier than the one in the card room—the dining room table glowed. My grandmother's pair of five-prong sterling candelabras flickered like torches, ornate and imposing on a green satin runner, casting liquid shadows upon the silver chargers. The dining room swam with the mingled aroma of the feast, and the boxwood centerpiece, laced through with holly whose branches Mom and Ella had pilfered from Elmwood Cemetery when they thought no one was looking.

"Now then, Finley," Miss Mycroft said, "tell me. You play the guitar?" She smoothed the napkin on her lap and spoke in a hearing-impaired voice unaware of its own volume. I knew Miss Mycroft only made conversation when she stabbed at any old subject just to get herself heard.

"That's right, Finley plays the guitar," Belle said, leaning forward from the other end of the table to answer her late daughter-in-law's septuagenarian sister.

"Well, that's lovely," Miss Mycroft responded, her frozen smile disproportionately pleased with what was in play. "How are you liking Memphis University School?"

Finley pivoted in his seat and started to say something. "I—"

"He's in his sophomore year," Belle shouted.

"What's that?" Miss Mycroft cupped a hand to her ear.

"Helen, Finley is in his sophomore year," Belle over-enunciated.

"Belle, Helen can hear for herself," the colonel barked. His irritated tone came so abruptly it felt like cold water had been splashed on my face.

I looked at Mom, who sat smiling, following along with the exchange as if it were completely normal. Embarrassed as I was for Belle, I was more curious about her reaction and couldn't stop myself from sneaking a glance her way. I thought it'd be perfectly reasonable for her to rebuke her sixty-year-old son, but Belle kept a serene smile and lowered her head as if suddenly interested in something on her plate.

Tucker Hudson rerouted the moment. He was the congenial sort, married to the colonel's daughter, Margaret, for almost six years and was obviously versed in the family dynamic. Tucker was the kind of tassel-loafered, buttoned-down guy "you could take anywhere" because "he comes from a good family," as my mother once claimed. Good-looking in a fresh-faced, nonthreatening way, he instinctually knew every functional conversational ploy aimed at social niceties.

Tucker leaned back and laughed with perfect timing. "Finley can't get a word in edgewise, for all the interest in him, can he, Millie?" He beamed his blues eyes at me.

I couldn't help but blush at the sudden attention.

Margaret glared steely-eyed across the table, a "how dare you attract the acknowledgement of my husband" kind of look.

"Finley, maybe you could play something for us later," Uncle Wick encouraged, rattling his Scotch on the rocks before draining the last swig.

"I'm not that kind of player," Finley explained. "I mean, I would if I were. I'm just not a soloist. I play in a band."

"Finley plays lead guitar," I clarified, even though I knew nobody at the table knew what that meant.

Tucker nodded, cool for the first time in his life, as if he knew about rock-n-roll, as if there were a world beyond the neat grid of upper-crust Memphis he knew something about. I mistrusted this sudden interest in Finley. The way everyone looked at him, with his angular face and his long russet hair, he may as well have been an alien at the table, dressed up like Bowie on the cover of *Ziggy Stardust*, for all the common ground he had with the colonel's conservative family.

Tito appeared carrying tongs and a silver biscuit box, from behind the green embroidered partition off the butler's pantry. She went to Mom's left, then circled the table one by one without the employment of words. The energy exchanged between Tito and the colonel spoke volumes. Tito bowed deferentially, and the colonel snatched for the tongs and dove in for himself.

"Thank you, Tito," I said when she got to me.

Her barely audible two-noted "Umm-hmm" carried her next to Finley, who looked up at her and winked.

Margaret and Tucker's two children sat in the alcove at the end of the dining room, where two high-backed settees faced each other, above a low marble table. Something about the graceful fall of the amber draperies cascading over the floor-to-ceiling windows caught the fascination of their little boy who, bored with his sequester, reached out and tugged one of the draperies from its hooks. Down the panel cascaded, top-heavy onto the table, upsetting two fragile glasses filled with apple juice. The sound of shattering glass on the tile floor made such a startling racket that everyone jumped.

Margaret rushed to the alcove, saying, "Oh, Posey, I'm so sorry" and taking a napkin, she dabbed at the spreading stain. Pulling her little boy up, she said, "Honey, are you all right?"

The colonel split the air with, "Don't placate that child, Margaret. Just look what he's done."

"Daddy, it was an accident," Margaret whined, leading her crying child out of the alcove by his hand.

"Go sit him in the card room," the colonel instructed. "For the love of God, does he not know any better?"

My mother stood. "Margaret, why don't we take him upstairs and get him out of those wet pants?"

"Posey, I said let the boy go sit in the card room," the colonel reiterated.

Finley leaned over to me and whispered, "Strap yourself in."

"He needs to learn about consequences," the colonel bellowed.

"He's not even *five*," Mom returned. "I'm taking him upstairs."

"You're not," the colonel stated.

Tucker moved his chair back. "Posey, I'll take him up."

"Underneath this roof, he'll go where I say," the colonel roared. "Ella?"

Ella materialized from behind the partition. "Yes, sir, Mr. Henry."

"Take this child into the kitchen with you," he said, and Ella didn't skip a beat. She reached her big callused hand to the child.

Just as he began to accept it, Mom said, "This is ridiculous. Here, come with me."

The sting of unbridled pride lit fire under the colonel's feet. He hauled himself up from his chair, threw his napkin on the table in a final statement, and left the dining room in a major huff.

"Well, I've never," Belle said.

"The child needs to be cleaned up," Miss Mycroft put in.

"Helen, Posey's taking him," Belle said, raising her voice.

Uncle Wick swiveled his head toward Ella. "Ella, do you have a second to get me another Scotch?"

"Yes, sir." Ella took his glass.

A cadence of sound effects resounded from the back hall—the back door opening and slamming, metal grate rocking, car door opening and thwacking shut, ignition firing, car backing out, sonic attrition as the car screeched down the driveway, attenuation to silence.

The colonel would be gone until after midnight, I figured.

"Dramatic enough for you?" Finley whispered to me, then pushed out his chair and stood.

"Merry Christmas," I whispered back.

I got up and walked through the butler's pantry. Entering the kitchen, I heard Ella muttering to Rosa Mae and Tito. "Mm-hm, hand to God, I ain't lying. When Mr. Henry moved in, he brought his clothes and his dog. All this here's Miz Posey's. He ain't got no bidness carrying on this away 'neath this roof."

"Where'd he go?' I asked Ella, startling her with my presence.

"He gone," she said, turning to face me.

Mom sashayed into the kitchen. She patted her hair and presented a smile in that way Southern women do when they're observing the art of denial. "Ella," she said, "I believe we're about ready for dessert."

On the weekends, Finley and I drifted to freedom from the enclave of Kensington Park because Mom didn't much care where we went. She rarely asked. We'd take to the streets of East Parkway on foot, then cross to Madison Avenue where Overton Square drifted in a misaligned pattern without a central plan. The Square was midtown Memphis's version of the French Quarter—a hodgepodge of novelty shops, restaurants, and hole-in-the-wall beer dives.

The musty scrambling of an aged bookstore abutted the record store Finley liked, which sold vinyl imports and homegrown recordings in plastic casings.

A head shop with flickering neon signage and paraphernalia for the illegal substance smoker was manned by its bearded proprietor, who would have been incongruous anywhere else, and an herbal tea and incense emporium called Maggie's Pharm lay up a flight of stairs behind T.G.I. Friday's. The Square was the pinnacle of urban grandeur to Finley and me. We were spellbound in our wide-eyed autonomy as we explored its corridors, trying to decipher a Southern culture in the midst of a bad case of growing pains.

In the mid-1970s, everything about the Mississippi Delta was in a rapid state of flux as native cities like Memphis tried to establish a new direction from the civil unrest of the turbulent '60s. Nowhere was this more evident in Memphis than in the music that sprang from its streetwise, shaggy-haired youth. In the '70s, Memphis music personified the search for identity from hidden alleyways where newly integrated venues lay behind unmarked doors found only by word of mouth. Inside the dark clubs lay the gritty underbelly to my mother's genteel Memphis, which Finley ferreted out in that serendipitous, inexplicable way that magically comes to boys in the process of finding their footing.

It was as if an invisible veil separated two discrepant worlds and, unbeknownst to Mom, Finley would sneak out at night, heeding a musical call as it beckoned from the tantalizing atmosphere. Although I always knew where Finley was going, I never once let on. I understood intuitively that Finley's creative promptings were piqued, that he followed his instinct like water seeking its own level. Upon the seething ground of Memphis's sultry palette of ribs and blues and racial strife, my brother had begun his search for identity, like a phoenix rising from the ashes of a burned Minnesota childhood.

At ten forty-five on a Thursday night, Eddie Dean scratched on my bedroom door. He'd let himself in through the back porch and climbed the front stairs like a sleuth in the night, only to find Finley's bedroom door locked.

"Millie," I heard him whisper through my door as I lay in my twilight sleep.

I rose heavily from my bed and opened the door.

"Hey, sorry," he said, looking at me in my long tee-shirt, then shouldering his way in. His denim jacket was worn punk-style, the collar popped up and the buttons undone.

"Just going through there," Eddie said, then he sidled alongside my other twin bed and disappeared through the bathroom door. Seconds later he reappeared. "Where's Finley?"

"I don't know," I said, crossing my arms over my chest, suddenly self-conscious.

"Is he already gone?"

"Gone where?" I asked.

"The Well. Is the car here?"

"I don't know." I went to the window between my twin beds and looked over the back driveway. "I don't see the car. I guess he's gone."

"Your parents asleep?" Eddie pressed.

"They usually are at this hour, and stop calling the colonel my parent. I can't even bring myself to call him my stepfather."

"Stop being a brat," Eddie said, although he was smiling. He stood with his hands in his pockets, furrowed his brow, then checked the watch on his left wrist. "Finley must have gone on ahead. Probably forgot I was coming." He stood for a minute, considering. "You wanna come?"

I didn't hesitate. "Yeah, where'd you park your car?"

"Out front."

"I'll meet you out there in five."

When the door closed, I scrambled. I threw on jeans and a sweater, went to the closet, retrieved a coat, slid into shoes, and stepped down the back stairs on tiptoe. Outside, the tip of Eddie's Marlboro sparked beneath the grinding of his boot. I got in his blue Chevy and closed the door.

Way down Madison, The Well had an unmarked door that matched the night color of the dark grainy sidewalk. The door looked battered, as did everything else about The Well. The club was situated on a shady, vacuous part of Madison that had little of consequence around it, and its name was apropos. There were no windows in the dungeon-like cavern, its walls were painted black, and its concrete floors were sticky from spilled beer. Something taboo and menacing hovered in the atmosphere, something earthy and prohibitive, the lure from the other side of the tracks, and you were cool if the bouncers looked you over and didn't find you lacking. Admittance had nothing to do with the drinking age and everything to do with a holier-than-thou, irreverent attitude, which Eddie Dean mastered. I walked through the door in Eddie's wake, my presence vetted and stamped with a day-glow X of approval on the back of my hand.

I couldn't find Finley because it was dark inside and it seemed everybody wore black. Black jeans, black leather jackets, black boots, as if it were the fashion statement of individuality, or the uniform of the too-cool-for-school nonconformist, even though it was the standard everywhere I looked. Four-deep at the bar and the air was so choked with smoke I couldn't make out anything over two yards in front of me. We weaved through the singular room where everyone was taller than me, larger than me, heavier than me.

Most people were focused on the stage, where a red filtered spotlight hit the back wall at a five-foot rise. I couldn't tell if a smoke machine was somewhere at the edge of the stage, or if the gray spectral waves drifting before the lights came from the smoke of the crowd. Once my eyes adjusted to the dim light, I saw five people on stage—four clad in black, the other red-golden haired, with an unbuttoned flannel shirt floating over a dark blue tee. It took me a second to realize I was looking at a dancing Finley.

I'd never seen anyone so unselfconscious, so much a part of a primal rhythm that it seemed he melded with something fluid, as if he were riding a dynamic wave of sound. The angle of his head indicated he actively listened to something whose parts were more important than its sum. He played lead guitar as if he were carrying on a conversation—call and recall, question and response—and the subtlety of his swaying stance was almost imperceptible to the audience, but I knew Finley well enough to know he danced to something he heard in his head.

Eddie gave me his Cheshire cat smile and nudged me with his elbow, then pointed to Finley. I shrugged in a who-knew kind of gesture, although in a way, I wasn't surprised in the least. My chest throbbed from the resonance of the bass and kick drum, in an angst-ridden, electric-guitar-driven, Moog synthesizer-infused song that pulsed like a proclamation of youth. The lead singer was spellbinding in his writhing—with a dark-haired, pretty-boy femininity. I wondered where Finley had met him because he wasn't like anyone he'd ever brought home to Kensington Park.

I stayed next to Eddie, pretending not to notice when he took a discreet hit off a joint passed down a zigzag line of strangers. Inside The Well, it was too loud to hear anybody talking. I had no idea what Eddie wanted when he screamed in my ear.

"What?" I screamed back.

"Over there," Eddie yelled, pointing.

"Where?"

"The guy that just walked in," Eddie said, narrowing his eyes.

I turned and saw an angular, painfully thin guy dressed in black, with metal chains hanging loosely from his belt. He was wildly gesticulating to the bouncer by the door, but they stood too far away for me to tell what was happening. There was no way I could have known he was the original guitar player in the band. Or that he'd arrived late to consequences, that Finley was on stage in his stead, or that his temper would flare to a degree that he'd take out later on Finley.

Eddie always knew when trouble was coming. He grabbed me by the arm and pulled me through the crowd to the side of the stage. I saw him trying to catch Finley's attention, but Finley was in his own world and oblivious.

Later, when we were out on the sidewalk in front of The Well, the trouble began. We were walking to our cars in the echoing stillness of the midnight hour on Madison. Few cars passed on the street and the wind snarled with the dry bite of winter. Finley put his guitar case down to shrug into his coat. None of us heard anybody behind us until the second the guitar player shoved Finley from behind, then swung an angry foot that kicked Finley's guitar with such force, it sent the fragile instrument flipping to the street. Eddie was on it quick as lightning, but it took Finley a startled second to register. He'd been jolted to unsteady footing, and when he turned around, Eddie was already on the guy, having thrown a punch to his face and now ducking and weaving with alley cat grace.

"Keep your boyfriend offa me," the guy yelled at Finley, his chin in the air as he lunged back from Eddie's reach. "I ain't interested in your boyfriend. I want *you*. Come on," he roared.

But Eddie was not deterred. He kept his dancing momentum and went for the guy repeatedly until Finley sprang forward, knocking the guy backward with a landed blow to the left side of his head. When the guy went down, Finley straddled him, pinning his arms to the ground overhead as he squirmed and kicked, head thrashing side to side while Finley yelled, "Give it up," and Eddie yelled, "Go for it, Finley. Kick his—"

The guitar player seethed, screaming filth and derogatory epithets toward Finley and Eddie.

"Finley, stop," I screamed again and again, and before I knew it, Finley had tumbled side over side, with the guitar player trying to pin him face down to the sidewalk.

Eddie yanked the guy's head back by the hair, freeing Finley to scramble up, where he next threw his nemesis down and kicked him in the side as he tried to rise, grabbing desperately for Finley's ankles, until two bouncers came running, one with a bully-club poised and threatening to swing, yelling, "Break it up. Now. I'll beat the life out of all y'all," while the other put Eddie in a bent-elbowed headlock pulling him out of the fray.

There was a gash on Finley's face where it'd hit the sidewalk, and his shirt was splattered with blood. He paced like a thwarted fighter nowhere near ready to quit, and his unbridled energy surged without recourse in a rage I'd never known he possessed. I was stunned and useless, acutely aware that I was unqualified to be in this testosterone-fueled chaos. I stayed in a delayed catatonia driven by shock, too horrified to register what had just happened. My cognizance of the fact that we were out on a school night without Mom's knowledge, coupled with the evidence of our crime all over my brother's face made me think there'd be no avoiding punishment.

But miraculously, we skated by undetected. Finley said days later that we'd gotten lucky, that one of the bouncers could have justifiably called the cops and it would have ended with a precinct call to Mom in the dead of the night. God only knew what the colonel would have done had he ever found out. He probably would have clenched his square jaw in that disapproving, passive-aggressive way of his, and then counseled Mom behind our backs to levy something severe. But I wasn't interested in imagining a worst-case scenario. I was too surprised to discover the sage-like Finley had a wellspring of rage he knew how to call forth with his fists.

13

Among the twenty-six houses in Kensington Park, one in particular stood out prominently because of the fifty-foot steps at the top of its sloping front yard. Surrounded by lawn velvet as a golf course, the five detached steps were made of weathered marble that complemented the sprawling columned veranda. Massive, symmetrical, and regal, the house's seven French doors were spaced evenly in front and covered in ironwork crafted in 1917, the year it was built. Limestone statuary punctuated the grounds with old-world European flair, setting the scene for the Northrup family, whose patriarch was named James Winslow, a prominent Memphis figure who had made his fortune from a successful chain of grocery stores throughout the lower Southeast.

The Northrups were our closest neighbor, so close that our yards were adjoined by a beaten path through the azalea bushes that J.W.'s daughter Lucy and I wore ragged after we'd fallen in cahoots. I spent many afternoons with Lucy in the exquisite house, which was tended to by a maid, a nanny, a butler, a cook, and a chauffeur. It had a fine mixture of eccentric opulence and relaxed Southern charm, and many of its rooms were large enough to park a plane. There were separate wings off the atrium for Lucy's parents, who appeared to me as different from each other as night and day. J.W. was serious and stolid and there was something authoritative and square about his steady short stature. He was sixteen years older than Twyla, his sensuous, dark-haired, doe-eyed wife.

As children, Lucy and I tiptoed across the Persian rug in J.W.'s well-appointed library, with its hand-carved mantel flanked by toile draperies and dappled green built-in bookshelves, on our way to find Twyla, who never turned us away. Twyla hustled us into her car and drove us out to what we called the sticks of Collierville, where the Northrup family farm sprawled like a fantasy on two hundred and thirty wondrous acres of woodland.

Inevitably, on the long road through the agrarian land, one of Twyla's three children would squeal, "Mamma, drive like an old lady," and Twyla would never disappoint. She'd scrunch her shoulders forward, her head barely higher than the wheel, and rock the steering wheel unsteadily to our rapturous laughter. She was an object of fascination in my early adolescence—one part Bohemian earth-mother, one part coiffed Southern belle.

I spent many carefree weekends with the Northrups in their pastoral wonderland. There were goats and peacocks, horses in a cavernous stable, and a rambling trail through the haunted woods all the way to a dam at the far end of the lake. A thirty-year-old black man named Cecil lived in a four-room, timbered house by the side of the lake with his wife, four kids, and an arsenal of shotguns. He was keeper of the demesne, master of all he surveyed, and he knew every inch of the woods and all its attendant dangers.

J.W. wasn't always in attendance, but when he was, the farm took on the aura of a country gentleman's estate—aged whisky on the porch in the late afternoon, and J.W. sitting with his cohorts, discussing the Civil War as if they knew all the players personally and it was still going on down the road. Intellects and Southern-landed gentry populated J.W.'s world. They gathered on the porch exchanging stories while Twyla had Cecil pull the horse and carriage round front and outfitted us in country costumes of patterned dresses and plumed hats. They then encouraged us to take to the woods on an adventure.

But J.W. had a side of him that was fun, albeit the ceremonious kind. He was the proud owner of a maritime cannon that was stationed permanently on the worn red-brick steps to the main house, built in 1852 as a country inn for travelers. On special occasions, such as the Fourth of July, a birthday, or any celebration deemed worthy, J.W. would gather the troops, hold forth with a short speech, and fire the cannon in a boom that shook the world.

On the night of J.W.'s last birthday in Kensington Park, he donned a tuxedo and hosted a party on the lawn, ostensibly to celebrate the turning of a year. All the guests, though wise to the truth of his failing health, went right along with the ruse. He and Twyla flew in oysters, crawdaddies, gumbo, and a jazz band from the heart of New Orleans, and J.W. made a memorable though brief appearance when the guests were well into their third and fourth drinks. Although he was a taciturn man, too dignified to mention the cancer laying waste to his body, he knew how to orchestrate an exceptional party. J.W. Northrup was not the kind of man to take to his sickbed when facing his demise, because he was old-world South. He was the kind to render a grand goodbye.

It seemed everybody in my sphere of influence was there that night, all ages from Mom's group down to their children, most of whom I knew from Hutchison and MUS. In the humid night air, the front and back yards were aglow in the thermal incandescence of torches and tea-lights, spilling over the environs in a gauzy halo of luminosity. On the wooden dance floor below the marble stairs, a stage held a ten-piece band who wore maroon tuxedos and rocked with swing and R&B standards. There wasn't a person in the crowd that night without a mixed drink in their hand, which the waiters kept coming.

My mother had once tossed up the line, "You know, people who don't drink are no fun," and in those pre-treatment days, before admitting a problem with alcohol was acceptable, my mother's group drank like there was no tomorrow. But it freed them up, relaxed their carefully caged images, and leveled the social playing field with a magnanimity that suspended their judgment, until the next morning. Never was there a group with more over-the-top women: they were beautiful, gregarious, and chimed like silver bells and took the lead in two-and-a-half-inch heels beneath knee-length cocktail dresses, spritzed heavily in clouds of perfume, while their husbands played second fiddle in complementary sport coats and ties.

At fifteen, I learned there's a fine line between cute and tacky in a Southern woman's dress. If my mother was any example, choosing a cocktail dress for a party wasn't something taken lightly. She was completely aware she'd be scrutinized—not in the moment, but on the back end, when a network of phone calls erupted to discuss the party the next day.

"Mom's looking for you," Finley said. He'd appeared beside me with an iced Wild Turkey in a tall plastic cup. He and Fatty Thompson had been over by the band, eyeing their equipment. A genial, likable fellow, Southern as the soil, Fatty was the son of Mom's childhood friends who had married the day after high school graduation. Fatty wasn't fat anymore, but he was before he slimmed down around age fourteen. His given name was Jared, after his father, but the whole world still called him Fatty because once a Southerner gets ahold of a nickname, it tends to stick.

"You coming out with us later?" Fatty asked me.

"Where y'all going?" I wanted to know.

"Down to the river. Eddie will be down there with a keg."

"She'll ride with me," Finley said to Fatty, putting an end to any other ideas. Every once in a while, when I least expected it, Finley slipped into protective-older-brother mode, and it flattered me.

"Where's Mom?" I asked, and Finley pointed to a group of circular tables draped in white linen up the yard. I'd been standing with a group of my girlfriends—Lucy and Tama and Cissy and Louise. We'd been watching our friend, Laurie, dancing in front of the stage with an older guy. We were at that stage in our youth when something like that was a big deal.

I turned and climbed the manicured berm of the lawn in the direction of the tables, where I came across J.W. standing on the steps with a gaggle of young girls, all my and Lucy's friends, who'd clustered around him, preening and posing for a photographer. The photograph would become one for the archives.

"There you are," Mom said when I found her. "Come meet Shelby. He hasn't seen you since you were two." Mom guided me by my elbow to an eight-top table, riddled with half-filled plates and diluted liquor in plastic cups, where her friends flitted and flirted like hormonal teenagers.

Shelby rose when he saw my mother coming. He was her childhood friend, now transplanted to Charleston, and he beamed at me in his lime-green linen jacket. "Well, Posey, she looks just like you," Shelby said as if I weren't standing right there.

I started to say I looked more like my father, but I spied the colonel snaking his way forward and decided to keep my mouth shut and take Shelby's offered hand.

"Millie, you having a good time?" the colonel asked, an anticipatory high note in his cheery voice. For one blind instance, he could have fooled me into thinking he cared.

"Yes, sir," I answered.

"I see all your friends are here. Finley's too."

"Yeah, most of them," I said.

"I remember Millie when she could fit in your hand," Shelby said to the colonel. "Posey put me up at the house in Wayzata, the one time I had cause to go to Minnesota."

"Do tell," the colonel encouraged. "When was this?"

"Lemma think back. When was that, Posey? Early sixties?"

"It was sixty-two," Mom said for a fact.

"I'm telling you, Posey was in hog heaven up there in Minnesota. The belle of the ball everywhere she went. You been back to Minnesota since you left, Millie?" Shelby turned his eyes to me.

"No, sir, not yet," I answered.

"Well, narrow escape you not being raised a Yankee, thank God. Better you're down here with your own people. Girls up there don't even make their debut."

"Not everybody knows how to do," the colonel said and laughed. When he was out in public, the colonel morphed into one of those genial, back-slapping guys with a ready laugh, and it made me uneasy. I never knew how to relate to his alter-ego, but I was certain of one thing—it'd be nowhere around in the morning.

Under the marquee down the yard, a commotion brewed. I saw a clearing spreading before the stage, so I tripped down lightly to see what was afoot. The band leader led a dignified black man in white coat and bow tie to the stage, where he began a low-throated rendition of "Ol' Man River" that reverberated from the depths of his haunted soul. I watched Finley chumming it up with a group of friends a few yards away, then the boom of fireworks rattled the sky in starlit intervals, with trailing streamers of green and gold set off in bursts of thunder.

Finley appeared at my right. "Ready, set, go," he whispered in my ear as a final round of applause thinned the crowd.

Eddie Dean's car was parked at the north end of Tom Lee Park, in plain sight of the Memphis/Arkansas Bridge, which straddles the Mississippi River and stakes its claim in skywriting in the flow of a graceful letter M. The ember of his cigarette glowed as he took off his jean jacket and laid it beside the twenty-gallon keg he had in the open trunk of his car. He looked up when he saw Finley and me approaching with Fatty and a girl he'd brought from the party close at our heels. Word had spread through our age group at the Northrups' party to meet down by the river, which was where we all went when we weren't ready for the night to end.

There was a certain spot in Tom Lee Park's mile-long riverside stretch that we never had to specify because we called it our own—that unobstructed grassy area right over the river, where we could hear the river bubbling past in its muddy opaque flow. The slamming of car doors clapped behind us as girls took off their heels to walk barefoot along the bluff in their thin party dresses and Hove perfume, procured in New Orleans. A breeze kicked up from the river to float the latest from the Isley Brothers from the stereo speakers in Percy's Jeep. Blankets were arranged and cups passed around in this starlit Memphis night, sultry and loose as a slip dress.

"You best cut that down before we get busted." Eddie nodded to Percy. "You don't have to cut it off, just cut it down to low."

"I've got a better idea," Percy said. "Finley, you bring your guitar?"

"Always," Finley said. He didn't have to be asked twice. He went back to the car and returned with his case, then sat down on a blanket, which was filled seconds later by a group of fawning girls.

Eddie paced around carrying a fifth of whisky. He was the master of ceremonies, the man on the case, and his eyes scanned the circumference out of habit because Eddie always liked to know what was happening behind his back.

"You might wanna quit flashing that bottle around," Allen said, cocking his head toward Eddie. "If the cops come, they'll haul you off to jail. Keg in your trunk and you flashing that around, it'll be all over."

"They wouldn't carry me off. I'm in with the boys," Eddie stated. "My uncle's on the force. Believe me, I've tested this one twice." Eddie leaned over and passed the bottle to Finley, who rested his elbow on his guitar as he took a good pull.

Out of the corner of my eye, I saw a button-down guy named Conrad Fahey sauntering over the bluffs toward us, carrying something in his left hand. He was captain of the MUS football team and an all-around star athlete, sacred by all at the school. Conrad was so good-looking, with his straight dark hair and chiseled features, he had God-like status with the girls at Hutchison. Two years ahead at MUS, Conrad had struck up a friendship with Finley because he had a similar musical aptitude. He played the drums with a natural-born rhythm that came from the same source as his athletic prowess.

"All right, now we're talking," Finley said smoothly, making room for Conrad on the blanket. Conrad lowered lightly for such a built guy. He settled a pair of goat-skin bongo drums on his lap and launched into a boom-ba-boom-bam, scatta-tap-tap, while Finley slid from a thrashing rhythm to a finger-picking lead. Girls sprang up from the blanket and swayed in barefoot two-steps, and Eddie produced a harmonica, which he played with sprightly personality. Round and round the whisky bottle was passed, and when it was spent, another magically appeared. Behind us, a handful of boys fanned out. They threw a football back and forth and arched it through the night air, yelling, "Give it here," and "I got it," before hurling it up again.

Conrad was close enough to Finley that he could see his unhealed cut from that night at The Well. "Wait a minute," Conrad said. "How'd you get that?"

"Don't worry about it, it's nothing," Finley deflected.

"Nothing?" Eddie butted in. "You should have seen him jump that low-life the other night at The Well. The guy came out swinging at Finley. It was way more than nothing."

"You jumped him? Why'd you do that? Didn't you swing back?" Conrad asked. He was a guy with experience, a guy who knew his way around a fight.

"Well, yeah, eventually," Finley said. "But the guy was going for my knees."

"Still, next time use your right hook," Conrad encouraged. The excitement in his tone was evident. He embraced the subject with all the enthusiasm of a coach giving a tutorial.

"I'm left-handed," Finley said.

"No, you're not, Finley. You're ambidextrous," I interjected.

"That doesn't matter, Millie. One arm's always gonna be stronger," Finley said.

Conrad rose to his full power and stepped a couple of yards away from the blanket. "Here we go. Get up, let me show you."

"Finley, don't be an idiot," Eddie said. "You're outta your league."

"No, I'm not. I can take him," Finley said. He delivered the line with such certainty that I believed him.

"I'm not gonna hit you, I'm just going to demonstrate," Conrad assured. "I won't make contact."

"No, come on. Go on and give me your best," Finley said.

"No way, Jose. I'll hurt you."

"Finley, need I remind you Conrad's an all-state boxer?" Percy warned.

"You think I care?" Finley said.

"I think you're *gonna* care," Percy answered.

"Oh God, here we go," Allen said as he stood on the sidelines, watching Finley bounce on the balls of his feet.

Conrad didn't move as Finley danced around. He stood eyeing his lanky frame with a bemused half-smile on his face.

Quick as an instant, Finley swung right as Conrad leaned back out of his reach. Finley came at him again, once, twice, a third time, but Conrad's feet never shifted.

"Come on, what's stopping you?" Finley taunted.

"Finley, I'm not gonna take you," Conrad said.

"Only one way to show me what you've got in mind," Finley said, swinging at Conrad. Then *thwack*, a landed blow from Conrad on Finley's face catapulted him backward to the ground. Getting up, Finley acted as if he took it in stride, but I could tell he was baffled. I knew Finley well enough to know the surprise on his face was there because he thought himself infallible.

14

In the spring of Finley's senior year, the outside world found its way to MUS through newly blurred parameters laid lax by the loosened grip of late-1970s Memphis. The boys wore their hair long, their collars unbuttoned, and their blazers undone. Most of the students knew where they'd be attending college the following September, and the overall energy of the graduating class switched to glide, in view of the light at the end of the tunnel.

They played Frisbee in the school's parking lot and loitered on the athletic field during free time, musing on what life would become after graduation. The world was their oyster; they had earned it, and to celebrate their pending freedom, Finley had taken it upon himself to organize a school-sanctioned music festival on MUS's grounds. Billed "Spring Fling," it was held on the Friday before graduation. There was no dress code that day, and the neighboring girls from Hutchison's upper school had been invited. They erected a stage in the middle of the athletic field, and musicians hot on Memphis's music scene came to the campus for the first time in their lives.

Finley acted as both emcee and intermediary at an event the likes of which had never been seen on campus, and because I was part of Hutchison's upper school, I attended what I saw as a blending of my brother's disparate worlds.

Finley stood lithely behind the standing microphone as both artist and academic, his long, side-swept hair rustling collar-length in the spring's gentle air. For someone with such a magnetic presence, there was something tentative about his awkward beauty. Something subtle and immature on its burgeoning way from adolescence to the full power he would come to own. But I saw signs in his self-possession. There was something so fitting about Finley standing on stage, and, as I watched him, it crossed my mind that I had been given a glimpse into his future. He seemed as relaxed as a lion in his den with all the musical equipment around him. And, for some reason, my eyes stayed riveted on his long, elegant fingers as they rested on the microphone. They were pretty fingers, thin and graceful as a ballerina's, God-designed for Finley's path ahead.

It's funny how you can know someone your entire life and never zero in on their beauty until you see them perform some inconsequential gesture, and suddenly you are awakened by it.

"Millie," Eddie Dean said as he sidled beside me, all long-legged and blond-haired, flashing his whiplash smile. "Who let you out of your cage?"

"Shut up, Eddie. What about you? Who let you cross to the other side of the tracks?"

"What, you didn't hear MUS lets in riffraff?"

"No, but I always knew you were good at weaseling into places you don't belong. Glad you wore Levi's and that natty green tee-shirt. You went out of your way not to blend in," I bantered.

Eddie hovered his blue-eyed gaze over me. "Come on. I'm part of this event's brass—Finley had me go get Furry Lewis."

I was duly impressed to think that anybody had been able to coerce the iconic country blues guitarist, now in his eighties, to come out anywhere, much less MUS. Everyone who followed Furry Lewis knew he hadn't played in public in far too many years.

"Finley had you go get him?" I asked, making sure I'd heard him right.

"Finley knows Furry. You didn't know that?"

"No."

"You don't know much, do you? Finley's tapped in with the powers that be. What you don't get is it's not that he knows them, it's more like they know him. Anyway, you seen Percy or Allen?"

"Not yet," I said. "But I'm sure they're around here somewhere."

In the crowd, boys and girls weaved in groups and pairs, strutting and preening in vibrant spring colors, casting anticipatory eyes to Finley on stage who now spoke into the microphone.

"Welcome to the first MUS Spring Fling. I'm Finley Crossan, and this is a seminal moment for MUS. The class of 1977 is bequeathing subsequent graduating classes a musical standard to uphold. And to show you all exactly what this standard is, let's get started. Ladies and gentlemen, I give you the Tommy Hohen Band."

Clapping and emphatic whistles erupted as five musicians from midtown Memphis took to the stage—three boys and two girls, all perfectly disheveled in their Bohemian cool, looking enviously incongruous on the staid playing field of the academically advantaged. They plugged instruments into amplifiers and tore through a five-song set of original songs. The girls singing back-up swayed in slinky, slithering movements, while Tommy Hohen switched between keyboards and an electric guitar, looking as compelling as a young Jim

Morrison in tight leather, ringing out melodic vocals tinged with rebellion in the kind of unselfconscious artistry that demonstrates the very viscera of the artist and holds up a mirror to everyone else, shaming them with what they are not. The John Byrd Band—an electric acoustic threesome who asked Finley to play with the band—came next. Finley played with rhythmic fluidity, and many in the audience saw his talent for the first time.

When Furry Lewis was helped to a straight-back chair on stage as the closing act, most everyone took photographs, capturing one of his last unpublicized performances. I was so proud of Finley, I was beside myself, yet couldn't abate the pangs of our pending separation, knowing as I did that he'd accepted a four-year scholarship from the University of Virginia. Brown University, as well as Stanford, had offered the same, but Mom tipped the scales in UVA's favor when she told Finley, "You can go to Brown or Stanford as a poor student, or you can attend UVA with money."

And so, come the end of summer, Finley would be Virginia-bound and I would be left alone with Mom and the colonel at 79 Kensington Park.

Somewhere in the first few months of Finley's absence, 79 Kensington Park changed frequency, giving the colonel's disapproving energy wide berth to expand unencumbered into every corner of the house. Every morning, the colonel rose with a list of things that were wrong. He'd take his dog outside and not notice Kensington Park's serene solitude. He didn't appreciate the birds, the flowers, or the majestic trees gracing the soft haven like fastidiously appointed art. His supervisory gaze gravitated to every aberration on the grounds, as if he were scanning for something to fix his irritation upon, which etched a permanent furrow on his brow and slapped lines around his lips from holding a permanent scowl.

"Posey," he roared one Friday morning, marching into the entrance hall from the driveway. "*Somebody* didn't lock the door under the portico."

I knew right away that "somebody" meant me.

"That be me, Mr. Henry," Ella called from the kitchen, which wasn't the truth at all, but I recalled Ella once telling me she had nothing to lose. "Good news is, I ain't got no dog in the fight round here," she told me. "At the end of the day, I gets my purse and goes home."

I sat at the kitchen table, waiting to leave for school, when Mom walked in and rolled her eyes. The colonel was four paces behind her, walking in tight, urgent steps as if a fire blazed somewhere in the house, begging to be put out. He bellied up to the counter, poured his second cup of coffee, scooted the coffee machine to some imagined rightful angle, then opened the dishwasher and rearranged it with a clatter, suggesting some lazy idiot had loaded it wrong.

Ella had an uncanny aptitude for keeping her back to the colonel. She ironed out pie crust on the counter with a marble rolling pin, and although she'd already flattened the dough within an inch of its life, she kept up the task with continued brute force.

Mom sat at the kitchen table and began constructing a list with pencil on paper. I was in a puss and couldn't hide it; the boy I currently had a crush on hadn't called when he said he would.

"What's wrong with you?" Mom glanced at my pout.

Ella answered for me. "It Friday, and the boy she eyeing ain't called for the weekend."

"Well, as Gaga would say, when he does call, tell him he's put you in your place, and you think you'll stay there."

"It's not that big a deal. We're not dating, we're just friends," I qualified, keenly aware the colonel was still in the room.

"It's always like that at your age, but I predict someday soon you'll be seriously dating. You have to figure this out now. You have to know how to play the game."

"Posey, don't teach her to play games," the colonel flared.

My mother ignored him, continuing on. "Gaga would also say, 'Put a higher price on yourself.' If you don't, nobody else will."

The colonel straightened from the dishwasher, glared at my mother, then clipped from the room and up the back stairs.

"A man ain't got no bidness in the kitchen," Ella said under her breath.

"Oh, who cares, Ella?" Mom said. "Let him think he's doing something."

The colonel returned moments later, carrying an armful of button-down shirts. "Not too much starch on these, Ella. Just the collar and cuffs," he instructed, putting the bundle on the counter.

"Yessir," Ella said, not meeting his eyes.

"Posey, I know I told you not to let Ella in my office," the colonel said, as if Ella had left the room.

"That's right. I know that." Mom said.

"I knows it too, Mr. Henry," Ella said. "I ain't been up there."

"Then how'd my chair get pushed up under my desk?"

"I did that," Mom said. "I'm getting the daybed up there reupholstered."

With a look that weighed whom to rebuke, the colonel levied his gaze from Mom to Ella then back again. "What for?" he challenged.

"It hasn't been done since Dr. Joe had it," Mom answered.

"Well, check with me before you settle on anything." The colonel wheeled toward the back door, leaving for work. "Ella, you want a ride home today?" he called over his shoulder in a voice suggesting either way, it would be a hassle.

"Yessir, I'd appreciate that."

"I'll be back after three," he said, and was out the door.

The second the colonel was gone, I looked at Mom with total exasperation. "Why do you let him talk to you that way?"

"What's it to me?" she said in all seriousness. "It's his short temper. I don't let it bother me."

But my stomach had tied itself into knots. The grating way the colonel talked to my mother got on my nerves like nails on a chalkboard. I couldn't figure out how Mom could stand it. If I were her, I would have taken the colonel's condescending attitude personally and it would have taken full restraint not to point out that his pettiness was childish and wrong. But that wasn't my mother's way, and I figured she was either way above it, or thought it was easier not to whack the beehive. But each hostile infraction I witnessed made me worry about a woman's position in marriage. I didn't know if a woman was supposed to act as if her husband was superior, or if my mother's way was all a ruse, designed to hoodwink the colonel into thinking she thought this was the case in an attempt at mollifying his inflated ego.

"But how could he not bother you?" I persisted. "The guy's angry all the time over nothing."

"Well, somebody's got to do the getting along," Mom said. "Honestly, Millie, you don't have to overthink everything."

"Miz Posey ain't got no real problem until he retire," Ella said, stabbing the crust with a fork.

"That'll be the worst day of my life," Mom said. "How many days in a row can you go shopping and then meet your friends for lunch?"

I took the easy way to Hutchison—out Union Extended to Walnut Grove, past Galloway Golf Course to the winding tree-lined residential lane of Shady Grove, where many of my friends lived in Southern Colonial houses set back from the street. I knew the area as well as I knew midtown. It was only a twenty-minute drive, and since I'd gained autonomy by driver's license, I spent much of my time out there.

On Fridays, it was mandatory to dress up at Hutchison because its educational process placed equal importance on the awareness of occasional appropriateness. Fridays carried a sense of ceremony. In the day's last period, the students assembled in the cavernous gymnasium, where the headmistress addressed the upper school from a lectern, followed by some form of entertainment, such as a performance by a talented student with musical ability, a demonstration of gymnastic prowess, or an inspirational address from an outside speaker, aimed at encouraging us to make something of ourselves by fashioning meaningful, contributory lives.

When school let out on Fridays, my friends and I made a beeline to the untamed acreage beside the Memphis Hunt and Polo Club on Shady Grove Road, where a group of boys from MUS would be waiting. The dynamic had been in play since the advent of MUS and Hutchison, and "the field," as it was called, was common ground, where the lines of hierarchy separating the upper school grades disappeared.

I was closing my car door when Emmy Sanderson came walking toward me from the edge of the field. A senior, Emmy was long-legged with dark tousled hair, two grades above me. She had a sister named Margo who was the same age as Finley.

"Did you hear?" Emmy said, when she reached me, "Finley's going to be Margo's escort at the debut this Christmas."

"I heard," I said. Mom had shared the news the week before, with such excitement it made it clear she thought it was the biggest deal in the world.

"When's Finley coming home?" Emmy asked me.

"In three weeks," I said. "What about Margo?"

"Earlier. She's having her dress made here, so she's coming home the second Mary Baldwin lets out."

But I wasn't interested in Margo's dress, nor the debut that would be held at the Memphis Country Club. All that mattered to me was Finley was coming home for Christmas.

15

Every December, my mother went all out. She'd have Murl wrestle yards of pine garland into the entrance hall and drape it languidly along the curving banister in flowing, elegant loops tied with generous taffeta bows of red floral ribbon bordered in gold wire. She draped garland over the downstairs mantle pieces, sylvan and pungent as a forest bed, scenting the rooms in an aroma so redolent it tickled the back of my throat.

Year after year, Murl hauled the fifteen-piece crèche down from the attic, and Mom arranged it on the two-tiered Oriental fold-out desk in the parlor. She centered a crimson-and-gold-patterned runner on the dining room table and topped it with a series of Herend candlesticks, arranged amidst pine boughs and holly the entire length of the table. I never knew how she procured it, but sooner or later a ten-foot tree appeared in the parlor—skirted in embroidered velvet and appointed with lights—before she invited anyone to assist.

She made a sacrament of Christmas each year, and would slide the big cardboard box marked CHRISTMAS in black felt-pen, from the little closet under the entrance hall stairs. Year after year, I saw my mother reach into the box reverently to produce the ornaments Finley and I made in kindergarten. She'd anoint them with diaphanous murmurs and coo a wistful succession of "I remember whens" and "y'all were so cutes." I'd stand in the entrance hall and watch her delicate gestures, realizing there was a side of my mother given to maternal nostalgia, and once I let that light in, all I wanted was more.

Her excitement was unbridled as she dressed to get Finley at the airport, his first Christmas home from UVA. The colonel paced downstairs, while I sat on the edge of her chaise lounge watching her slide on lipstick two winter shades deeper than her customary color. She'd asked me twice if I wanted to ride along to get Finley, but I knew it was to be her moment. That it would be better unshared. I knew she'd stand anxiously at the gate when Finley disembarked, jumpy as a bird dog, craning her neck to spot him. Then she'd break through the crowd and cling to him for dear life.

I was sitting on the sofa with Eddie Dean when Finley came swinging in, wearing his gray three-quarter coat from Brooks Brothers, all long-haired and collegiate-cool. He covered the card room in four sweeping strides and gave me a hug that lifted me off the floor. I was beside myself to have Finley home, as he edged between me and Eddie on the couch, then reached over to squeeze that funny area above my knee.

"Quit it," I squealed, but didn't mean it. He could have slapped me upside the head in that moment, and I wouldn't have cared.

Even the colonel seemed elated to have Finley home. He gave him a good-ol'-boy back pat and let ring a jolly, "What can I get you to drink?" Surprisingly, in four short months my brother had risen in the colonel's estimation. He'd left just as familiarity was starting to breed contempt, but here he was now, an honored guest.

"Finley, let's go tomorrow morning to get your tux," Mom began, settling in with a drink in her hand and watching Eddie erupt in laughter. "What's so funny, Eddie?" she asked, because she hadn't the slightest clue.

Eddie smirked at Finley, then answered. "What's the saying? You can't make a silk purse out of a sow's ear?"

"Shut up, Eddie," Finley said, but I could tell he thought it was funny.

"When's this?" Eddie continued. "When do the girls 'come out'?" he said, spinning the phrase.

"Night after tomorrow," Finley told him, slipping a knife through the double-cream Brie on the coffee table, then smoothing it over a Carr's table wafer.

"Mind if I ask why?" Eddie pressed.

"Not at all. In fact you probably should, you lowlife. Somebody needs to explain civility to you," Finley said, popping the round cracker into his mouth.

"It's a tradition," Mom stated.

"But what's it for?" Eddie tried again.

"The girls are being presented to society, of course," Mom explained.

"Then what's society going to do with them?" Eddie looked at me.

"How would I know, Eddie? Ask Mom," I said.

Eddie looked at Mom, his eyes focused and wide. "Then what happens?"

"Well, then it means—" Mom began, but Finley cut her off.

"Basically, it's a big party, wherein everyone goes to the club and drinks for the entire night. Not any different than anything else that goes on around here. They're just wearing better clothes."

"Oh, Finley, hush up," Mom chided. Then switching the subject, she added, "I meant to tell you there's a rehearsal at the club tomorrow at five."

"Okay," Finley said. "I'm not sure what there is to rehearse. I mean, how hard could this be?"

"Very, if you don't know where to go and when," Mom said. "And you should call Margo to tell her you're in town."

"I will," Finley said.

"Millie, we'll pick up your dress after we get Finley's tux."

"Can't you just pick it up for me, Mom? Do I have to go with y'all?" I asked.

"Yes, you do." Mom said.

"But I was going over to Cissy's house," I tried to protest.

"Well, call and tell her you can't come. I'm sure Cissy needs to get ready for the debut herself. She'll understand."

"So, all the swells will be there," Eddie surmised.

"Every club member with a daughter who is of age," the colonel said. "My daughter, Margaret, made her debut eight years ago."

Eddie stood and buttoned his wool pea coat. "Well, I'd love to stay and learn more about proper etiquette, but I ain't got the time. It's nice to see y'all. Finley, give me a call after you make your debut. Be sure to dab on a little cologne behind your ears before you put on your cummerbund," he said with a wink.

In the kitchen, Finley regaled us with his class descriptions and expounded upon his assessment of campus life at UVA. I could feel the glow of Mom's pride enshrining Finley like a beatific spotlight, altered as he was from his life's expansion. Afterward, I followed Finley up to his room and sat on the floor, as I always did whenever he played guitar. As I watched his fingers glide over the frets like spindly spider legs, I thought that God Himself had made Finley for the explicit purpose of coaxing the instrument's highest potential, and considered the best way to articulate the question ricocheting in my head.

"Why do I have to go to the debut?" I began. "I don't understand what it has to do with me. I'll probably be the youngest one there."

"No, you won't," Finley said. "Your age group will be there. Cissy's going." He glanced up at me. "Quit looking like it's the end of the world. We have to do this kind of thing every once in a while, so quit pouting. Your resistant attitude is upsetting Mom."

"But what's it got to do with me?"

"You're her daughter, that's what. In a way, it's really about her. You're her reflection. Your presence helps her project a unified front. Lets everyone see she's a good mother. You should try to understand the psychology behind it.

Most of what Mom does concerns appearances." He looked at me again. "But I'm not telling you anything new. Anyway, you'll be making your debut in a few years, so you best become one with the idea."

"Why does everything always have to be about Mom?" I asked, assuming Finley had the answer.

"It just does, so do yourself a favor and stop challenging her," Finley said.

At sixteen, I was beginning to wrestle with the gnawing impression of what I interpreted as my mother's superficial world, and it left me conflicted, for I had yet to arrive at the stable ground of my own identity. It seemed to me my mother cheated herself of half her potential by being overly concerned with appearances, which I judged as a shallow existence. I planned on living a bigger life, and didn't realize I was in the early stages of my own self-absorbed self-discovery, which found me challenging anyone who tried to paint me into a corner.

I had a low-grade guilt concerning my mother, which festered like disloyalty, and before I understood it as a predictable adolescent phase, I became disproportionately defensive over my mother's directives. It seemed she tried to mold me into her replica when I wanted to find my own way. With my tenuous skills of articulation, many words and gestures unwittingly came out sideways, spawning an unnamed uneasiness between my mother and me that was so uncomfortable, we both pretended it just wasn't there.

"Let me put it this way—it's not just about Mom, it's about popular opinion," Finley said. "Haven't you noticed the name of the game around here is what everybody thinks? You're only as good as how others consider you. For God's sake, Millie, don't bang heads with Mom on this one. Just put on a dress and go."

A wide, red carpet rolled down the front steps of the Memphis Country Club, which loomed large in columned splendor on mansion-lined Goodwyn Street. I teetered up tentatively to the marble foyer, wearing silk stockings and kitten heels for the first time in my life. Down the maroon-carpeted hallway, regal and hushed as hallowed ground, oil paintings of past MCC presidents hung sentry on antique ivory walls. Maids in black uniforms carried drinks on serving trays, and bow-tied waiters manned bars in discrete rooms tucked away like solemn libraries at the left. I walked between Mom and the colonel, stopping so often on the way to the ballroom that it took forty-five minutes of chatting and air-kissing to get there.

The ballroom's hardwood floor had steps at the end that rose to a stage partitioned by heavy burgundy curtains. I knew somewhere behind them, Finley waited with Margo, ready to offer his arm. A cloud of celestial women in colorful midwinter gowns floated in a sky of tuxedoed men, scenting the room with their perfume, as their feminine voices rang in the swirling eddy of this see-and-be-seen world. There were so many at the club's biggest night of the year that the beautiful people overflowed from the ballroom, into the red room, the men's tap room, the dining room, and the bar area overlooking the golf course.

Inside the sanctuary of the ladies' locker room, women perched upon upholstered settees, freshening their lipstick. They cooed over the other's dress, every one of them lit with a flame so bright it lifted the room. It was a secret society, the ladies' locker room—a refuge from the presence of men, where the ladies recalibrated themselves, reinforcing all that goes into being the type of woman both part and parcel to society, and wise enough to know that, collectively, they are pillars of a way of life so integral to Southern decorum that without them, no one could find their way.

I joined the flow of ladies from the locker room back to the ballroom, where the air was charged with rustling anticipation. Above the stage stairs, a soft spotlight cast a corona from top to bottom. Once or twice, the curtains fluttered as if in trial run. When they parted, a hush lowered over the room, and all eyes turned to the man in white gloves who held a proclamation on parchment beginning with a salutary "Ladies and gentlemen."

One after another, fifteen young women emerged in the second-most-important white dress of their lives. Each wore a personally designed, no-expense-spared coming-out dress, their hair so glossy it cast a shimmering auric field all the way to their satin shoes. It was the role of the escort to show off these seraphic creatures in a gait so well-rehearsed it would spur the envy of a military cadet.

I watched in wide-eyed awe as names were formally announced: Miss So-n-So, daughter of ... escorted by ... One after another. I thought people would clap after each name was called, but the gravity of the occasion would not be cheapened by such a gauche display until its conclusion, when the spell was shattered and the mood shifted to celebration.

In the middle of the disassembled aftermath, Finley stood tall, his coloring a stand-out against the black-and-white tuxedo he somehow wore differently than every man in the room. Margo clung to his arm with a swinging propriety, all blonde and smiling in the attenuating spotlight.

But she was no match for the thunder-stealing presence of Finley. When the orchestra began to play, Finley and Margo were the first to move to the center of the dance floor. I watched in abject surprise—my brother had gone out into the world and learned how to waltz without telling me. I could have watched all night, but Margo's father made a chummy shoulder-tapping display out of cutting in just as my mother went taffeta-swishing to Finley.

I looked around for the colonel, not because I wanted to know where he was but because I wanted to know where he was not. Then I looked at the ear-to-ear smile crinkling my mother's heart-shaped face, then went in search of my friend, Cissy Enright.

Cissy didn't appear any more comfortable dressed up than I. We had both been instructed by our mother to wear heels, so we balanced at the dining room bar like newborn foals testing our footing. I'd spent many summers at the country club pool, and had gone to dinner in the red room enough to ensure that every club employee knew me by name.

It seemed to me the black employees were in it for life. They were a constant, a mainstay, a militia ruling the grounds in uniform, charged with the task of preserving all as it should be. They allowed no misstep from my age group, no running in the halls, no display of entitlement, no back talk. And because they knew to whom we each belonged, we were accountable to these dignified guards who laid boundaries with one displeased look.

Yet they treated me with an air of deference because I was Miz Posey's daughter, and although I knew in my bone marrow that the obeisance was completely unearned, as I grew to maturity, I came to accept the decorum of the South without judgment, as it was shown to me by those who had been in the milieu way longer than I.

"What can I get you, Miss Millie?" Benita queried, standing behind the bar in her white-collared black uniform topped with a flounced pinafore—the kind the staff wore at night.

"May I have a Coke, please, Benita?"

Benita presented a monogrammed cocktail napkin on the bar, filled a highball with ice, then shot it through with Coke from a hissing hose.

"Y'all gonna get out there and dance?" Benita asked. "I see your brother cutting a rug."

"I've got to learn how to walk in these first," I said, looking down at my shoes.

"Yes, you gotta learn to walk the walk. Every one of us does," Benita confirmed with a nod.

Cissy and I were still standing at the bar when we spied Finley and Fatty Thompson sneaking outside to the golf course. I crossed to the bay window to look out, but the blazing interior lights obscured the view.

"Come on," I said to Cissy, "let's follow." We weaved past the ballroom to the coat checker's Dutch door, then walked down the front stairs and circled around back to the golf course. From a distance, I thought the group of eight or so were standing in the night air smoking cigarettes, but when I drew near, I smelled the heady cloud of sweet-burning pot. I knew every one of them standing in the cluster. They were laughing and passing and holding highballs as if they owned the grounds.

"That's one for the books, Finley," Allen was saying, his earlobes pink in the winter wind. "How long were you locked up?"

"Just overnight. I was used as an example. The cops don't mess around in Charlottesville."

Percy's voice rode the white puffs of his breath. "What'd they charge you with?"

"Inciting a riot."

"All by yourself?" Allen asked.

"They had to get somebody at S.A.E. They're always watching fraternity rush." Finley cut his eyes to me. "Millie, keep this one low."

The boys laughed and postured like young bucks in tuxedos, ruling the night with their own agenda, as Memphis' old guard carried on in the club unaware. Somebody passed me the joint, but Finley intercepted. "She's too young," he said, even though I'd already lurched back with revulsion.

Percy passed around a bottle of Visine, and the boys tipped their heads to the sky, sniffing audibly then straightening up, before filing back inside, where they all headed straight to the bar.

It wasn't until two days later that I learned Mom already knew about Finley being thrown in jail. I'd missed the late-night call five weeks before from the bail officer in Charlottesville. Finley had caught a lucky break with the timing. The colonel was marching his dog outside at the exact moment the call came through, and Mom didn't feel the need to divulge the facts after she'd handled it.

But the colonel eventually found out, a week into Finley's Christmas break. He'd come down to the card room promptly at five to find Finley and me sitting with Mom, waiting. He knew very well it was beneath our mother to fix her first drink, but for one uneasy moment, he stood between the open cathedral doors that separated the parlor from the card room, then he entered, holding an envelope in his hand and a scowl on his face.

"What's this?" he began, his hand shaking the paper.

"What's what?" Mom said, straightening out of her recline.

"What's this credit card charge to Charlottesville's office of corrections?"

"Well, you can see what it is, you're holding it in your hand," Mom returned.

"It's mine," Finley volunteered. "It was nothing."

"Nothing? Then you pay the fine. A thousand dollars bail?" He thumped the paper for effect.

"It was all for show," Finley downplayed.

"I'll write you a check. I put it on the Visa because I had to," Mom interjected.

"You had to, and didn't tell me?" The colonel glared at Mom with a look that would have caused a lesser woman to tremble.

"I'm telling you now," she said, meeting his eyes.

"Fix your own drink," the colonel said before he wheeled out of the room.

I looked at Finley. "I don't get it."

"What's there to get?" Finley shrugged, all devil-may-care.

"What, now you have a record?" I asked him.

"No. I'll just be going to court, and it'll probably be dismissed. I'll get the bail money back."

"Arrested for inciting a riot? How does someone single-handedly incite a riot?" I asked.

The colonel returned to the doorway. "If you think you're using the car while you're here, you can think again," he spat, glowering at Finley.

"I won't ask," Finley said as the colonel turned his back and stomped into the parlor.

"Finley, you can use the car," Mom whispered. "Just don't talk back. You can see his dander's up." She stood at the bar, measuring Scotch into a silver one-ounce jigger, which she then splashed over ice. She picked up the soda bottle and poured it into her highball, then picked up the Scotch decanter and topped off her drink. Settling into her chair in front of the fireplace, she crossed her right leg over her left, then tucked her left foot beneath her. Taking a quenching sip, she set her glass down on the side table, waved her feminine hand, and said, "I'll talk to him later."

"You'll talk to me now." The colonel reappeared. He sat facing Finley. "You go all the way to UVA on scholarship, and this is the first thing you do?"

"It wasn't the first thing I did," Finley said.

I shot a look at Mom, and saw her wince.

"Don't you get smart with me," the colonel snapped. "You're out there like white trash brawling in the street, ruining your chances in college, but that's up to you. This is really between you and your mother, but I have to live with her. I'm telling you one blame thing, you better sort yourself out now. Posey"—he pivoted—"if you're going to hide things from me, don't come to me later worried about your children." With that, the colonel rose and clipped out of the room again.

"You think he's gone this time?" Finley said to me, in a flat deadpan voice.

"I seriously doubt it," I said.

Finley looked at Mom. "Why'd you have to marry this guy?"

"He's good to me," she said, completely unflustered.

"You could have had anybody in Memphis," Finley stated. "What you did was take the first firm offer."

"After your father, who was no picnic, I was just thrilled someone was nice to me. He'll go anywhere, which your father never would."

"That's enough?" I asked. "You married him because he'll go places?"

"Look, Millie, I've had the one great love of my life, and it turned out it wasn't exactly a trip to Paris." She picked up her drink and took a good swallow. "I still can't believe he's dead, but I'm telling you, it was the best thing that could have possibly happened to him. He'd screwed up his life so badly." She set her drink down and paused as if considering. "Your father left us all penniless. I couldn't get to the trust Dr. Joe left me for years. Comes a time when a woman has to get practical."

"What's your financial arrangement with him?" Finley ventured.

"I own this house, and he pays the upkeep. I pay for my clothes and my children, and he pays the other bills."

"All right. I'm just glad you own the house," Finley said.

119

"Well, he wanted to buy it from me. Half of it, if I wanted. But I think I'm better off owning the house. Things are just fine, but do let me add it'd be exceedingly convenient if you'd keep your scholarship and not get thrown out of school," she said. She raised her brows over the rim of her glass and gave Finley a nod.

16

Finley bought a secondhand car that Christmas, and since I had another ten days of Christmas break before school resumed, asked me to ride to Charlottesville with him. We took to the road in late December, relieved for both the excuse and the means to travel away before anything else hit a head. Finley started the four-door cream-colored Volvo. "Good Lord, get me out of here," he said, pulling out of the driveway. "Mom standing there crying like I'm going off to war. I don't know what I did to deserve this dramatic go-round."

"You got thrown in jail," I volunteered.

"Good point," Finley said.

"Now that the colonel knows, Mom's got to live with the fallout," I added.

"No wonder she was tearing up. Now she's alone with him. I'll give her this, she can handle him. He's such a jerk," Finley said.

"I know. He's a control freak."

"It's all fear-based, believe me," Finley said.

"Fear-based? What do you mean? What do you think he's afraid of?"

"Anything being out of his control. Guys like that can't stand anything ambiguous. He goes about life troubleshooting on the front end and overreacting on the back. It's completely reactionary, a complete inability to handle most situations because he won't acknowledge a middle ground. He's got to take the guesswork out of everything by labeling it as either black or white. Gray's too tall an order. He's got to have certainty, which is missing the entire point of life."

"Oh, okay, so now you've got the point of life? What's the point, Finley?"

"Mastering the ambiguities of life is the entire point of existence," Finley said. "It's the hardest task any of us will ever be called to do."

Through the window, I watched the part of I-40 that crosses the Tennessee River, halfway between Memphis and Nashville, flow from stark flatlands to gently rolling hills. It flitted by in staccato images of twisted oaks and fallow farmland, with an eerie sense of history that crawled the stretch known as Music Highway. I'd never been this far east of Memphis, and could feel the air lighten, as if I'd shrugged off the spectral influence of the Mississippi River's pervasive consciousness as we careened out of its reach.

"You want to know why Mom was crying?" I asked. "It's because she misses you. It hasn't been any fun at home since you went off to school. You know she worships you. She's always telling me she can't figure out where you came from because you're so smart."

"Ah, come on, that's not true." Finley darted a glance my way.

"I'm not making that up," I said.

"When'd she say this?"

"I don't know … she's said it a million times."

"Hmmm," Finley considered. After a few contemplative beats, he said, "I'm not all that smart."

"Yes, you are, Finley. You're smarter than me."

"No, I'm not. You're smart, Millie. You just don't care about school. Not everybody sees the merit in school, but as long as you have to be there, you might as well learn something. That's the only difference between you and me—I like the challenge."

"Because you're competitive."

"It's not intentional. Might just be a predilection that guys have by nature."

"Yeah, well, I definitely don't have that," I said.

"You kind of do," he stated.

"Where am I competitive?"

"With Mom," Finley said, his tone unflinching.

"No, I'm not. What are you talking about?"

"You have to be. It's your subconscious defense mechanism because she's competitive with you. Don't tell me you don't know what I'm talking about."

"Finley"—I lowered my voice—"I don't know what you're talking about."

"Tune in, it's beneath the surface, you're already in it. It's inherent in age. You're coming into your power, and she's losing hers. Look, it's not just you. Mom's competitive with all women."

"Gosh, Finley," I said. "Do you have to psychoanalyze everything to death?"

"Dirty job, but somebody's got to do it," he said, disarming me with a wink.

We crossed the Cumberland Plateau between Cookeville and Crossville, then dropped into the Tennessee Valley, stopping at a gas station-slash-diner on the outskirts of Knoxville.

"Come on, let's go in." Finley swung out of the car and pushed through the diner's glass door, a string of metal bells jangling at our entrance.

High from the checkered linoleum floor before the counter, red vinyl swivel stools rotated in furtive turns, and heads twisted to sneak a peek. Finley caught the eye of a waitress and pointed to one of the red Naugahyde booths, then slid in with a suctioned squeak. The fluorescent lights made my eyes squint and the smell of foul grease hit me in my queasy stomach. Fried eggs and links, burgers, hash browns, and simmering onions jumbled on the griddle, emitting a mingled steam so acrid it peeled the wallpaper above the shelf, on which rows of heavy crockware were tainted a yellow-cream. In back, a woman pushed a wheeled plastic bucket by a mop handle, leaning over its press with her ample bosom to wring it out before sloshing it to the floor.

Finley turned the metal spikes of the table's jukebox. "You got any quarters?"

"In the car," I said. "I'll run and get some, if you want."

"Yeah, do that. We do nothing without music," he said, scrutinizing the play list.

But I didn't make it to the car, for the second I pushed through the diner's glass door, there on the sidewalk was a thin tri-colored dog, medium-sized and matted. It seemed skittish with indecision over whether to draw closer or scuttle away, yet its eyes remained fastened on me, fearful yet somehow longing, its body taut and prepared to spring at my slightest move.

Finley saw me through the window. He came out to the sidewalk with his brows furrowed, his eyes assessing. The dog scampered back the second he opened the door then turned quickly to face him, its body crouching then rising, maintaining a wary aloofness, yet remaining engaged.

"Don't walk toward it. It's scared. Just stay still," Finley said, kneeling. "Let's see if it comes. Right now, it doesn't know if it can trust us."

I sat on the sidewalk facing the dog. "You think it's lost?"

"I don't know. Kind of looks like a collar imprint there. See where the hair on its neck is lying down? It might be abandoned, which is worse. There's nothing worse than having a home, then all the sudden you don't. Means you spend the rest of your life in need and searching. Poor thing, you can tell it wants to come closer, so it's not entirely afraid, it's just uncertain."

The air remained undisturbed from Finley's subtle movements. He put a silencing hand over the string of bells and opened the diner's door. "This anyone's dog out here?"

The waitress behind the counter walked forward, her rubber shoes sticking with each step to the door. "She's a stray comes 'round here because we feed her."

"You sure?" Finley asked.

"Yeah, son, I'm sure," she said. "You 'bout ready for that club you ordered? How long y'all gonna stay out there with that dog?"

But Finley didn't move until he'd devised a plan. "Somebody has to assume a leadership position here. Someone has to take care of this dog, give it safety and structure. It can't just drift around." He put his hands on his narrow hips, looked down at the dog, then turned his face to my waiting eyes. "Don't you remember how disoriented Inky and Ike were when we got to Memphis? Those two were never the same."

I eased up close enough to Finley to feel the whirring wheels of his mind in motion, a kinetic amalgam borne from his specific internal crucible, which made him the most unusual of men. Finley had the unique ability to resist the compartmentalization of a problem. He had a gift for synthesis, the melding of opposites, the merging of clashing forces. He approached every quandary with the certainty of solving a mathematical equation, and could see the sum of its solution before the distraction of its parts. He paused and looked back at the dog. "All right, we'll take her with us to Charlottesville," he concluded. "I'll take her to a vet, then bring her home. I can take care of her."

The collie mix settled easily on a blanket the waitress gave us with gratitude when she saw me coaxing the dog to the back seat of Finley's car. We pulled away from the diner and set out toward the middle of the Appalachians in Bristol, where the mountains are so heavenly, they reflect the color blue. Each time Finley tilted his head to the rearview mirror to look at the dog, I'd turn to look too. Then Finley and I would meet eyes and smile knowing we'd made the right move in bringing the dog home. Once we got to Roanoke, we dropped into the Shenandoah Valley, then on into Staunton, where we headed east over the Blue Ridge Mountains, then entered the piedmont of central Virginia, where Charlottesville lay scholarly and homespun, like lord of the manor in a blue-blooded country estate.

Finley lived in the lawyer's cottage of a rolling demesne, in the wooded outskirts of Charlottesville. It was an old-growth area so clandestine and untamed, with its multilayered treetop canopies, it seemed enchanted. It was an area that unhinged my imagination from the moment we set upon its labyrinthine paths to scratch our way beneath oak and elms shot through with dappled sunlight. The stone cottage was earth-toned and tucked in a graceful hollow beyond the view of the estate. Comprised of one large room, a makeshift kitchenette, and a sunken bathroom that looked like a russet-brick outhouse, it had a wood-burning fireplace, floor-to-ceiling double windows, and a solid oak ladder that climbed to the loft overhead.

"You take my bed, I'll sleep up in the loft," Finley said as we entered the cottage. I put my suitcase on the full-size bed and looked around. Everything in the cottage melded effortlessly in one muted color scheme. The walls and floor were faded brick, and the unadorned windows seemed to coax the winter land inside to soften the space, where auburn sisal rugs lay strategically, and an oak table with four matching chairs stood two yards before Finley's bed. There wasn't much else in the cottage, beyond the books and the yellow legal pads Finley habitually used. They were arranged on a four-tiered bookshelf, beside his arsenal of musical equipment: three guitars, a Marshall amplifier, a four-track, a turntable, and two three-foot speakers. Outside, a circular parking space made of scattered gravel had a path that veered from an angle into the sodden, spent fields, littered with bare trees in the gray December air.

Finley stood feet planted wide, his arms across his chest, like a captain on a prow surveying the horizon. "I see deer around here all the time," he told me. "They walk right up to the front door."

"Cool," I said, imagining those balletic creatures traipsing softly toward Finley's door like an otherworldly visitation. It seemed fitting in this harmonious, sylvan setting, where everything seemed gauzy and surreal. I looked down at our new companion. "Where's Tramp going to live?" I asked, using the name Finley had chosen for the dog.

"Inside and out. She'll be all right. I'll take her with me as much as possible. When I can't, there's a caretaker here who can look in on her. I never lock the door. He lives over there in another cottage and has two dogs of his own. The people who own the house are only here part-time. I've thought this through—she'll be perfectly safe. For now, I think we should give her a bath."

The next morning, we took a clean Tramp along while Finley showed me UVA's campus. We walked her on leash through the lawn of Academic Village, then climbed the stairs of the columned Rotunda, where red-brick walkways stretched out before in a herringbone pattern, like a pedantic optical illusion. We took turns watching Tramp while the other walked in the Gothic Revival

Chapel, where wooden pews warmed in the cloudy half-light through stained-glass cathedral windows.

Trailing through the gardens, we set out for what Finley called "the corner" because he wanted to go to the university bookstore. The sky was a historic steel gray, and as I walked beside Finley, I was taken by the weightiness, the erudite Jeffersonian gravity of the University of Virginia's environs. There was something austere about the suburban school grounds; as a whole, the combination of the landscaping, architecture, and adjoining sidewalks had a sobering quality that leveled my mood.

There were trees everywhere, and students glided past with pensive eyes and pocketed hands, as if contemplating the meaning of existence. I felt frivolous and ungrounded by comparison, for they seemed to be the chosen few, in the initial stages of launching meaningful lives. I knew without question that Finley belonged here, that his life had come into focus, after having outgrown Memphis and everything else unsupportive of whom he would become. I walked along, mirroring his casual ease, and stood out on the sidewalk with Tramp when he disappeared inside the bookstore to buy another stack of legal-sized paper. When Finley emerged, a blond-haired, blue-eyed young man walked alongside him. He was tall and compact, with apparent athletic grace in the sinewy way he glided forward. He was so startlingly vibrant and golden that, at first, I didn't know where to look.

"This is Luke," Finley said, coming to a stop. "This is my sister, Millie," he continued, presenting me with the sweep of his hand.

A sly smile that told me he knew something about me crept beneath Luke's aristocratic, slightly flared nose. "Luke Piedmont," he said, offering his hand. "How was the drive from Memphis? Finley tells me y'all found a dog."

I had to pull myself out of the awkward, inarticulate stupor that had come upon me by this arresting, dazzling young man. I could feel Finley looking at me as if he were waiting for me to say something—anything—and somehow managed to stammer, "Yes, this is Tramp."

Luke ran his hand the length of Tramp's back and scratched her behind her tufted ears.

"So, Friday night," Luke said, continuing a conversation with Finley that must have originated in the bookstore.

"Okay," Finley returned. "How'd you book that?"

"My brother's the bartender on the weekends," Luke said. "There's a guaranteed audience. Millie, how long you here for?"

"Until Monday," I said.

"Great, so you're here almost a week." Luke looked down at me as if pondering. He ran his hand through his sun-streaked hair, which fell in a pallet of metallic gold. "You old enough to drink? No, wait, you're under eighteen, right? Might be a problem, but I'll ask my brother to get you in."

"Get me in where?" I asked.

"The Mineshaft," Luke said. "We're playing there Friday night."

"What?" I looked at Finley. "You're playing?"

"Yeah, we've got a band," Finley said as if it were obvious.

"Your brother's the master of covert maneuver." Luke cuffed Finley on the back. "Careful of this guy, he leads a double life."

"Shut up, Luke. It's not like she doesn't know I play guitar," Finley said.

"Finley was born with a guitar in his hand," I said to Luke.

"Yeah, well, I was too. Only I don't play anywhere near as well as he does. Anyway, for the next few nights, we can rehearse at my parents' place. I'll call you about the time," he said. "Nice to meet you, Millie. Guess I'll be seeing you."

I watched Luke amble away in his khakis and white Keds sneakers with navy blue rims. He looked like he'd just crawled off a Southern California beach—like one of the Beach Boys, touched in that endless-summer way that brimmed with unselfconscious vitality. "Where'd you meet him?" I asked the second Luke was out of range.

"Oddly enough, walking across the university's lawn. He was whistling a tune with such perfect pitch, I stopped him. Luke's our singer."

"Does he go to school here?"

"Mm-hm, Luke's from Virginia. He grew up in Staunton, which is only about forty miles away. He's right, we'll need to rehearse. You don't have to come if you don't want to, but you're certainly welcome."

I wanted to go without question, and we drove to Staunton the next night with Tramp in the car. We rolled through the paved hills of Mary Baldwin College to the residential area where Luke had grown up. Behind his parents' symmetrical Colonial Revival house, Luke stood waving in the doorway of a miniature replica. Inside, two collegiate boys looked up as we entered—one behind a drum kit, the other perched on a wooden stool, fingering a bass. Finley introduced them as Gene and Eric, and both were almost as good-looking as Luke.

I wasn't the only one affected by the appearance of the band, who called themselves The Facts. Four nights later at the Mineshaft, it was standing room only, and eighty percent of the attendants were screaming girls. Beneath white-hot lights on a high-rise stage, they stood three in front of the dark-haired Gene's drum kit: Luke in the middle, flanked by Finley and Eric. They wore skinny ties and white button-down shirts tucked into Levi's, as they layered harmonies in four-four timing around Luke's voice, which was thick and textured.

His voice had a quivering, adolescent quality tinged with longing, which gave the impression of intimacy. A little-boy-lost kind of quality that made every female swoon. Girls swayed, their arms wrapped around each other's waist, rising on tiptoe for a better view, and singing along to the band's original songs. As I stood wondering how all this had evolved without my knowledge, a voice shouting in my ear startled me. "Aren't you Finley's sister?"

"Yes," I answered, taking a step back to bring a young woman into focus.

"I knew it, you look just like him. I'm Caroline." She was tall and willowy, with chestnut hair cut in a shoulder-length pageboy and a heart-shaped Scandinavian face.

"I'm Finley's girlfriend," she announced, tossing her silky hair back with a swing of her head.

"You're *who*?"

"Caroline," she said loudly. "My last name is Lindquist."

"I'm Millie," I said.

"I know," she said. "I've been looking for you. Finley didn't tell you I'd be looking for you?"

"No," I said, taking in her long thin legs and flouncy short skirt, which she'd paired with a blue-jean jacket, black tights, and leather clogs.

"Typical Finley," Caroline laughed, but there was no trace of offense in her voice. In that moment, I had no way of knowing I was standing before the love of Finley's life. No way of suspecting the handprint she'd leave on his everlasting soul. She held a plastic cup of beer, which she extended to me, but I deflected with a shake of my head.

"Smart of you," Caroline said. "Don't start too young. I'm already an alcoholic." She took a savoring sip and laughed in such a winsome way, it lessened the nettle of her words.

I knew a thing or two about alcoholics, and this bright, wispy creature standing before me didn't fit the profile, whether she was kidding or not. I wondered how much Finley had told her about our father. I'd get to the bottom of it, once Finley confessed he had a girlfriend, which he got around to later that night.

Finley and I stood at the edge of the open field, at the far end of his driveway. It was well past midnight, and we were letting Tramp sniff around as we huddled in our coats against the biting air.

"You didn't bother to tell me about Caroline," I said like an accusation.

"Mother Superior, please forgive my sin of omission," Finley said, but the look in his eyes told me my tone was justifiable. "Come on, you know I was going to tell you. I only met her two months ago. It's new, but I really like her. Guess where she's from?"

"Where?"

"Minnesota."

"You're kidding."

"No, swear to it. She's from Lake Minnetonka," he said.

"Unreal."

"I know, what are the odds?"

"Slim," I said.

"That's exactly what I think. It clearly implies you can't discount like attracting like. Maybe I'll bring her home during spring break, depending on what's going on with the band. She hasn't seen anything of the South." Finley walked a few crunching paces into the dew-encrusted field beside the driveway to keep an eye on Tramp. There was enough light from the waxing moon to see clear around us, but Finley had brought a flashlight and swept it like a spotlight, illuminating Tramp's movements.

"Depending on what's going on with the band?" I asked.

"Yeah, we're not fooling around. I want to take this to the top," Finley said in all seriousness.

"I believe you," I said, and in that split second, of course I did.

17

It all tumbled upon me like the dawn of awakening, and in that second, I suddenly knew there was no other future for Finley. He'd take his entire being and apply it to the arts, and he'd create something beautiful and groundbreaking, something that could only be fashioned by his inexorable intelligence and intuitive grasp of music. Of course he would. It was all so obvious, I wondered why I hadn't thought of it before. "Where'd y'all get the name for the band?"

"Luke and I came up with it. There's a lot you can do with a name like The Facts—here's The Facts. What are The Facts? Give me The Facts. I'm already naming albums."

I could just picture it; they'd be in the center of popular music. They'd have songs on the radio while they toured the world. Because when Finley said he was going to do something, he did it. They were already touring the college circuit—the universities closest to UVA, such as Mary Baldwin, Clinch Valley College in Wise, Virginia, Hollins College in Roanoke, Randolph Macon in Lynchburg, and James Madison in Harrisonburg. Even the Citadel in Charleston. Caroline had said that what I witnessed at the Mineshaft was typical of the band's popularity.

"You're not kidding. I get it," I said.

Finley tucked the green-gray tartan scarf Mom gave him for Christmas into his coat and shook his head. "I'm not kidding in the least. It can't be that hard to do, not if you garner an impressive-enough following. What we'll do is create a brush-fire, like a grass-roots movement. Just look at the Beatles. They were turned down repeatedly by every record company they approached. It was their fans that pushed them over the line in the end. You can't argue with a fan base. If you've got one big enough, the record companies will come to you."

"How does a record company find you?" I asked.

"They have relationships with club owners everywhere. They just keep on top of who's creating a draw. If they hear enough about a band, they'll send an A&R guy to see for themselves."

I looked sidelong at Finley, getting ready to ask a question.

"A&R stands for artist and repertoire. They're like scouts, then they act as a liaison between the record company and the band," he answered my thought.

"Don't y'all do covers? How'd everybody tonight know your songs?"

"We never did covers. We wanted to come out swinging with originals," Finley said.

"Who's writing the songs?" I asked.

"Primarily Luke. The guy's like Lennon and McCartney rolled into one. He's unbelievable. I'm better with arrangements. Anyway, Luke's been playing solo around here since he was seventeen. We have similar musical sensibilities."

"Does Mom know about the band?" I asked.

"No. No point in telling her until we have something worth talking about."

I stamped my freezing feet to get the blood flowing and stifled a yawn. "You about ready to go in?" I asked.

"Okay. Come here, Tramp," Finley called to the side of the field. "Tramp?"

"She's over there." I pointed to a patch about four yards away.

Finley walked toward her and kneeled, calling. "Any dog you've rescued is going to come," he said over his shoulder, and he was right.

Tramp came bounding up readily, and we all went inside for the night.

From the loft above, Finley whispered, "Millie? You asleep?"

"No," I said.

"You mind if Caroline hangs out with us tomorrow? It's your last day, so it's up to you. I'll be taking you to the airport early the next morning."

"No, not at all," I called back, moving over in the bed to make room for Tramp. "Here Tramp, come up," I called, patting the bed, and Tramp jumped up and settled in. "You know what, Finley? I could really get used to having a dog."

"Fat chance of that happening as long as you're living at home," Finley said with a laugh.

Caroline Lindquist had an annual pass to Shenandoah National Park. We put Tramp in Caroline's secondhand Mercedes and drove a half hour out I-64 to US 250, heading for the Rockfish Gap entrance to the park. Finley wanted to show me a particular waterfall, so we navigated the Skyline Drive along the crest of the Blue Ridge Mountains, stopping at various lookouts over wooded vistas, now turned a sallow ochre in the damp winter season. When we reached an area called Big Meadows, we parked the car and started walking downward, toward Dark Hollow Falls.

Caroline was nimble as a cat, with an eager way of walking, as if springs were in her hiking boots. She showed every sign of adoring Finley—fitting her hand into his with such ease that they seemed right together, as she led us along the trail. Even the red in Caroline's hair matched the undertones in Finley's. When they walked side by side, she was a complementary five inches shorter than Finley, and I thought if ever there were a girl for him, it's this vivacious creature bouncing at his side.

Caroline gushed with enthusiasm to be showing me the park. "It's easier going to the falls than it is returning," she told me. "It'll be all uphill coming back, but it'll be worth it." She pointed northwest. "See all that down there? It's Hogcamp Branch, the source of the falls. Come on, it's incredible."

And it was. We climbed down for what must have been a half hour, and sat on the rocks near the frothing cascades, which were flowing to full capacity from the recent rains. The sun caught the tree branches at such an angle that prisms of light reflected on the water, and as the water barreled down, its roil amplified off the canyon like rolling thunder. Tramp settled onto the blanket that Caroline spread out, and Finley reached into his backpack and handed out bottled water. I tilted mine above Tramp's lapping tongue, and looked just in time to see Caroline sneaking a sip from a flask before she zipped it inside the lining of her down jacket.

Mist from the falls permeated the air, and I lay on my back, looking through elm limbs etched like latticework across the sky. I turned over the name Dark Hollow Falls, thinking the name was appropriately eerie. Anything could happen in this remote echo chamber, and there'd be no one around to report the worst. I started to construct a list of worst-case scenarios, but for whatever reason, I kept thinking of ghosts.

"Finley?" I began, my mind a kaleidoscope of free association. "Remember that night in Kensington Park when the portrait fell off the wall?"

Finley tossed the backpack to the side and looked down at me. "When we'd just moved? Yeah. Why?"

"Did you ever tell Mom?"

"No. What made you think of that out of nowhere?"

"What portrait?" Caroline asked with interest.

I sat up. "The big oil portrait of our grandmother's grandfather."

"It fell?" Caroline asked.

"Yeah," I said. "On the front stairs. A ghost did it. At least that's what Finley told me."

Finley looked at Caroline and started to explain. "Somebody committed suicide in the house before my mother's family moved in," he said. "The house feels kind of haunted."

"Are you saying there's definitely a ghost?" Caroline sounded fascinated.

"Maybe," Finley returned.

"Forget all that," I said in disbelief. "Finley, you're just now telling me somebody committed suicide in the house?"

"What, Mom never told you? She told me," he said.

"That doesn't surprise me from her, but from you, it does." I said.

"I tell you everything on a need-to-know basis, Millie," Finley said. Looking at Caroline he added, "My sister's a bit skittish over ghosts and such. She's always been afraid in the house we grew up in. Anyway, the portrait fell off the wall one night and scared her. Probably an accident waiting to happen, but who knows?"

"And you never told your mother about a ghost knocking something off the wall? Why not?"

"In our family, it's rare to have a conversation of any significance."

"Well, I'm going to your house then." Caroline said. "In my family, there's way too much."

Caroline Lindquist was the letter-writing sort. She wrote me letters in colored pen with swirling cursive, and dotted her I's with smiley faces on light-green stationery with butterflies on top. Two months after I'd met her, she mailed me a pair of clogs just like the pair she had and in my size, since I mentioned I liked them. She wrote me once a month and included photographs of herself and Finley with their arms around each other in various settings—Caroline and Finley at a barbecue, Caroline and Finley at a night club, Caroline and Finley side by side on a sofa, with Finley playing guitar and Caroline's worshipful eyes aglow in rapture. With each missive, she asked when I'd be returning to Charlottesville, but I had no plans. School was in full swing, I'd be going to Florida with Cissy's family for spring break, and I'd fallen in love for the first time with a boy named Aiden McNair.

I fell into an obsessive love with Aiden. The first time I saw him, he was playing point guard for the MUS basketball team, in a triumphant game against Briarcrest during my sophomore year at Hutchison. I was a MUS cheerleader—an honor bestowed to a group of girls from the private schools in Memphis by the yearly election of MUS's student body. I was captivated by Aiden's airborne fluidity as he ran coltishly up and down the court. There was something mysterious and inaccessible about his dark good looks. He was beautiful in a poetic, feminine way, with long black hair that swept to the side and downward-sloping eyes the color of cobalt.

Aiden lived in East Memphis and was part of the group of boys and girls with whom I spent every weekend in high school. I had no idea Mom knew anything about Aiden's family, until she sat in the card room one night and held forth with her opinion.

"Well, dating is one thing, Millie, but I'm telling you, if you ever marry into that crazy family, I'm going to kill you," she said, then sipped her Scotch.

Her declaration only encouraged my attachment.

Aiden's mother was from Memphis gentry, the scion of moneyed, prominent people of German descent who owned a string of high-end car dealerships throughout the Mid-South. Her name was Adelaide, and she looked like a statue with hammered facial features and a long frail body so paper-thin it seemed the mere act of walking across the room might be her undoing. She was habitually sick with one ailment or another, which she gratuitously described in minute detail, as if it would somehow commiserate with the delicate blue blood that ran in her veins.

From his mother, Aiden inherited his tall frame, chiseled features, and aristocratic bearing. From his working-class Scottish father, his easy temperament, love of the arts, and *joie de vivre*. It was said in some circles that Adelaide McNair had married beneath her, and in others that theirs was a marriage of convenience, but the allegations were never verified in the discreet society of Memphis's old guard. Yet there were rumors, people alluded, and there is nothing more damning than Southern suspicion when there is no proof either way.

The McNairs lived in an ivy-covered Tudor estate behind a circular driveway. A limestone fountain spewed cascading water in front, and a tumbling garden swept through ten manicured acres in back. The interior was a three-floored repository for collectible antiques, with every muffled room appointed with impractical décor. Upon entering Aiden's room for the first time, I was stunned by its uselessness. There was no indication whatsoever that a boy inhabited the space. No posters on the walls, no athletic gear lying about, no records strewn beside a stereo. Instead, the room was a sterile, deafened arrangement comprised only of a twin bed and side table, with a chest of drawers and a solitary high-back chair. Aiden's room had all the charm of a sanatorium, which told me all I needed to know about his family dynamic, wherein his mother obsessed over orderliness to such a compulsive pitch that there wasn't a misaligned pen in the house.

But being at Aiden's house was better than being at mine because my friends were afraid of the colonel. And the McNairs' basement had its own parental-skirting entrance, which was accessible from a series of concrete stairs off the back driveway. Precious little inhabited the basement—a sofa, a stereo, and a television—but because most of our friends lived in East Memphis, it was the place we all congregated after school. We were a group of teens who acted as a touchstone for each other, a support system in our coming of age, and we did everything as a pack. We called the boys by their last names— Hoolighan and Anderton, Van Houghton and Emory—and all of the girls had nicknames—Cecille was Cissy, Patricia was Patty, Louise was Weezie, and I, of course, was Millie, for Camille. We were a clique that gave each other the bedrock of clan alliance, a mainstay we relied upon that came to serve as a standard by which we measured friendships for the rest of our lives.

18

It was two years before I saw Caroline Lindquist again—when Finley brought the band to Memphis, two days after Christmas.

I was standing in the kitchen with Ella when The Facts pulled up in the driveway of 79 Kensington Park. They arrived in two cars: Finley and Caroline in one, Luke, Gene, and Eric in the one that pulled a U-Haul loaded with musical equipment.

Much had transpired in a short year for the band. They'd recorded a handful of songs on a four-track in Luke's home studio and were receiving airplay five times a day in seven Virginia counties. Every song they produced became the stations' most requested, and they were repeatedly featured in local magazines, while they packed clubs to capacity throughout the college circuit. As co-managers, Finley and Luke had decided the time was right to take things to the next level, so they scheduled a week at Ardent Recording Studios in midtown Memphis, and at a discounted rate, since it was during the holidays.

Ella stood at the back door shaking her head. "The colonel gone be thrown a fit, you don't get that U-Haul out from 'round back. You know how he be 'bout that driveway," she fussed at Finley.

"Well, that's a fine way to greet me, Ella. Come here and give me a hug." Finley leaned in, squeezed Ella in his arms, and stepped back to clear a view of Caroline. "This is my girlfriend, Caroline Lindquist."

"Nice to meet you," Caroline beamed. "I've heard so much about you from Finley."

"Well, I'll be," Ella intoned. "Finley, run up tell Miz Posey y'all here. She thought y'all wouldn't be coming till this evening."

"I'll do it," I offered after hugging them both. I bolted up the back stairs and called for Mom. Opening the bedroom door, I breathlessly announced, "They're here."

"They're here?" Mom dashed to the mirror to apply her lipstick. She was in such a tizzy, she let the colonel's dog escape through the bedroom door. Barking and frothing and general pandemonium broke loose as the dog made a mad dash to the top of the stairs.

"Millie, either get hold that dog or run fetch me a gun," Ella shouted from the bottom of the stairs.

"I'll get it, Ella," Finley said, mounting the stairs. He grabbed the dog by the collar and dragged it into the bedroom, where Mom hustled forward, extending her arms.

"Y'all are early." Mom peered over Finley's embrace. "Where's your girl?"

"Downstairs. Come on down and meet her." Finley turned to lead the way.

In the kitchen, Ella dropped lemon wedges into a pitcher of freshly made tea. Luke, Gene, and Eric sat at the table, while Caroline stood waiting for Finley's return.

"Here she is," Finley said. I watched Caroline and Mom hesitate in a mutually awkward moment, neither quite knowing of whom he referred.

Dressed in a navy Ann Taylor pantsuit and gold costume jewelry, Mom was the first to regroup. "I feel like I know you already, Caroline," she enthused.

"So nice to meet you, Mrs. Henry. I feel like I know you too."

"Mom, this is Luke. That's Eric, and this is Gene," Finley introduced.

"My, what a good-looking group," Mom said, looking one to the other. "Welcome, boys. We're so glad to have you here."

I saw Luke blush, but then he was completely unaware of the impact he had on people, and color rose easily to his cheeks. "Thank you, Mrs. Henry. We're glad to be here."

"Call me Posey. Ella, did you offer them a beer?"

Ella glanced at the kitchen wall clock. "It not but four in the afternoon," she exclaimed.

"I'll take a beer," Finley said, going to the refrigerator and pulling out a six-pack.

"Finley, did you bring Tramp?" I asked, hoping he did.

"No, she's with the caretaker. She'll be fine. We'll only be here a week." He sat at the table and pulled Caroline onto his knee, where she perched tentatively, glancing around as if to check if it were acceptable.

"Let's go into the card room," Mom said. "Y'all bring your drinks."

I could sense the scanning eyes and cautious steps behind me as we walked through the parlor to the card room. Under his breath, Luke whispered, "Geez, Finley, you didn't bother to mention this."

"Mom, Luke's afraid his uncultured country behind is going to break something in here," Finely joked. He could always be counted on to revert to sarcasm to lighten the mood.

"Now y'all are more than welcome to stay here if you want to. We have a guesthouse out back and two guest bedrooms upstairs." Mom sat in her chair and crossed her legs.

Finley paused at the bar. "We're renting the house by Ardent I told you about. I've already paid for it, but thanks anyway. Mom, can I fix you something to drink?" Finley asked, and I realized he was just as unaccustomed as I was to the sight of Mom in the card room without a Scotch in her hand.

Mom looked at her wristwatch. "Oh no, that's sweet of you," she demurred. "I'll wait for the colonel. He'll be here by five. Finley, tell me about Christmas night. I want to hear all about it." She looked at Caroline. "It was so strange not having Finley here for Christmas."

"Everybody else's parents said the same thing, but the band had to seize the opportunity," Finley explained.

"It was a complete sellout," Caroline added. "They had to turn people away at the door."

Mom seemed surprised. "Oh, Caroline, you were there? You didn't go home?"

"No, I stayed in Charlottesville."

"Didn't your parents mind, honey?"

"Caroline's parents are divorced," Finley interjected. "She hates her stepfather."

"Where's your father?" Mom asked, a concerned look on her face, but I knew her well enough to know she wasn't concerned at all. She was weighing, measuring, judging. Whatever Caroline's answer would be, it would tell Mom all she wanted to know.

"Minneapolis. He's a doctor. He's married to a nurse and they just had a baby," Caroline said, fidgeting in the leather wing-backed chair.

"They had an affair," Finley contributed. "One of those stereotypical office romances. The hero-worshiped doctor and the sultry younger nurse. Her dad's a jerk anyway."

"You've met him?" Mom raised her eyebrows at Finley, punctuating her rhetorical tone.

"I don't have to meet him to know he's a jerk. Nothing anybody ever does is good enough." He gave Mom a direct look. "He's one of those."

"Caroline, do you have any siblings?" Mom continued.

"I have an older brother," Caroline said. "We used to be close, but we're not really close anymore."

"He's a jerk too," Finley stated.

"Oh, come on, Finley. Everybody's not a jerk," Mom said.

"This guy is. He just moved back to Charlottesville. He went to UVA Law, moved to Minnesota, couldn't get a job, and now he's moved back. He's pompous and supercilious."

"He's a jerk," Luke said, to the obvious pleasure of Gene and Eric, who nodded their agreement.

"Gene, go on. Tell Mom the guy's a jerk," Finley prompted.

"He's a jerk," Gene confirmed.

"He's not all that bad," Eric said. "He's best friends with Caroline's old boyfriend. He just doesn't like Finley, that's all. It's complicated."

"Love always is," Mom sighed.

Ella came into the card room. "He fixin' to come home, y'all best get that U-Haul out from 'round back." Her eyes swept the room. "Y'all got enough in here?"

"We're fine, thank you, Ella," Mom said. "And boys, I think Ella is right."

Finley stood and turned to Eric. "Here, Eric, throw me the keys. I know how to back down the driveway." He and Caroline followed Ella out of the room, then Caroline returned carrying a wine glass.

"There, darling, help yourself," Mom said, nodding to the wine decanter on the bar.

I looked through the card room's windows to see Finley closing the car door at the exact time Eddie Dean pulled up in his Chevy. Eddie got out of his car and the two greeted in that half-effort, noncommittal back-patting way guys do—not wanting to give it too much lest they seem gay, but enough to express they were happy to see each other. Eddie pulled out a pack of Marlboroughs from his wool pea coat and lit a cigarette as they walked up the driveway. Seconds later, they walked in the card room.

"Oh, Eddie," Mom lilted, rising to her feet. Eddie held out his arms in a come-hither gesture, which always made Mom shine. She kept her hands on Eddie's shoulders, then stepped back, smiling. "You keeping out of trouble?"

"Absolutely not. Wouldn't want to break character," Eddie returned. "You mind this cigarette, Posey?"

"Not at all. You know I used to smoke," Mom said.

"Until the colonel paid her ten thousand dollars to quit," I qualified. "Now she just sneaks behind his back."

Eddie reached in his coat pocket. "That right? Posey, you want one? Ella indicated he isn't here."

"Well, yes, I believe I will. Thank you, you sweet thing." Mom accepted the cigarette with an inflection so coy, I thought she was flirting.

Eddie winked at Caroline as he lit Mom's cigarette. "I aid and abet this house," he said, which was Finley's cue to make introductions all around.

Smiling through his introduction in that sly, winning way of his, Eddie took off his coat and flopped down heavily in the chair across from Mom. "You hear Fatty's having a party on New Year's Eve? Y'all going?" Eddie's eyes swept over the group.

"I don't think we should, but it's a tough call. We're scheduled at Ardent on New Year's Eve and New Year's Day," Finley said.

"Oh, come on, let's go," Luke said. "I'm not going to miss meeting a guy named Fatty."

"Finley, go on and go," Mom encouraged. "What's one night?"

"Yeah, Finley, who would want to work all night on New Year's Eve, then be there early the next morning?" Eddie added.

Without skipping a beat, Finley said, "John Hampton, the producer I took great pains to hire and was lucky enough to get. We're not here to party, guys. This has to take priority over everything." The conviction in Finley's voice silenced the room, and I saw Luke look away as if duly reprimanded.

Gene and Eric nodded their compliance, then Mom took over the airwaves by sashaying to the bar, where she swiveled with a hand on her hip and said, "Now who'd like another drink?"

That night, a crash the likes of which I'd never heard jolted me awake at one in the morning. Dazed, I sprang up in bed, the back of my neck crawling in concert with my fluttering heart. I scanned my bedroom, trying to locate the source of the sound, when I noticed the crescent-shaped light coming from beneath the bathroom door by my other twin bed. My mind made no rational connection as it tripped through the possibilities of an intruder, the colonel's dog, or a ghost like the one who'd knocked William Porter off the wall, on its way to kill me. The key to Mom's door turned with its click-rotate-click, the door creaked wide, and then the colonel stood front and center in my bedroom, the hall light a beam behind him, and Mom over his shoulder, hastily pulling on her monogrammed robe.

"What's going on in here?" the colonel erupted. I shrugged my shoulders in a "deer in the headlights" gesture. "I didn't do anything," I defended, looking at Mom.

Another crash followed by harsh whispers catapulted Mom to the bathroom door, and she pulled it wide open. Because Finley stood blocking the entrance, I had a hard time seeing around Mom. I scrambled to my feet for a closer view. Caroline knelt on the floor, retching into the toilet. Finley held a white washcloth to his temple, stained red from the blood running to his jaw.

I cut around to Finley's room from the hallway. Shattered glass lay like cut diamonds along the baseboard by the closet. Something had hit with such force it made a nick in the wall. I looked through Finley's entrance to the bathroom and saw Mom bending over Caroline, who heaved violently from deep within her interior. Fetid and putrid vomit the color of pink molten earth splattered everywhere with alarming reach. Its width and breadth reached both the sink and the sides of the wall in a harum-scarum pattern that bypassed the toilet and was so revolting, it looked like a mass murder had taken place. I stood horrified but fascinated as the colonel removed himself from the scene, leaving us all to play out the rest of the night by our own devices.

"Leave me alone, get out of here," Caroline wailed in a voice so devoid of consequence there seemed no consideration beyond the moment.

"Finley, Millie, go on now," Mom directed. It was clear she'd be taking charge. She had one gentle hand on Caroline's shoulder while the other held back her matted hair.

Finley closed the bathroom door, still pressing the cloth to his temple. He looked at me with a levity so penetrating, it bolted my feet to the floor. "She's drunk," he said to my questioning eyes.

"What happened to your head?"

"She threw an ashtray at me. Twice."

"What'd you do to her? I thought y'all were spending the night near Ardent."

Finley started to answer when the bathroom door jerked open, and Mom ushered Caroline through to the sitting room across the hall.

"Millie, run get Caroline something to sleep in." I looked at Mom for a resistant second, thinking Caroline was only going to throw up all over whatever I brought. A wrangling production then took place in the sitting room as Finley pulled the marble table in front of the sofa bed out of the way.

I gathered pillows and a comforter from my bedroom, while Mom stripped a rag-doll Caroline down to her skivvies.

After we settled Caroline into bed, I thought it would be the end of it all. That Caroline would pass out and be humiliated in the morning. But the night continued when I heard the back stairs creaking a few hours later. I rose in the dark and weaved my way down them lightly to find Caroline sitting at the kitchen table. She'd found the gallon jug of Martini and Rossi white wine in the refrigerator, which the colonel bought on the cheap and served to guests, and which Mom let slide because she thought people didn't really care what they drink, as long as it got them tipsy.

"That stupid Finley." Caroline glared as I pulled out a chair at the table. "Everything's always about him. Your brother's such a control freak, he's unbelievable."

I knew better than to ask Caroline to elaborate in her drunken outrage. There was such hatred in her eyes, it didn't even surprise me when Finley took her to the airport at noon later that day.

We never discussed the episode amongst ourselves. Mom swept the scene under the rug, and Finley was too busy at Ardent to come to Kensington Park until the night before the band left to return to Charlottesville. But Ella had something to say about Caroline, no matter how she tried to comb its hair. I assumed she'd found out through Mom because Ella had ultimately been the one to clean up the bathroom. She stood at the kitchen sink, two days after Caroline left, wringing out a wet cotton cloth and mumbling to herself as if I weren't sitting there.

"Gots to watch your step with the company you keep," she said. "Mmm-hmm. I seen this one over and over. A body gets to be my age and ain't nothing new." I watched Ella as she wiped down the kitchen counter. I kept waiting for her point, but she seemed more intent upon cleaning the counter in broad, circuitous strokes.

"What're you talking about?" I finally asked.

"Ways of the world," she said, stopping to face me. "People oughts to know better than to go tying up with what they already seen ain't no good. That Finley must be crazy as a road lizard and blind as a bat too. I thought he too smart to have to learn the same lesson twice."

But it wasn't Ella's involvement in the aftermath of Caroline's drunken scene that made her wise to the facts. Later on, Ella told me it was Eddie Dean who'd come swinging through the back porch a few days later and opened up the refrigerator to help himself to sliced ham, mustard, lettuce, and provolone cheese, before he made his way to the breadbox and then had a seat to assemble a sandwich. He'd accepted the plate Ella pulled from the cupboard and laughed when she wrinkled her brow and demanded he get himself a napkin, saying, "Shame on you. You raised by wolves? What you doing here, anyway? Finley won't be here till later on."

"I know. I saw him last night," Eddie had said. "I was just in the neighborhood, thought I'd drop by."

Ella narrowed her eyes on Eddie. "Go on then. What you know I don't, but should?"

On a soft Saturday morning in April of my senior year, I looked through the oak branches outside my bedroom window to see Lucy Northrup picking her ginger way through the dense shrubbery separating her family's property from mine. I took the front stairs to the entrance hall, unlocked the door to the portico, then rounded out to the brick steps before the front door.

"You seen this?" Lucy held out an oversized, oblong magazine.

I shook my head.

"Look here, you won't believe this. Finley's in it," she said, opening the magazine from where her finger separated its pages.

"What? Where'd you get this?" I looked down at the full-page photograph of The Facts.

"I subscribe," she said, handing the magazine over to me. "It's Andy Warhol's *Interview* magazine. It's about the trends in popular culture." Her eyes found mine. "Millie, this is huge!"

The bold block caption read, "The Facts: The East Coast Version of the West Coast Sound." There was no attendant article, but I knew the mere presence of the band in the magazine was news enough. The boys were dressed in black blazers, white Oxford-cloth shirts, and black skinny ties. The staged photograph looked to have been taken with a fish lens and exaggerated the nonchalant looks on their faces, their eyes off-center from the camera as they leaned casually against a concrete wall.

"You didn't know?" Lucy asked. And when I shook my head, she added, "This magazine's worldwide. Here, you can keep it. Go show your mom."

I would have rushed to Mom's room immediately, but the colonel was still home. But I knew he'd be leaving for his daughter's farm in the country any minute, as he did every Saturday morning. Now that they'd been married for a while, Mom no longer pretended she was the sporting kind, so the colonel went on alone to Olive Branch, Mississippi, and Mom was mine for the asking, if I could bulldoze my way to a window of opportunity when she wasn't on the phone.

Once the coast was clear, I rapped on her door four times. I'd been standing in the hall impatiently, listening to the tail-end of her conversation, waiting for the cue of her heavy sigh followed by "Well, all right then," as if she'd exhausted every conceivable angle of gossip and it'd taken the wind right out of her sails.

"Yes?" Mom called.

"Can I come in?"

"Come on in," she answered.

I turned the crystal door knob to find her sitting with her legs crossed on the edge of the coral-patterned bedspread that complimented the chaise lounge across the room. It was her habit to rise every morning and fully dress in a combination of tailored attire and coordinating necklace and clip earrings. It was her allegiance to civility, a daily procedure dedicated to conducting herself as a lady to the manner born, for my mother was not a woman in conflict with herself. Her image was manifest from her clear vision of whom she'd decided to become.

"You going somewhere?" I asked.

"No," she said, rising. She walked to the chest of drawers, where she produced the ring-bound daily planner in which she wrote the left-handed lists that kept her life in order.

"Look at this. Lucy just brought it over." I handed her the magazine, already opened to the page.

She set her planner down and studied the page. "Well, I have never," she said in a voice that made me wonder if she understood the significance. "They have a manager? It says right here, management by Linda Horowitz. I thought Finley was the manager."

"Finley and Luke are, last I heard," I said. "I have no idea who Linda Horowitz is."

"Well, I don't know what's going on over there. If I don't ask the right questions, I don't get the whole picture. Since I'm not a musician, I never know what to ask." She sat on her vanity table's bench and faced me.

"I don't either," I said.

"He's excelling at school, which is all I care about. Whatever he's doing on the side is his business," she said as if concluding further discussion.

"Mom, this is bigger than the side. This is what Finley wants to do with his life. They want to be like the Beatles."

"Well, no doubt they will be, if Finley's involved. I don't know how he does it." She shook her head. "But I know one thing, everything he does turns to gold."

My mother had a mixture of pride and baffled amazement when it came to Finley's achievements. On the one hand, she gave herself credit as his parent, but on the other, she couldn't grasp how Finley had grown beyond her own limitations to actualize a character with which she couldn't identify.

And I, too, had familial pride over Finley. I was both intimidated and inspired to think I was cut from the same cloth. By this time, I'd decided I wanted to be involved in the music business, since music made up such a large part of my existence as a by-product of growing up with Finley. It was a time in American music when radio laid the soundtrack of my generation, and I aspired to being the DJ on the air, playing the songs. Because Finley had walked headlong into his ambitions, I blindly assumed I could walk into mine just as easily.

"I'm going to call Finley," I said, turning to go to my room.

"Well, let me talk to him after you do," Mom said.

Finley answered the phone on the third ring. "I just saw *Interview* magazine. Lucy brought it over," I said.

"Cool, huh?" Finley sounded excited.

"Yeah, incredible. Why didn't you tell me?"

"You'll probably get it in the mail on Monday. I wanted it to be a surprise."

"Well, it's a surprise, Finley," I said. "Who's Linda Horowitz?"

"She's our manager. We signed a management deal with her three months ago."

"Meaning what?"

"Meaning she'll take us to the major labels. Meantime, she's all over publicity. The woman's tapped in. She's the one who got us into *Interview*," he said. "It's all going to be a build."

19

I was privy to The Facts highlights, but not the painstaking minutiae of their climb to success through the following years. What I learned of it, I heard over the phone. Geography and the disparate aims of our individual paths set Finley and me in different orbits that intersected only once a year when we'd make like homing pigeons and return to 79 Kensington Park for Christmas. He returned home to be my escort the winter my girlfriends and I made our debut, and I'd gone to Charlottesville with Mom the June he graduated from UVA "with distinction."

I remained in Memphis after high school graduation to study communications and fine arts at Memphis State University, and began a radio career that progressed slowly and incrementally. While I paid my dues, I led a life centered on work and tempered with what became an on-again, off-again relationship with Aiden, surrounded by the regular company of the group I'd known since high school. I acquired a typical midtown apartment down East Parkway—a vaulted-ceiling, hardwood-floor one-bedroom flat with built-in shelves, arched doorways, and plenty of old-world charm. It was close enough to Kensington Park that I could blow in to see Mom and Ella, then scuttle on out before the colonel arrived on the scene. I talked to Finley often enough on the phone, usually about his band and popular music.

Two years later, as the hyacinth and azaleas in the front yard bloomed, and the yellow jonquils bordering the length of the driveway sprang forth to nod their two-toned heads like the salutary tip of a hat in the spring breeze, Finley and Caroline came pulling into Kensington Park with a seven-year old Tramp in the back. When I'd heard they were coming, it seemed an untimely visit from what I knew of everything going on with the band.

A subsidiary label of Warner Brothers Records had come to the table due to The Facts' regional popularity, and I'd learned they'd be sending the band to a recording studio in upstate New York. From what I understood, Finley's dreams were coming true. It would just be a question of time before the world knew of The Facts.

The cathedral doors to the gazebo were open to the late-afternoon air, wafting the fragrance of trellised jasmine inside and scenting the card room.

I was sitting on the sofa when Finley entered in that sauntering walk of his, followed by Tramp and Caroline.

He'd grown a beard, which surprised me, so much so that the first words from my mouth were, "That beard makes you look like a Viking." The beard was fiery red, and not just slightly. It seemed a freakish genetic throwback of prickling amber that verged upon orange, and it made Finley's face appear more rounded. And he'd gained a little weight, which made him seem more imposing. Studying him, I realized Finley cut a figure so reminiscent of Dad that it reached into my emotional archives with evocative fingers and accessed a part of my soul I'd thought would lie dormant forever. He was losing the hair on the top of his head, but the sides were tufted with undulating waves of Celtic gold protruding beneath the baseball cap he wore backward.

Considering the motivation behind the cap, I suspected there was vanity involved, and while the camouflage may have seemed reasonable for any man newly twenty-five and losing his hair, on Finley it seemed out of character. He leaned back as if he inspected me and said, "Long hair looks good on you." He cast his eyes upward. "And it's clear to me you swiped all the hair from our gene pool."

One smile from Finley flashed my way and I forgot all else. Whenever Finley smiled at me, it was like an inside joke, and it anchored me to my place in the world.

Mom hugged and sputtered and carried on as if she hadn't seen Finley in ages. She fluttered her hands across his back, kissed his cheek, and asked what he wanted to drink.

I could tell the colonel wasn't of a like mind. He stood steady at the bar and cut to the chase. "Finley, so what are your plans? How long will you be staying? You going to keep that dog in the house?"

Finley tilted his head and shot me a wink, then sidled his six-foot-two-inch frame shoulder to shoulder with the colonel. He picked up a highball, filled it with ice, then measured Scotch into a jigger. He held two fingers up to Mom with his eyebrows raised, then threw in another ounce of Scotch, which he topped with a splash of soda. Handing it to Mom, he sat and patted the sofa for Caroline to light beside him.

I drew my arms around Tramp and said "sit," then stroked her coat until it shined. Tramp emitted a deflating sigh just as the side door banged open and a chiming "Posey" came ringing from the back hall.

"It's Uncle Wick," Mom said, rising. "He'll want a drink."

"I hope I'm not too late for cocktails." Uncle Wick entered with an enthusiastic smile. "Finley!" he exclaimed. "I didn't know you were home. How are ya, you rascal?"

Finley rose and offered his hand just as I glanced out the cathedral windows and saw Eddie Dean. Finley saw him the exact moment I did. "What is this, mental telepathy?" he said.

"I told Eddie we expected y'all today," Mom volunteered, and after we heard the side door open and close, Eddie was before us in an instant.

"Y'all are predictable," he said. "Colonel, I'll have a vodka-tonic. What's happening, Millie-Billy-Filly?"

"Everything at once," I said.

"Percy and Allen are coming later," Eddie announced.

"Later? What'd you do, issue invitations?" Finley said, but I could tell he was happy.

When the phone rang, I picked it up to hear Lucy from next door. "What's going on over there?" she asked. "Y'all having cocktails?"

"Come on over," I said.

"I'll be there in fifteen."

"Lucy's coming," I said to Mom.

"Oh good, the bride-to-be," she trilled.

"What's this? Lucy's getting married? When?" Finley asked.

"She'll be a June bride. The wedding will be out at their farm."

"Well, she's fulfilled her mission in life," Finley said with deadpan sarcasm. "Millie, you're lagging behind. How's that thing with Aiden you've had going on for far too long?"

"Shut up, Finley. Lucy's been dating Lee for longer than that," I said.

"I only wish her father were here to give her away," Mom said, taking a sip. "I loved J.W. so." She set her drink on the side table and stood. "Excuse me for a minute, y'all. I'm going to put out hors d'oeuvres."

When she returned, Allen and Percy were trailing behind like ducks in a row. Percy carried a round silver serving tray and Allen carried a brown paper bag.

"Here, Posey, I brought the good stuff," Allen said. He lifted a bottle of bourbon from the bag and set it on the bar. I saw Mom's entire body bristle, and a forced smile tightened her face. "Oh, how sweet of you," she managed to say, but something in her tone dripped falsely.

At eight thirty that night, Finley, Caroline, and I joined Mom and the colonel in the kitchen. Ella had left a chicken casserole on the stove, and Mom put it in the oven to warm while I set out placemats and cutlery on the round marble table.

"Caroline, you want some wine?" Mom asked as if she'd never been around the bend with Caroline on the subject.

"I'd love some," Caroline said, which sent me to the row of glass cabinets in the butler's pantry to get one of Gaga's Waterford stems.

"Well, I'm telling you, I have never," Mom said, by way of introducing a new thought in her head.

"You've never what?" Finley asked, pulling out a chair.

"I've never been so offended in all my life." She placed a hand to her chest as if to steady her heart.

"Over what?" I rose to the bait.

"Over Allen waltzing in here carrying his bottle in a brown paper bag. I've never seen anything so tacky. I've thoroughly lost my regard for him. Doesn't your age group know any better? I'm worried about all y'all. Finley, I know I taught you better than that."

"What, you think Allen made some kind of statement?" Finley asked.

"Well, of course." Mom looked at him with her eyebrows raised to the middle of her forehead. "He might as well have come right out and told me I serve cheap liquor."

"An unpardonable offense," Finley qualified to Caroline. "It'd be okay if Allen picked up an axe and threatened any of us, but he can't insult Mom's liquor. I know you don't know these things, but in the South, them's fightin' words."

"Oh, I get it," Caroline said, taking a good sip of her wine.

"Mom, Allen wasn't trying to be rude," Finley said. "We're all just alcoholics in training who have yet to master the cultural necessity of liquor etiquette. We'll get there eventually."

Later, in the upstairs sitting room, I helped Caroline unfurl the sofa bed. There'd be no sharing of an unmarried bed under Mom's roof—never mind that she knew Finley and Caroline were living together in Charlottesville. And rather than put Caroline in my old bedroom, which joined Finley's, Mom parked Caroline across the hall, the better to drive home her idea of appropriate separation.

"I guess I better be getting home," I said. "I'll go say bye to Finley."

"He's on the phone with Luke," Caroline said. She paused as if thinking something through. "Have you heard anything about what's going on with all of them?"

"No, what?" I stood in the doorway and crossed my arms, eager to hear.

"Finley and Luke aren't getting along. It's kind of a contest of wills." Caroline turned on a table lamp and sat on the bed. Leaning down, she heaved her suitcase up from the floor. It was the hardback kind with a brass button latch.

"How big of a deal is it?" I asked.

"Big enough that their drummer quit the band. He got tired of the internal conflict. Finley and Luke made him feel like he had to pick sides. He's been straddling the fence on whether to go back to school anyway."

"So it was like forcing him to a conclusion, and he opted out?" I asked.

"Yes," Caroline said. "It's a shame, really. But you can't fight with Finley, as you probably know. He always has to have the final word, and can be so overbearing. I love him, but if you add his ego with his intellect, there's no winning with him."

"You're not telling me anything I don't know. I never have a chance with Finley."

Caroline laughed and gave me a conspiratorial wink. "I can relate, but in Finley's defense, I don't think he realizes how confrontational he can be. And Luke is kind of the opposite, but if you push him, he'll push back. He calls Finley a perfectionist, but to hear Finley tell it, he's doing everything on behalf of the band. I don't think Luke sees it that way. He thinks Finley's just controlling, that everything has to be his way or else it will fall apart. In the meantime, I swear, Millie, you ought to see how popular they are. People swarm to see them. You wouldn't believe it."

"What are they going to do without a drummer?"

"That's why we're here. Finley knows someone at Ardent who plays the drums. He's going to try to get him to move to Charlottesville. The band's in a bit of turmoil right now, but the good news is they don't have to be in the studio for another five months. Still, they better get someone quick because their manager will be sending them on a tour of the Southeast to generate a bigger fan base." Her face brightened. "They'll be playing Memphis in a couple of months."

I already knew this part of the band's story, that Warner Brothers Records had a subsidiary label that gave The Facts a contract, and that they'd be touring soon. "Bad timing," I said.

"Exactly," Caroline said. "I'm sure it'll all work out, but for now, it's a war zone."

"How is that for you?" I had to ask.

Caroline avoided meeting my eyes as she rummaged through her suitcase.

"I mean, are y'all getting along or what?" I half expected Caroline not to answer. It would have been understandable if she didn't, so I was surprised when she responded so quickly.

"We've been fighting," she said. "I know I'm partially at fault. I don't do well when people don't take me at my word. Finley always thinks I have some hidden agenda, so I get defensive. And to make matters worse, my brother lives close by, and he's almost as controlling as Finley. The two hate each other, and I'm caught in the middle." She stopped for a minute, lifting a nightgown from her suitcase. "Don't get me wrong. Finley's the funniest, most unique, creative guy I've ever known. I just think he's stressed out over the band because music gives his life so much meaning. He thinks his whole life hinges on the success of the band. Everything's complicated," she said. After a pause, she added half-heartedly, "I'm sure it'll all work out."

I crossed the hall to Finley's room and stood outside the door, listening to see if he was still on the phone. When I heard no sounds coming through the door, I knocked.

"Yeah?" Finley said.

"Can I come in?"

"Of course," he said.

Tramp came wriggling up when I opened the door. Her nose was lowered and her ears lay back as she swished her lowered tail in greeting. I leaned down to scratch her neck. "I'm going to get going," I said. "I just wanted to say goodbye."

"Okay. Did you tell Caroline goodbye?"

"Yeah, I helped her pull out the bed."

"Maybe you can spend some time with her tomorrow. You're free in the afternoon, right? I need to be at Ardent around twelve thirty."

"I can do that," I said, then straightening, I added, "Caroline told me about the band."

"She did?" Finley seemed surprised. "What'd she say?"

I had a seat on the chair by the tall chest of drawers. "Something about discord." I figured I'd start with that, to see if Finley would fill in the gaps.

Finley darted his eyes at the door, then back to me. "The immediate problem is we need a drummer. Can you close the door?" he asked, his voice low. "All right, go on and say it," he said after I sat back down.

"Say what?" I asked.

"Come on. It's not as if I don't see you watching Caroline. I always know what you're thinking," Finley said.

What I wanted to say was, "All right, she drinks too much and I have a little baggage on the subject," but Finley was looking at me in that blue-eyed, scrutinous way of his, and I wasn't in the habit of challenging him. If he wanted to carry on with a girl who drank like a fish, then I wasn't going to say anything. I always figured he knew what he was doing. I decided to steer the conversation elsewhere. "She says you and her brother hate each other."

"We do," Finley said as if it were a matter of fact. "He doesn't have the full story on his sister."

"So what's the story?" I asked.

Finley rose and went to the walk-in closet, where his suitcase was open on the floor. Coming back, he handed me a Xerox copy of a letter he'd written. "This pretty much explains it." He handed the letter to me.

"You want me to read this now?" I asked.

Finley nodded.

I settled back in the chair and began to read.

Dear Michael,

While I empathize with the pain and frustration you must derive from the current status of your relationship with Caroline, it still hurts me that you are not large-minded enough to refrain from using me as a scapegoat for the fact that your sister—and by extension, your relationship with your sister—is not in the shape that you might like at present. If you want to use someone as a psychic punching bag, it might serve you to get some facts first.

I was aghast as I turned the pages of the letter Finley had composed, which addressed a list of disparaging accusations levied against Finley and chronicled the nightmare of Caroline's alcoholic episodes: the drunken scenes in public, binges in isolation, face punches, thrown coffee mugs, kicks in the groin, the intervention of security guards, and threats of eviction. And then there was a heart-wrenching flipside to the tenor of the letter as Finley explained Caroline's behavior—her shameful appeals for forgiveness, promises made and broken, frantic pleas for Finley to stay by her side. Finley wrote he would continue to try to help Caroline as much as he could, for as long as he could because, despite everything, he thought she had the most breathtakingly beautiful heart in the world.

I handed the letter back to Finley.

"Before you say anything, I'm already on it," he said with resolution. "I'm encouraging her to go somewhere and get help. This is definitely bigger than anything I can do."

"How long has this been going on?" I asked.

"Years," he answered. "I think it's time to take this to the next level. Since she's from Minnesota, I've already looked into what she needs to do to check into the treatment center that Dad went to."

Out of all the three quarter of a million words in the lexicon of the English language, Finley had casually chosen three—Minnesota, treatment, Dad— that, when used separately, are completely innocuous, yet when strung together in one sentence had an impact that dropped the bottom out of the emotional sinkhole I'd been tiptoeing around since Dad died. He'd inadvertently made reference to the subject of Dad as if we'd had some running dialogue, when of course, beneath the shadow of Mom's example, the subject had remained tacitly taboo.

20

Mom's idea of how to entertain Caroline while Finley was at Ardent was predictable. I'd been working the entry-level midnight-to-six air shift at the radio station on Beale Street, and because my days and nights were turned around, I'd gone home after work, taken a nap, and then put on a dress to have lunch at the club and go shopping afterward. Finley was still at the house when I walked into the kitchen at noon.

"You're not going to say anything about what we talked about last night, are you?" he said as I slid into a chair at the table.

Ella glided back to the butler's pantry like a specter. She was the director of central intelligence in Kensington Park—she who knew all—but kept her shoulders squared, her mouth shut, and her gaze straight ahead.

"I'm not going to bring it up out of nowhere, especially with Caroline sitting there. You know I'd never do that. Does Mom know about it?"

"Entirely debatable," Finley said. "Depends on if you're talking about specifics or the big picture. I'm pretty sure she's got the big picture, she's just not saying anything."

I nodded. "No surprise there," I observed. "Anyway, I'm not going to bring anything up."

Caroline appeared looking delicate and lovely in a green and pink sundress cinched at her small waist, with skinny straps on her thin shoulders and a skirt that floated two inches below her knees. Her frame had the long, narrow essentials of a cat-walk model: nothing superfluous, nothing in excess.

"If you have a sweater, you should bring it," I said. "Mom's taking us to the red room in the club. The air conditioning will be on full blast."

"What y'all gone do with that dog?" Ella reappeared carrying a small copper watering can. She'd been tending to Mom's orchids on the window ledge above the pantry sinks.

"I'll take her out before I go. She'll be all right in my room," Finley answered.

"Let me know when you do, I needs to get in there and clean," Ella said.

Mom came in the room and chirped, "Y'all ready? Let's get a move on."

In the club's red room, so named for its tasteful burgundy carpeting, we sat at a center table, the better for Mom to receive her peers. Caroline and I sat tearing the cellophane wrappings from the basket of Melba toast on the linen-draped table, and wielded stainless-steel knives to smother it with chilled butter encased in small gold envelopes.

When Benita came to the table, we ordered iced tea and poured packets of Sweet'N Low into a brew so strong it went down like battery acid. Between the Cobb salads and the discreet signing of the membership check, we talked to everyone in that room of well-dressed lunching ladies who approached the table one after another, their jewelry jangling, their smiles flashing, punctuating their "don't let me interrupts."

Mom was at her finest on such occasions. I'd never seen anyone so practiced at the art of graciousness. She exuded an effortless, genuine charm that sprang with the perfect amount of lilting inflection as she delivered lines pertaining to just how thrilled she was to see each manicured friend standing over our table. You could have timed each exchange with a stopwatch. There seemed to be an implicit, aggregated understanding of just how long it's appropriate to engage in social niceties before one is considered intrusive. It made each interplay feel like a waltz that began with "So good to see you," and ended with "Give my love to the colonel," before they sailed away on their daytime heels.

"Well, I think we should go over to Laurelwood," Mom said, folding her linen napkin and placing it on the table just so. "Mimzy called me this morning. Her bookstore is hosting an author, so she's begging all her friends to come. I want to run into James Davis while we're over there. Finley's birthday is coming up. Millie, you should also get him a present."

"I will. Let's go to the bookstore first. James Davis is a men's store," I clarified to Caroline. "Laurelwood is a shopping center just up Poplar."

Sometimes the most innocent of gestures can have unintended consequences. Sometimes you think there will be no consequences at all to something as benign as the selection of a birthday present, and maybe I should have trusted my intuition. At the time something momentarily held me back from buying the book for Finley because I couldn't be sure of his reaction to M. Scott Peck's *The Road Less Traveled*, and at the time I thought Finley might judge me for my selection.

If you give someone a book, it implies you're in alignment with its premise, that you've read it and given it your stamp of approval, but that wasn't the case. All I knew of *The Road Less Traveled* was that it dealt with psychology and spiritual growth. At the time, I had no idea where the subjects converged. I only thought psychology dealt with the science of the mind as it relates to human behavior. Since Finley was so erudite, I thought the book might give his mind something to chew on. I thought he might take the book back to Charlottesville, put it on his bookshelf, and get around to glancing through it when he had nothing better to do.

And there sat M. Scott Peck wearing a gingham coat, behind a card table in Mimzy's Bookstore, where there were only five people in line.

So I got in a line I never should have, to buy Finley a present I wish I'd never given.

I don't know how it evolved that Eddie Dean took me to Lucy Northrup's wedding out at the farm in Collierville, other than Aiden and I were on the outs. I didn't consider it a date, and I'm sure Eddie didn't either, but he held the door for me when he picked me up in his Chevy, wearing a white dinner jacket and black bow tie. I gave him the once-over and an obligatory, "Don't you look nice," before I got in the car. I figured I had to say something. I hadn't the heart to tell him he looked like part of the staff.

Five o'clock on a June afternoon, and the meandering gravel driveway of the Northrups' farm was bordered in torches, which Cecil would light once the sun set. There were so many guests arriving simultaneously that Twyla had sent the horse-drawn carriage out, decorated nose to back wheels with white carnations, to carry guests to the grass in front of the house, where an arched trellis of white jasmine canopied the brick walkway leading to the brick steps before the front door. Twyla had the foresight to engrave on the ivory-and-gold invitation, "Ladies, wear flat shoes, we'll be standing on grass," which sent Mom and her friends into a phone networking tizzy that went on for weeks prior.

I stood to the side of the walkway holding a glass of champagne, when Uncle Wick stepped to the bricks, wrangling his bagpipes in full Highland dress. Lucy appeared behind him on the arm of her younger brother, who wore a tuxedo. He looked like a younger version of his father, and a hush silenced the crowd as the piercing pipes tested then erupted in wailing procession as the three made a promenade to the groom at the top of the steps.

I caught the eye of Reverend McAlister. He rocked on his heels as his robe flowed behind him, then cast his eyes about in a poignant pause as Lucy's younger sister arranged the hem of the wedding dress. Puffed to full power, the Reverend belted, "Dearly beloved, we are gathered here today in the presence of God to witness the union ..."

Fatty stood beside Allen and Percy. He smiled at me and tipped his glass. At the ceremony's conclusion, there were cheers and clapping, doves and butterflies, and J.W. Jr. fired the cannon to clapping oohs and ahs.

"Come on, let's go get a drink," Eddie directed.

I followed him around back to one of the stationed bars on the grass.

"I forgot to tell you that I called Finley yesterday morning. Caroline's in treatment in Minnesota. Did he tell you?" Eddie asked me.

"No, but thank God," I said. "It's been a long time coming. I've been worried about her."

"About her? I'm much more concerned about Finley." Eddie ordered a bourbon on ice, then looked at me square on. "What's he trying to do, save her? Doesn't he have enough going on without this? The band is on the brink of fame, for pity's sake. What kind of idiot would hang on to a troubled chick? I've always said that for every girl that's crazy, there are a dozen more standing in line that aren't."

"Says you, Eddie. Finley's in love. You ever been in love?"

"Why would I want to weigh myself down?"

"You're twenty-six, Eddie. Join the real world. You can't be a kid forever."

"Oh yes, I can," Eddie returned with total conviction. "I'm keeping that wolf at bay as long as I can. Things start getting complicated the second you let someone in." He was so charming, with his long dusty-blond hair and wicked smile.

I stood there thinking he had a point, because there stood Aiden across the lawn, acting like he didn't know me. I smiled at the bartender and handed him my champagne flute for a refill. "Anyway, did Finley say how long Caroline will be there?"

"She's doing hard time. She's in for ninety days. Probably be in a halfway house after that. Me? I'd rather stay drunk. And Finley's all into it. He says the Serenity Prayer is the most profound wording ever arranged. 'God grant me the serenity to accept the things I cannot change, the courage to change the things I can, and the wisdom to know the difference.'" Eddie rolled his eyes. "Yeah, profound maybe, but I take it at surface value. To me, it means nobody can do a dang thing about much, so roll with it." Eddie took a swallow of his bourbon and set his glass on the bar. "Y'all were never religious, were you?"

"No, not really," I said. But the image of Dad sprang to mind and wrapped its arms around me in such a way that it dampened my mood. I didn't feel like explaining to Eddie that Dad was deeply spiritual in his own way, that his way of interpreting life had instilled in me a spiritual awareness that transcended definition. My understanding was inexplicably personal, and I harbored it like a secret, knowing that Dad's imprint was mine alone to carry, that words would forever fail in any attempt to describe the internal navigational system I walked around with, which Dad had installed. It gave me a way of being in the world, as if Dad were still beside me, watching and guiding. It made me think that when people die, they really don't go far; they just take up residency in your body, and walk around under your skin.

That night, after the rice was thrown and the carriage spirited away the newlyweds to a waiting limousine on Collierville Road and I was home dozing in bed, I was visited by a memory that came to me in a half-dream. A young Finley and I sat digging in the earth in the woods of Minnesota. Dad sat solemnly against a tree trunk watching, letting us find our way in the burial of a bird Finley had unthinkingly shot with a BB gun. "There's no justification for the taking of life," Dad had said, as distraught as I'd ever seen him. And it wasn't so much that he was distraught over the bird, as he was over Finley's failure to fathom the full impact of what he'd done.

"All life is of equal value," Dad said. "You have no superiority over anything that lives, and there is no life up to you to take. It's up to God, however you choose to see Him. You both need to find your way with the subject. I'm not going to tell you how my mother tried to indoctrinate me with her Catholic views but they didn't take." He rested his elbows on his bent knees and cradled his forehead in his hands.

I looked over at Finley, who'd set his trowel down beside him, just as tears came streaming on their way to his quivering lip.

"I know it'll come to you when you're older," Dad said. "But I can tell you right now that what you do to others, you do to yourself. Just as what you do to yourself, you ultimately do to others. You have to see that everything's connected. None of us is an island. That bird you shot had a family, Finley, think of that."

Finley looked pleadingly at Dad. He was so ashamed to have disappointed him that he didn't construct a rebuttal, and I sat hanging my heavy head, thinking about that little bird's family.

21

The Facts arrived in Memphis the same night I sat for my portrait with Julian Enzo and the colonel's gun went off upstairs. It was the month of July, and the humidity came panting and oppressive through the screened doors of the card room, all opened in the futile hope of limping a breeze inside to stir the damp, lifeless air. I was nervous and self-conscious under Enzo's furtive scrutiny. The tendrils of hair on the side of my head clung to my temples, and the back of my neck was wet beneath my long hair.

Julian Enzo was a tall, elegant portrait artist from the genteel side of the Delta, with plantation manners and feline grace, who spoke haltingly and deliberately in an aristocratic accent that rolled out two beats after he weighed each word. He didn't intend to intimidate, yet people sat up a little straighter under his assessing gaze because he was reputed to have associations with the highest standard of beauty and form, which made many people excruciatingly self-aware. Everyone knew he had painted the portraits of Eudora Welty and Gloria Vanderbilt.

Under normal circumstances, wrangling him into the card room to sketch me would have been no easy feat, but my mother had been introduced to Julian at a cocktail party, and the two had formed a mutual admiration society. This led to the only job she ever secured; she became his curator, which basically involved introducing Julian to all of her friends.

I couldn't fathom where in the house Mom would hang a life-size portrait of me, but I had come when expected, wearing a candlelight ivory sleeveless dress. And although I hadn't been much in the habit, I'd accepted a glass of wine gratefully when Mom handed it to me without asking.

"I'd love to hear a little something about you, Millie," Julian purred, pencil in hand. Because his chin was lowered to his sketchpad, he cast his eyes up to look at me through his round-rimmed glasses, loose on the tip of his nose.

"I'll be twenty-three in October," I said.

"Hmm?" he said as if to say go on. "What do you like to do? Do you have a boyfriend?" ... to which Mom let out a "Hah."

"Kind of," I said because Aiden and I were still on the outs, and I'd recently started seeing a boy named Curtis, who came from a disreputable background, according to Mom. She'd known of Curtis' mother from decades ago, and dismissed her as a "torch singer" who once sang in shady bars down by the river. But Curtis was fun and exciting, with a self-assured manner, a sly pirate smile, and an irreverent sense of humor. He reveled in the fact we didn't come from the same walk of life, showered me with besotted attention, and called me his uptown girl.

For months, I'd resisted his advances when I'd see him at a rustic bar on the outskirts of Overton Square called Huey's, where my age group congregated on weekends. He'd appeared attractively dangerous and unpredictable when he brazenly walked up to me unintroduced. He said he'd been watching me around town for years and knew something about me, then astonished me further by saying we knew a handful of the same people, which I couldn't fathom because people from the neat grid of Memphis society I'd been raised in didn't test its perimeters.

"This one will pass, please God," Mom said, and I could feel my cheeks raising scarlet as Enzo swung his gaze from Mom to me. "He makes me wish she'd get back together with Aiden, if that tells you anything."

Enzo used his gentle hand to slide his glasses up the bridge of his nose. "Are you athletic in any way? Tennis perhaps? Golf?"

"Sometimes I take ballet class at Memphis South. I like to take long walks, if that counts. I played soccer in high school. That's about it," I said. "I don't know if this makes me athletic, but I've always kept moving."

The colonel burst into the card room and sat down heavily once he'd poured himself a drink. Looking at Mom, he boomed, "Posey, you ready for a sweetener?" Mom daintily held out her tall empty glass, and he rose again to his deliberate feet.

Enzo cleared his throat, reminding us of his purpose. "Are you working?"

"I work at the radio station on Beale Street," I said, watching his nimble fingers glide along in wide sweeping arcs across his pad.

The colonel handed Mom her replenished glass and stood at his full height. "I'm going to take the dog out," he announced.

Moments later, I looked through the glass doors and saw the two in the yard—the colonel walking with his drink in his hand and his dog submissive at his heels. Julian Enzo folded his pad and produced a Polaroid camera.

"If you will indulge me, perhaps stand over there in front of the fireplace … yes, that's fine … and fold your hands in front of you as if you were holding a bouquet … yes, beautiful, thank you." Julian hummed as he aimed the camera. Presently he lifted his eyes. "Well, this ought to do it," he said, looking at my mother.

"Julian, stay and have another drink," Mom suggested in her way of offering an invitation one couldn't refuse.

Julian draped his long, languid body in the chair across from my mother, legs crossed felicitously, in his European white shirt and summer suit.

The colonel, having taken his dog upstairs, came back into the card room. He reached down and took the glass from Julian's hand. "Julian, what are you having? Let me get you a refill."

"Vodka-ice, thank you," Julian said as the pinging of ice hit the low, shallow glass.

The colonel took up occupancy in the wing-backed chair and settled in, though it seemed to me he was a fish out of water. Julian and Mom had so much to talk about. They were eager with each other, enthusiastic and encouraging. They were purveyors of the same language, which gloried in the discussion of people, the intricacies of their decorated homes, their parties, and whom had said what so jocularly that it couldn't go without repeating. They basked in each other's company in such an exclusive manner that, after a while, the colonel saw the writing on the wall and went on upstairs.

"Well, I certainly hope we didn't chase him off," Julian lilted.

"Oh no. If we did, he'd have said something." Mom dismissively waved her hand. "Julian, I'm thinking of having a facelift. What do you think? I'm sagging a bit down here." She placed her hands on her cheeks and lifted up.

"Well, Posey, I think you should do whatever makes you feel good. And if a woman has the kind of looks you do, she wants to preserve them." He took a long sip of his drink. "Yes, I'm all for a facelift. Just make sure you go to the best."

As they continued discussing who they knew who had had a good facelift, boom came the pandemonium that shook the air, freezing them both for one confused second as their bewildered eyes locked.

"What was that?" I said. "Was that a gun?"

Mom uncrossed her legs in preparation to stand, then crossed them back as she reconsidered. She leaned back in her chair and sighed. "Well, that's it. He's done it. He's killed himself," she said. "I'm not going up there. I don't even want to know."

"I'll go up there," Julian said. He got to his feet and I did too.

"I'm going with Julian," I said.

Mom stood. "Oh, for pity's sake."

We walked through the parlor and cut up the back stairs to find the master bedroom door closed. Julian knocked twice, while Mom and I stood behind him.

"Colonel," Julian tested, "everything all right in there?"

"Yes, not that it's any of your business," came the reply over the bark of his surly, snarling dog.

Mom reached around Julian to open the door. We found the colonel standing with his back to the window, a can of gun oil and a cleaning rod lying beside the gun on his bedside table, the dog panting at his feet, and a hole in the opposite wall.

"What in the world are you doing?" Mom erupted. "You scared us half to death. I thought for sure you were dead!"

I'd never seen anyone so embarrassingly out of character in a red-handed moment as this Lieutenant Colonel Commander, caught flagrantly irresponsible.

Just then the back door opened and closed, and a cacophony of layered voices came reaching up from downstairs as all four of The Facts clattered into the back hall. They'd only be in Memphis for two nights before continuing with their tour of the Southeast. We'd known they were coming that night, but hadn't known the exact time.

"Mom?" Finley called from their midst.

"Shhh," Mom ordered everyone in the room. "Don't say anything. Let me go down first. Julian and Millie, go down the front stairs. I'll see y'all back in the card room." She threw both hands up in a declarative move. "And whatever you do, don't say a word."

I figured I should stay quiet for the moment, but I smiled as I made my way down the stairs with Julian in front of me. I now had the goods on the colonel. And fortuitously, the episode had exposed him for being humanly flawed. I kind of liked this new information. I kind of liked being asked to safeguard his iron-fisted image. I had surreptitiously seen him treading the edge of vulnerability, however fleeting the moment would last, before he snapped back like a rubber band.

And I knew a chance for change when I saw one, and curiously, it made me soften toward the colonel. It made me want to crack the armor of my resentment, put down my braced attitude, now that we'd joined in momentary cahoots. This glimpse of his humanity gave me hope for some kind of connection, because I'd grown exhausted by the years of tiptoeing around him. In the room, before we all departed as Mom ordered, I had met his eyes for one unvarnished moment of transitory truce, then turned and left the room.

I have an indelible picture etched deep within me that's so evocative it affects me physically every time I call it to mind: Finley on stage with his band under three roaming lights of red, yellow, and green, before an adoring crowd of eight hundred at the Omni New Daisy Theater on Beale Street in Memphis. They were evenly spaced on the stage, wearing white shirts and black skinny ties, looking so collegiate as to be edgy, so full of dancing enthusiasm and youthful vigor as they threw their spirits around the room and affected the swaying crowd with a passion for life that overflowed at peak capacity. Never before had I been in witness of a moment so mind-alteringly surreal as to seem fated by a beneficent universe, which had conspired through thick and thin to bring Finley to that stage. He stood to the left of Luke Piedmont, holding his electric guitar so effortlessly it seemed a part of him, and he played it as if it were the only means of communication this lifetime would ever afford. Riotous applause ricocheted from wall to wall between each of their six opening-act songs.

I was beside myself to see my brother so rapturously in his center of joy that I could barely contain myself. I felt a part of it all—from dream to fruition, and standing there looking up at Finley made me think there is justice in this world, if one identifies what gifts they have and puts them to use. In that moment I had proof, for there stood Finley, blue eyes glowing beneath a spotlight as the music moved through him in the midst of his dream come true. This is a vision of my brother I can access from the depth of my being, if I'm feeling strong enough, a moment so ecstatic and pure it might persuade the hand of fate to reconsider, to reach back into the netherworld and hold Finley on that stage forever, his life stretched out before him.

Parking my car in the back driveway, I saw the silhouette of Ella through the dotted swiss curtains of the kitchen window. Before I reached for the back door, it opened, and there stood Ella, her hand on the door, a purse on her lips.

"The colonel done lost his fool mind. I see they done rearranged the furniture upstairs to hide that hole in the wall, 'stead of gettin' it fixed."

I stepped on the ornate iron grate Dr. Joe had commissioned for the landing and walked into the back hallway. "Maybe he doesn't want to be reminded he mishandled his gun every time he looks at the wall. If they spackle it, they'll have to paint the whole room. Maybe it's just easier." I shrugged. "I don't know, Ella."

She followed me into the kitchen. "He cheap, that's what he be. Too bad that gun didn't hit that dog."

"Where's Mom?"

"She upstairs on the phone with Finley. Been up there with the door closed for high near an hour."

I'd exchanged a few rounds of brief letters with Finley, but it'd been two and a half months since I'd heard his voice. The band had occupied all his time in Upstate New York, where they'd been recording their record. I wanted to hear the details, so I picked up the phone in the hall. "Hey, Mom, I'm downstairs. Finley?" I said.

"All right, I'll hang up now," Mom said. "Finley, keep in touch."

"Hey, tell me what's going on. My radio station's still playing 'Don't Go Out,'" I said, referring to The Fact's single.

"Man, it's been incredible. You're not going to believe who they brought in to play on 'Five-Forty-Five,'" Finley said.

"Who?" I asked as the catchy notes of a song Luke and Finley had cowritten came to mind.

"Todd Rundgren."

"My gosh, Finley, unbelievable. You're talking lead guitar, right? I thought you play lead."

"Well, I do, but come on ... Todd Rundgren. I'll gladly take a back seat for him. I'll send you something when I get a copy. Right now, I have to go. I've been on the phone with Mom for too long and I've got stuff to do. I promise I'll call you next week."

"Okay, but wait. How's Caroline?" I managed to squeeze in, my voice dropping to a whisper.

"I'll let Mom tell you. I have to go."

"You told Mom about Caroline?" My voice returned to normal.

"I kind of had to," he said. "Listen, I'll talk to you later. I really have to get off now."

"Okay, talk to you later. I love you."

"Yeah, love you too," Finley said.

I walked into the kitchen and sat at the marble table to wait for Mom. We'd be going to a Doncaster showing at a private residence on Goodwyn Street, in one of the early 1900s mansions lining the stretch of road parallel with the Memphis Country Club's golf course. It happened every year on the second Thursday of September in preparation for the coming holiday season. Mom and her friends would smell like flowers and move like queens as they perused the exclusive line of English women's couture, only shown in the living rooms of private houses by select invitation.

The click of Mom's heels brought me to my feet. "You ready to go?" I asked.

"Not yet, let me get a cup of coffee."

Ella produced a cup and saucer as Mom sat in a chair across from mine.

I didn't know how much Mom knew about Caroline, so I cautiously framed my question. "I just asked Finley about Caroline. He said I should ask you."

"Oh, God." Mom rolled her eyes. "I can't say if I'm glad or not." She glanced over her shoulder at the retreating Ella. "Thank you, Ella." She positioned the cup in front of her. "And I'll just have—thank you," she said as Ella returned to place Sweet'N Low and a pint of half-and-half beside the cup.

"Glad about what?" I asked.

"Finley and Caroline broke up."

I couldn't have been more shocked. "What? When was this?"

"It sounds like the moment she left treatment. I assume you know about that."

"I do. Eddie told me and then Finley wrote me about it later."

"Well, Finley's still trying to hang on, but I don't know how he thinks he'll do that. She's going to stay in Minnesota."

"Unreal," I said, still taking it in. "Is Finley okay?" I looked up at Ella, who stood behind Mom with her fists planted on her hips.

"Of course he's okay. He doesn't believe she really means it. He seems to think she doesn't know her own mind, so he fully intends to straighten her out. I told him the first thing that happens when someone quits drinking is they make everyone around them miserable. Oh, they apologize, but they also manage to slip in that you're a big part of their problem. Your father never did that. Thank God, he took responsibility. But he was one of the rare ones, believe me. I've seen this number many times. When alcoholics aren't being insufferably confessional, they're preaching about how everyone else needs to quit drinking." Mom set about preparing her coffee. "Once they sober up, they look around and decide everyone's an alcoholic. Sooner or later they cut everyone out who was with them while they were drinking. The only friends they have in the world are the ones they find in AA meetings, which they go to for the rest of their lives. I told Finley there's not a lot of hope here. Lord, deliver me from a recovering alcoholic." She sighed before taking a sip from the cup. "The fun's over, as far as I can see. Dead as a doornail. I can't fathom why he wants to hang on. Just because she screwed up her life doesn't mean he has to screw up his. I told him to do himself a favor and let her go."

"He don't know that dog don't hunt," Ella said with a deep frown and a dip of her chin.

"That's right." Mom looked over her shoulder. "That's just about what I said, Ella, but you can't tell Finley anything. He's the kind who has to figure things out for himself."

Mom was right. Finley spent an inordinate amount of time figuring things out for himself. Part of Caroline's treatment was to hear in writing from those affected by her alcoholism. Finley had been sent a questionnaire asking for the details of Caroline's alcoholic behavior, as well as how it affected him.

He embraced the process of examining his part in Caroline's alcoholism with fearless, soul-searching abandon, which he shared with me right about the time he got his hands on the Al-Anon program. It was as if a light descended upon Finley, illuminating his interior spaces. He looked at the history of our family dynamic in a way that explained his subconscious reason for becoming involved with Caroline in the first place. On the phone, he spoke to me of our "internal maps," and said our frame of reference regarding normalcy was skewed because of Dad's alcoholism and Mom's denial. He said he was processing everything and may not come home for Christmas, which I accidently let slip as Mom started making her holiday plans. Finley was lit by a fire that wanted to save me from ruin, so he introduced me to the findings of Adult Children of Alcoholics. It didn't bother me that it was over my head or that the subject had yet to affect me.

But that all changed when Finley wrote Mom a letter that came on the heels of an unpleasant phone conversation they'd had, and it started an avalanche.

Dear Mom,

I would like to sincerely apologize for the things I said on the phone the other day. It was wrong of me to use words which distort the truth of what I really feel. I lost control of what I was saying. If I could change what happened, I would.

I feel it would eclipse the main point I would like to get across at this time, that I am sorry I said hurtful things, if I were to offer too detailed of an explanation of why I think our conversation went as it did. At the same time, I feel I would be remiss if I didn't at least explain my part of it in brief.

I am going through some fairly predictable emotional upheaval with respect to my relationship with you and Millie and Dad. Although emotionally, of course, I would like to share my feelings with you all, my rational mind, as well as my intuitive mind, tells me that it is best that I keep my feelings to myself. This would prove a next-to-impossible task if I were to come home for Thanksgiving and Christmas because much of what I am feeling these days involves you all.

Put another way, I was thinking of not coming home specifically because I wanted to avoid scenes such as the one we experienced on the phone. I do not want to address why I believe those scenes would be inevitable, but at this juncture, I believe they would be.

Later, that will not be the case.

Unfortunately, Millie told you what I was thinking (and I do not blame her) before I had a chance to discuss it with you. I want to emphasize the word "discuss." I was never planning to just say "I'm not coming home." I wanted to see if you could talk to me and understand why. If you couldn't understand, I might have thought it better just to come. I don't know. Anyway, that was my thinking.

I am sure you and Millie must find it awfully dramatic of me to be so emotional about my family. I feel I can safely say that, until recently, (increasingly in the last year and reaching a peak as of late), no one would have found it more distastefully dramatic than I.

It probably comes as no surprise that I have always believed that I didn't possess any particularly strong feelings about anyone in our family one way or another. I've only recently begun to realize what a ridiculous lie that is. It's a subconscious stance I needed as a child to get by and I never discarded it. I didn't choose it. I didn't author it. I just felt it. It's called denial and it isn't working anymore.

There are some other stages after denial that I believe people go through before they arrive at true acceptance (emotional) and not just understanding (intellectual) of the effects of trauma on their psyche. I do not believe these stages are going to be pleasant, but I intend to grow through them nonetheless.

If these stages are dealt with at the proper time, the process needn't, in my mind, be a protracted one. If they are dealt with years or even decades after the traumatic events, as in my case, it can take a long time.

Although emotionally I might be moved to, I don't think it's right for me to try to get anyone in our family to accept my way of dealing with issues or even to convince anyone that there are any issues. That's up to each of you.

But I think I should be supported and not belittled for following my own road (whether to my face or in my absence), and hopefully respected for having my own conception of reality, since at least it is arrived at each day with a lot of care and an overriding effort to do the right things for the right reasons.

Love,

Finley.

"His own road," Mom exclaimed after reading me Finley's letter in her bedroom on a November morning. She tossed the letter on her bed with a quick flick of the wrist, as if its pages were suddenly too hot to handle. "What was the name of that book you gave Finley? What road was it about?" She turned and glared at me.

"*The Road Less Traveled.*" I paused to gather my thoughts. "So ... did you belittle him? What did he mean by that?"

Mom gave me one of her looks. "I only told him that if he sits around and dwells on his problems, they only get bigger. I think he's being self-indulgent."

"Mom," I said. "Come on. He and Caroline just broke up. He's probably going through a phase."

"A phase where I'm to blame," she shot back. "The joke's on me. I just thought I was going to have children and everything would turn out fine." She retrieved Finley's letter, then folded it and tucked it in the drawer of her bedside table.

"When did y'all fight on the phone?" I wanted to know.

"About two weeks ago. He ended it by hanging up on me. I wasn't going to call him back after that." She sighed so deeply I watched the draperies to see if they'd billow under the weight of air. "Now he's going to screw up Christmas."

22

That Christmas season, my mother soldiered around the vacancy of Finley by performing her customs as if nothing were amiss. She was a one-woman circus throughout the entire month of December, receiving a flurry of friends who dropped by delivering presents, and after checking her schedule in her daily planner, rushing out to deliver her own. She'd started constructing a gift list in early October, in her illegible left-handed scrawl, which stretched into the hundreds. She scratched a notation to the right of each name to remind her of who had sent what the year before, so she wouldn't make the faux pas of regifting the giver. Her list stayed on the console in the back hall between the phone and a sixteen-inch Imari bowl, filled to the brim with Christmas cards she'd received from all over the country.

She and the colonel threw a cocktail party for sixty, and they were guests at countless others. The rhythm of her life went on that December as usual, but I noticed a strain in her tight smile and a force to her uplifting demeanor when the colonel's daughter brought over her family for Christmas Eve dinner. Belle arrived wrapped in a mink stole, and Miss Mycroft tottered in her wake. Mom and I were both distraught over Finley's absence, but whenever anyone mentioned it, Mom put a sanguine lilt to her voice that could have melted butter and exclaimed, "Well, he's just so busy with his band. I think it's wonderful what he's doing. He'll be home as soon as he can," which made everyone think everything was fine.

But I wasn't fine. Without Finley there, I felt like an only stepchild faking revelry in my own house, outnumbered by the colonel's family and irritated with Finley for abandoning me. My only solace was that I'd requested a short vacation from work and I'd be driving to Charlottesville to see The Facts play on New Year's Eve.

I packed my duffel bag with all the enthusiasm of a traitor on his way to the Tower of London instead of three days in Charlottesville with my brother. Mom acted as if I'd chosen sides and decided to abscond to opposing forces. She had a knack for underhanded manipulation. She combed its hair so well it made me question my interpretation of her motives when she called to wish me a safe trip.

"Are you all packed?" she asked when I picked up the phone.

"Just about," I said.

"Well, you better get a move on if you plan on getting to the halfway mark before it gets dark."

"I'll be leaving in about an hour."

"Be sure to call me when you get to—where is it, Johnson City?"

"There, or maybe Knoxville. I don't know, I'll see. I promise I'll call you."

I heard her release a sigh. "Well, I'm glad he's speaking to one of us," she said. "But it certainly doesn't seem to bother you that he's not speaking to his mother."

"Mom, don't be like that."

"Don't be like what? It's the truth. He didn't bother to call me on Christmas Day. He invites you up there, and up you go, but he doesn't feel moved in the slightest to call his mother." I knew my mother well enough to know the exasperation in her voice was my invitation to comment.

"You didn't call him either," I said.

"Yes, I did. I got his answering machine. I didn't leave a message, but he knew it was me. I know he knew it was me. He was probably sitting right there."

"Well, call him again. What's the big deal?"

"You're treated the way you allow yourself to be treated, that's the big deal. No child of mine is going to treat me this way."

"All right, fine, be that way. You still want me to come by and pick up those boxes to take to him?"

"No, I've changed my mind. At this point I wouldn't send him switches and ashes. Let him sit himself over there in Charlottesville and think about all the horrible things I've done to him. Suits me to a screaming T."

"Well, I don't know what else to say," I said. "I should get going."

"There's nothing more to say. I'm just surprised he's letting you come, since you're part of his dysfunctional family. I'm just unappreciated and misunderstood by my ungrateful children, that's all. Dysfunctional family ... I don't know where he came up with that phrase unless it was something he read in that book you gave him. And don't you let him talk you into hating me while you're over there."

"Mom, Finley doesn't hate you."

"Yes, he does."

"No, he doesn't. Anyway, I love you, Mom," I said.

"Well, that's one of my children. And don't you dare tell Finley I'm over here suffering."

"I won't."

"Unless you think you can knock some sense into that fool head of his. I'll leave that up to you."

The winter had beaten the fields around Finley's cottage to a sodden exhaustion. The grounds were lackluster and depleted, the trees stripped and eerie in an aromatic environment as pungent as a wet dog. Finley stood in the marled gravel driveway without a coat when I scratched up the road. His flannel shirt flapped over a navy tee as he guided me forward in semaphores, then opened the car door when I came to a stop.

"It's about time," he said, smiling down. "Come on in. I want to play you something." The eagerness in his voice drove me straight inside, where I put my duffel bag down and sat on his unmade bed, then leaned down to pet Tramp. "Okay," I said, "what is it?"

"You ready?" he asked.

"Yeah, I'm ready. What am I listening to?"

"Four songs we recorded in the studio. I want you to hear how it's going." Finley pressed play on the reel-to-reel stationed by his bookshelf. I started to stand, but he said, "No, stay there. The sound will be better if you stay where you are." The force of his blue eyes arrested me. He stood beaming down as if willing me to hear what he heard, feel what he felt. But I already knew I'd love it because Finley and I were on the same page.

My appreciation of music had come as a consequence of growing up with him. Not only had I learned to interpret music beneath his tutelage, I came to understand the myriad elements of its life force, that at music's core is a celebration of life. To listen to music with Finley was to be infused with his passion. And, as I listened to the songs, it seemed to me the band had reached a higher bar. The essential pop structure they were known for was there, but they'd added the vibratory undertones of synthesized keys. There were layered harmonies and crisp dynamics and, always, the driving force of Finley's guitar.

I looked at Finley, smiling my approval, and couldn't help but notice he paced around the cottage, picking up this and straightening up that. I was halfway to asking him to just sit down, because he made me nervous, when he switched off the reel-to-reel and swung into his gray, three-quarter coat.

"Come on," he said, "let's get out of here."

"Can we bring Tramp?" I shrugged into my coat, then followed Finley out to the car.

"Yeah, if you want," he said, opening the car door. "As long as you're willing to keep an eye on her. I've got to go over to Luke's apartment and pick up some equipment. He has a little terrier that hasn't been socialized enough, so if it's outside, you should probably keep Tramp in the car. I don't want a dogfight."

"So, we're not going over to the studio behind his parents' house?"

"No, Luke has a place in town."

I slid in the passenger seat of Finley's car and settled Tramp between us.

"All right, we're not going to talk about me and Mom, okay," Finley said in more of a statement than question as he pulled out of his driveway. "But I'd bet anything she read you the letter I wrote her."

"Yeah, she did. But if you don't want to talk about it—"

"I don't." Finley cut me off. "I'm just going through some stuff she doesn't understand. Or if she does understand, she doesn't want to talk about it."

"It's not that she doesn't want to talk about it, she just doesn't want to be blamed," I said.

"I think it's better if we don't talk about Mom. If you're not open to talking about our family dynamic either, then that's fine too."

"Finley, it's not that I'm not open. I just feel kind of ambushed. I mean, all of a sudden you've got some intellectual take on what you say is our family dynamic, when it was enough for me to live through it. I mean, since I can't change the past. I just accept it, that's all."

"Okay, fine. I hope it works for you," he said.

"Okay," I said more defensively than I intended. I looked at Finley and saw that his jaw was set tight. "Can I ask about Caroline? I know y'all broke up, but are you still in touch?"

"Yeah, we're in touch. She's at a sober-living facility in Minneapolis."

"For how long?"

"She doesn't know. I talk to her every few weeks. She doesn't know her plans because she's taking it one day at a time."

"What, she can't make a plan beyond a day? She can't even come down for tomorrow night?"

"It's a commitment to recovery. Once you're in sober-living, that's it. Recovery comes first." He spoke as if what he'd said was obvious.

Words sprang unbidden from my lips. "Dad never went to sober-living."

"You see where that got him," Finley said. "Maybe if he had, he wouldn't have relapsed like he did. His personality was such that I'm surprised he even went to Hazelden in the first place."

The words stung. Finley had never said a disparaging word against Dad and neither had I. We'd both been in the habit of leaving that dog tethered up safe and sound in the backyard.

"Look, Millie, I know I just hurt you." He threw me a sideways glance. "Alcoholism is a sad disease. Have you ever looked at any of the literature? I've had cause to because of Caroline. I view the disease as a complex interaction between the agent—meaning alcohol—the environment, and the individual. Each case and its attendant symptomology is inevitably as unique as the individual and his environment. I don't think Mom helped Dad one bit. It's not as if she curtailed her cocktail hour. Dad went to treatment, but I don't think it permanently took. Until treatment takes, alcoholism is like any other terminal disease, be it cancer, leukemia, or whatever. The road to untreated alcoholism is just sadder by virtue of its sheer avoidability. Dad never did live up to his own potential, which I believe was limitless." He shot me a look that told me he was right about all this. "Anyway, it's time we stopped acting like Dad was perfect."

"I think Dad was okay at the end. It kind of took," I rationalized.

"Yeah, well, who knows what would have happened had he lived," Finley snapped.

"And another thing," I lobbied, "who ever said Dad was perfect?"

"Who ever said anything? That's my point with Mom. About the only thing she said to me after he died was that it was the best thing that could have ever happened to him because he'd screwed up his life so bad."

I thought Finley was being unfair and cruel. I didn't like the way he levied such a final judgment when Dad wasn't around to defend himself, so his words hit me as disloyalty. I didn't want to argue with Finley, and it was unfamiliar, uncomfortable terrain to hear his opinion, while I felt so differently. I backed off and changed the subject. "Why do you always have to drive home a point? Mom already knows everything. She was the one married to Dad. It's her story, not ours."

"That's where you're dead wrong. We're the ones who will suffer in the long run."

"Finley, I'm not suffering."

"That's because you're in denial. You won't look at the facts. We were basically cheated of the most significant relationship most people ever have in life. Parents are the center of a child's universe. Under normal circumstances, they're the complete foundation. Aren't you ever envious of your friends when they talk about their normal fathers?" Finley looked at me as if it were a foregone conclusion I was. "I can't even engage in a conversation about Dad with any of my friends." He drew in his breath and softened his tone. "Look, Dad let us down. It'll affect all our relationships for the rest of our lives—probably yours more than mine."

"Why mine?"

"You'll get married someday. I don't know if it'll be Aiden or whomever. You don't seem capable of letting Aiden go, even though he's clearly not the one for you. In my opinion, you're wrestling with the issue of stability, having been deprived of it with Dad. This is deep-seated stuff, Millie. Relationships are problematic enough as it is: they're chaotic and complicated, and although nobody ever gets up in the morning and says, 'Today, I'm going to screw everything up,' they get screwed up just the same. To top this off, you don't have a normal premise from which to relate to a man. If you think the colonel is some kind of male role model, he's not. His hostile presence just gives you something to defend against, which is going to color any intimate relationship you'll ever have with any man. You're going to have to work this one out someday. I'm pretty clear it'll come around to haunt."

"Well, I don't think there's anything wrong with acceptance. And I don't hate the colonel as much as you think I do. I mean, it's kind of like this—I've got a dog. It may not be the best-looking dog, it may not be the fastest, or the smartest dog ... but it's *my* dog."

"Okay, fine," Finley said. "As long as we're reciting platitudes, go on and accept the devil you know. Time will tell where that'll get you."

We pulled in the alley beside Luke's apartment, a faded ivory Victorian house, sectioned into four units, with blue-gray shutters and a raised veranda. I took Tramp out of the car and watched her sniff around the front hedges while Finley went inside. Moments later, the front door flew open and Luke came laboring out, his muscular arms wrapped around an unwieldy tweed amplifier.

"Millie, I'm glad you're here, give me a hug." Luke set his burden down and gave me a cheek-to-cheek embrace, which immediately caused the color to rise to my face, which was how I always reacted whenever I saw Luke. "Can you flip the trunk? We're taking this amp tonight." He heaved the amp back into his arms and walked ahead of me. "Did Finley tell you our manager's coming down with the head of the record label from New York?" he asked over his shoulder. "Charlottesville's never seen a New Year's Eve like the one they'll see tonight."

"I didn't know that, but cool." I reached under the front seat and found the release for the trunk.

"They're bringing someone down to film it too. Linda Horowitz keeps telling us to get used to the buzz."

"How long are y'all going to be playing tonight?"

"Probably an hour. We'll be doing all the songs on the record. It's going to be a pre-release thing. We should have the record finished by February, and it'll be out soon thereafter." Luke positioned the Fender amp in the trunk and snapped it shut.

"Sounds meant to be," I said.

"That's what Finley keeps saying. Y'all sound just alike."

"I can tell Finley's excited. Actually, he seems kind of hiked up."

"Yeah, I was going to mention that," Luke said, slowing his speech to his cultured Virginia drawl, which sounded a little to the left of Canada. He ran a hand through his hair and turned to face me.

"Mention what?" I looked at him, waiting.

Luke took his time saying what he had to say, and when the words came, they were measured. "Look, Finley's the last guy who needs it, and it's probably my fault, but I think he should lay off the blow."

"What?" I had not expected this.

"I'm not saying it's out of hand. More than half of everybody I know does it. It's just that Finley's an extremist as it is, and on blow, his Type A personality is heightened to exaggerated proportions. I find him difficult to reason with, let's just say that. He's putting the band under a lot of stress."

I could only imagine what this meant. I thought about what Caroline had told me a few months earlier regarding The Facts' inner-band turmoil, and wondered if Finley had been tampering with cocaine back then or if she'd only been commenting on his personality in general. And now here was Luke telling me something similar, which made me think that the consensus was that Finley is difficult.

"I'm not sure what to say," I said, crossing my arms and steadying my stance. "I had no idea. I can't influence Finley one way or another about anything. He follows the beat of his own drum, but you know that. Anyway, let me ask you something. Why do you say it's probably your fault?"

Luke cut his eyes from my face to a spot in the yard, as if there were something important happening a few yards away. He took his time answering me, but I wasn't going to say another word until he did. "I tend to have it lying around," he eventually said. "Guess I'm kind of culpable. Sorry, Millie. I should have known better, what with your family history and all, you know."

I wanted to deflect the family implication because it made me feel tainted. "I'm not going to say anything to Finley out of nowhere," I said.

"Well, all right. I just thought … maybe." Luke shrugged. "But let me articulate my concern. Finley's been under a lot of pressure. He's the one shouldering most of the responsibility on behalf of the band, which I appreciate, but if he's doing blow now … the question is, what's going to happen if he looks to destress by doing other drugs? Intellects like Finley tend to reach for the edge. It's like this earthly level of consciousness isn't enough for a guy like him. He has to reach for more, know what I mean? I think this business with Caroline has set him off. He's all over the place."

"Maybe he has good reason," I said.

"Maybe, but I don't know why he still keeps in touch with her. I wish to God he'd just get over her. She's the last thing he needs at this point in time."

Finley came out to the yard carrying an armful of cables. "What?" he asked pointedly, looking quickly from Luke to me. "You gonna help me in there or what?"

Luke and I exchanged looks in silent complicity.

My anger, which exploded later that night, started building from there.

23

I was terrified in the dingy motel room thirty miles outside of Charlottesville—a godforsaken stretch of I-64 West, an eerie, shadowy extension beyond the reach of street lights, disturbingly deep in unsavory darkness. I'd driven posthaste in a flight of un-self-governed anger, which catapulted me in a flash from Finley's cottage straight to my car, where I'd scratched a fishtail on the damp gravel for good measure. I didn't care that it was two in the morning. I didn't care about the success of the night, the multitude of fans, the record people from New York, or the bad timing of my first serious fight with Finley.

The fight started the way most do, predicated on a backlog of feelings that had nothing to do with the matter at hand. I'd said nothing when Finley had pronounced me in "arrested development" over our family earlier that day, but I'd carried his hurtful words around in my chest, where they were compounded and exacerbated by Luke's revelation that Finley was doing coke, until they morphed into the first excuse I had to lash out at Finley.

My eyes bounced back and forth from the door to the bedside table, where a beige telephone sat beside a laminated card of dialing instructions tucked halfway beneath a copy of The New American Standard Bible. My blood pulsed so heavily it gave me second thoughts. I almost called Finley because I felt so unmoored, but then I remembered that I sat on the edge of a brown tacky bedspread in a seedy motel because my only refuge in life had turned against me.

I replayed the night over and over in my mind: a filled-to-capacity New Year's Eve crowd singing along beneath strobe lights to music so loud it rattled my bones. I'd met The Facts manager, Linda Horowitz, who stood authoritatively with her arms crossed over her ample chest in black pants, black shirt, and serious blazer during the show. She said we were lucky to see the band in a venue such as this before they lit a fire throughout the rest of the country. I stood beside her during most of the show, only able to nod a greeting over the music to her colleagues from the record label.

After the show, the four boys paced and swayed like decompressing track competitors fresh from the finish line. Towels draped from the back of their necks as they stood in the backstage anteroom. A line of fans queued in the hallway, pressing to draw near, so each one could offer a congratulatory handshake and share in the boys' afterglow. Because I couldn't get to Finley, I shouldered my way to Luke and Eric. Eric gave me a brotherly squeeze, but Luke leaned down and kissed me square on my mouth, and somehow, I returned it.

I saw Finley's smile turn down, and in what seemed like seconds, he was beside us. In one swift movement, he jerked Luke by the arm and said, "You can do that to anyone else, but you can't do that to my sister."

Luke faltered, and I was so mortified that I couldn't get out of there fast enough. Finley had taken an innocent moment and made it into something sordid. I weaved through the hall with my head down, then descended the stairs to the main room where I found a telephone.

I took a cab to Finley's cottage, arriving long before he did. He never locked the cottage door, so I walked in, almost tripping over Tramp, who whined and wagged her tail by the door. I took her outside to the icy field across the driveway. I'd never seen Finley put a leash on her when he took her out on the property, so I hadn't bothered to look for one. I walked beneath a starless sky whose clouds were so dense and low, they blocked out the moon. I could hear Tramp rustling around before me and followed her lead, twig by breaking branch, through degradations of land and shadows. At the far right of the field was a small gully, wet and worn from entrapped leaves, impacted from the erosive runoff of winter rain and snow. Tramp was rooting around in the marshy declivity before I could call her off, which explains why she was covered in mud when Finley came swinging home.

"You disappeared without telling me," he began, walking in the door. He took one look at Tramp and the muddy tracks on his floor, then set his guitar case down and snarled. "What have you been doing?"

"I took her outside," I started to defend at the tone of his voice.

"Did you bother to put a leash on her?"

"No, you never do."

"I swear, Millie, you never think anything through. Here, Tramp." He leaned down, took her by her collar, and guided her through the door.

"Yes, I do," I said, following. "Why do you have to say never when it's just this one time? And I did think it through. Somebody had to take Tramp out. You weren't even here."

"I wasn't here because I obviously had stuff to do. Sorting out Luke was one of them, no thanks to you. Just look at her. Now I'm going to have to put her under the hose."

"It's freezing outside. Why don't you take her in the shower?"

"Do you have to contradict everything I say?"

"Finley, I'm not contradicting you. It's too cold outside. Come on."

"And what in the world were you doing cozying up to Luke like that?"

"I wasn't cozying up to anybody. What's wrong with you, Finley? Is this the cocaine talking or what?"

"What the—" he began.

"Luke told me, so you don't have to hide it."

"Look, Millie, I can do whatever I want."

"Yeah, well, so can I, so shut up about Luke. It was nothing, and I can't even describe how much you embarrassed me. You would have thought I took my clothes off from the way you were acting."

"Well, that would have been next," Finley said, his eyes glaring mad.

"Yeah, well, thanks for everything, you maniac. I'm getting out of here," I said without thinking. Because I didn't mean it. I didn't mean it at all. I wanted Finley to stop me right there. I wanted him to see how mean he was being and reconsider. Maybe even apologize. But he didn't.

"Fine. Suit yourself," he said. He casually uncoiled the hose from the side of the cottage as if he had more important business, which infuriated me.

I stormed out, spent the night in the motel room, and drove back to Memphis the next morning because I wanted to get Finley back. I hoped he'd stayed up worrying about my safety, and wanted him to know that it was his fault—that if he was going to be such a jerk, then there would be consequences.

I thought I was calling his bluff as I left, that he'd cry uncle any second. But later it crossed my frantic mind that I might have trapped myself in a snare of my own making, because Finley never made a gesture toward me until after I got home.

Four months after Finley and I had our fight, I tried to explain to Mom what was happening with his band as she and I sat in the kitchen. Neither Finley nor I had mentioned our skirmish to Mom, nor had we mentioned the scene to each other. There'd been no residual animosity. Neither of us held the other at bay with a grudge. Instead, Finley made a joke that diffused all resentment.

I'd just woken up, when the phone rang in my midtown apartment at seven o'clock on a Tuesday morning, three days after I'd high-tailed it out of Charlottesville. Startled into action, I rushed to answer the phone.

"Hello?" I said, prompting what I thought couldn't be good news at this early hour.

"And another thing," Finley said, laughing.

It was enough to return us to grace.

Mom looked up as I entered the kitchen. "Well, I talked to Finley this morning, but I'm just not smart enough to understand what's happening with the band," she said, scraping low-calorie margarine on her Weight Watchers toast. She'd recently started a diet. She'd told me the day before that her weight had crept up to one hundred and twenty-three pounds and, if she didn't lose three pounds quickly, she'd have to break down and give up the cocktail hour a few nights in a row.

It was a Friday morning in April, and I'd driven over to Kensington Park after substituting for the six-to-ten morning show. I'd committed to helping her plant geraniums out back in the etched concrete planters circumvallating the swimming pool. This was the kind of shared activity I reveled in because there was something so incongruous about my mother's engagement in a domestic mien of any capacity. She'd wear canvas gloves and a wide brim hat because she said the sun would turn her Scotch-Irish skin to leather. "Millie," she'd once said, "If I turn into one of those drooling, senile old ladies in a nursing home with liver spots on my skin from the sun, just pick up a gun and shoot me."

I thought she'd picked this Friday morning to plant geraniums because of her standing Friday appointment at the beauty parlor, which would undo any damage from her hair-flattening hat, but she told me the real reason was that the colonel wasn't around to comment. She was wise to his habit of micro-managing the most mundane of affairs, and was a master of planned deflection.

"Here's what Finley told me about the band," I said, pulling out a chair across from my mother. "Their record label is going through reorganization because the president of the label they were signed to had a heart attack and died on the Concorde flying over to Europe. The entire company is going through an overhaul."

"So, let them go through an overhaul," she said with a dismissive wave of her hand. "The boys' record is finished, right?"

"Right. It was ready to go, but the thing is, they were signed to a subsidiary label of Warner Brothers. When a label goes through an overhaul, what it means is they look at the numbers and tighten everything up. Since the record wasn't even out, the label decided not to pursue it. They're not going to include it in their catalog because it'd be like taking a chance on the unknown when they already have enough acts to handle. In short, they're not going to invest in anything that isn't already in the works. Finley says The Facts fell through the cracks of reorganization."

Mom put her butter knife down on the side of her porcelain plate at an angle just so. "So now what?" she asked.

"They'll get the rights back and put the record out themselves, I guess. Finley says that's an option. What they want to do is create a fervor with the record that'll entice another label to sign the band. They have a lot of fans on the East Coast. I don't see how they could miss."

Arranging a cloth napkin on her lap, she smoothed its edges to a fluid drape. "Well, I don't understand," Mom said again. "But I'm not going to worry about it. Finley always lands on his feet. Oh, Ella, there you are."

Ella came in the kitchen carrying a coffee mug and a feather duster. A damp rag draped on her left shoulder, and the soles of her off-white rubber shoes puckered on the tiled floor in a suctioned cadence. "The colonel done left his mug up on his desk," she said, setting it down in the sink.

"Doesn't that fall into his off-limits zone?" I said. "Maybe you should have left it up there."

"Millie, don't be sarcastic, it's unbecoming," Mom said. Between Finley and me, she'd heard so many underhanded comments about the colonel that she no longer feigned reprimand.

"I'm not being sarcastic. The colonel laid down that law years ago, didn't he, Ella? He'll keep that one up till the day he dies."

"He too mean to die," Ella snapped. "Miz Posey, you can run put that dog up, so I can get in the room."

"Okay, give me a minute," Mom said.

"The colonel's not as bad as he used to be, Ella. I will say that," I said.

"He getting old," she said. "Y'all done wore him out."

Mom scoffed. "Old? He'll outlive us all. His mother's ninety-two. His family lives forever. They're hardy as cockroaches. He'll take a date to my funeral, then remarry within the year, which will give his daughter something to get mad at all over again."

"You still seeing that boy, what's-his-name?" Ella said to me.

"You mean Curtis? No, not anymore. We're just friends."

"Oh, praise Jesus," Mom said with a dramatic exhale. "I didn't raise you to consort with the likes of him."

"Mmm-hmm," Ella said, nodding. "You lay down with dogs, you get up with fleas."

"Come on, y'all. Curtis isn't that bad. Ella, you only met him once, so why do you say that?" I looked down at the table. "Besides, I never said I was going to marry him. Aiden and I are seeing other people, so what's the harm in getting to know someone else?"

"He ain't your kind." Ella pursed her lips.

"What happened?" Mom said.

"Nothing happened, it just fizzled out. No big deal."

"Does that mean you're getting back together with Aiden?" Mom asked.

"I don't know. I don't have a crystal ball. All right, probably so."

"Finley claims you don't have a normal frame of reference when it comes to men. He thinks it explains your mercurial relationship with Aiden. By the way, those are his words, not mine."

"Finley told you that? What are y'all doing talking about me behind my back?"

"Look, nobody talks *with* Finley. All I do is listen. He wants me to go to something called The Forum. Fly over to Oregon or somewhere to sit with a bunch of strangers so that he and I can learn how to talk to each other."

"What?" I said.

"You gone go, Miz Posey?" Ella asked.

"No, I have no intention of going. I'm still mad at Finley for not coming home Christmas. If he wanted to talk, he should have come then. It's all I can do not to yell at him every time we get on the phone, but that would only give him the chance to bring up my shortcomings again. If he'd let me, I'd just pretend it never happened." She looked at me over the rim of her coffee cup as she took a last sip. "You know, there's a lot to be said for pretending."

24

When I was in my early twenties, I lacked the self-awareness it takes to understand the full implication of the romance I had with Aiden McNair, even though Finley kept telling me the romance was symbolic. I wasn't introspective enough to question the drama Aiden and I played out, and I didn't consider our dynamic an indication of my unhealed wounds. I didn't think I had any wounds, which was a concept so antithetic to Finley's point of view that it became a point of contention between us.

I wasn't interested in Finley's psychodynamic perspective; all I knew was I had a difficult time staying with Aiden and a harder time being without the blue-eyed boy I'd met at sixteen. To me, Aiden was part of my family. He was one part brother and one part beautiful boy I was lucky to know. But a subplot of need ran through me, predicated on the longing for Aiden's constant verification, and no amount of love he could give me would ever be enough, because deep down, I didn't trust love's endurance. So I was cagey with the fear of Aiden's abandonment, and in my immaturity I'd try to push him away before he could do it to me.

But Aiden didn't push me away. He asked me to marry him when we were both twenty-three. And while Finley remained in Charlottesville holding his band together, I walked into a marriage completely unprepared.

Mom forgot all about her threat of killing me if I married into Aiden's crazy family. She hadn't a care in the world beyond staging my January wedding, the planning of which sent her into spinning exhilaration and landed her on center stage. She couldn't wait to set the Memphis phone lines ablaze with the news that her daughter was getting married. She aimed a spotlight on what she considered my crowning achievement at such an angle that it eclipsed me completely and highlighted her. That I was getting married meant she could hold her head high because she'd raised someone normal, and she was thrilled with the opportunity to showcase this fact by orchestrating an extravagant wedding.

I knew Mom meant business when she solicited Julian Enzo's involvement. She'd summoned me to the card room for the cocktail hour on a Wednesday in early July, and I entered to see Julian with a charcoal pencil in hand, his keen eye above a sketch pad teetering on his crossed knee. He stood when I entered and stooped elegantly to kiss my left cheek, dressed in his pressed blue Oxford-cloth shirt and three-pointed handkerchief, monogrammed in contrasting navy. His sweet sylvan cologne mingled with the bouquet of flowers he'd brought me—fuchsia and hydrangea, with reeds of limber narcissus, tied with a translucent bow.

"I can't tell you how thrilled I am for you," Julian drawled in an inflection that took me straight to a plantation's verandah, where jasmine hung from trellises behind white wicker furniture, and any minute now bourbon in a crystal decanter would arrive on a silver tray, topped with a sprig of mint.

"Pardon my appearance," Julian sputtered in his paradoxical Delta accent, which scratched like shards of glass tearing through silk. "Your mother and I have been up in the attic—"

"Where it's hotter than the hinges of hell," Mom interjected.

"Yes, but there's an entire history up there. I've never seen such an array. You could decorate another house with the furniture. We could scarcely make our way around."

"That's nothing, Julian. I'll have you know half of Gaga's furniture is gone. She gave it all to Rosa Mae. I drove Rosa Mae home not long before Gaga died and recognized every stick of furniture in her living room. Gaga set her up to the point that Rosa Mae lives better than we do."

Julian nodded, a look of comprehension on his classic face. "Well, that's how things were in your mother's day, Posey, but times have certainly changed, especially among the younger generation. It's a completely different dynamic now. I'll tell you a little story," he said. "My ex-wife said I simply had to get rid of our Beulah, who's twenty-five and had grown so comfortable with us that she won't get dressed anymore. But I said, 'Mary-Liza, I can't get rid of Beulah, she keeps my brushes so beautifully.' I did go out and get her a white uniform, which she won't wear. But the other night we had a party. I told Beulah I'd get the drinks if she'd tend to the hors d'oeuvres and so on, you know. Later I heard a commotion in the powder room, all this banging and clattering and jangling around. I had no idea what it was, until Beulah appeared in the living room wearing a black uniform and gold bedroom slippers, with all this jewelry on—turquoise and strands and strands of fake pearls and I don't know what-all," Julian said, fluttering his hands down his chest. "She marched right into the center of the party carrying a tray and said, 'Hors d'oeuvres is served,' and not a one of us raised an eyebrow. We're all so afraid of offending, we don't know how to ask for anything anymore."

"Listen, Julian, I no longer ask," Mom said.

"But Posey, it's different for you. You're so polished that working for you raises status, of course. You're so divine, nobody can do enough for you. I'm sure it's Ella's joy to make her Charlotte Russe for your parties. She likes to do for you."

"Well, it helps that Ella's pushing seventy," Mom said. "She told me she's happy to let the young ones take whichever stance they choose. She says she's just happy for the work."

Julian turned his eyes to the dress. "Anyway, Millie, we did locate your mother's wedding dress. There may be a stain near its hem, but we can probably fix that, if you'll try it on for us."

"That's a champagne stain. After I married your father, Gaga wadded the dress up and threw it in a box in the attic. It's been there ever since," Mom explained.

"Well, that lace is something you can't find anymore. Millie's smaller than you, Posey. I'm sure the hem can be somehow tacked under. Posey, you wore a crinoline under the dress, right?" Julian walked to the settee before the fireplace and lifted Mom's wedding dress from the coffin-sized cardboard box. The dress unfurled with a swish as Julian held it up.

"Yes, that was what people wore in my day. It made everyone's waist look smaller." A look crossed Mom's face, one that said she'd slipped into a memory only she held. "When I got engaged, Gaga put me on a train to Chicago to buy that dress," she said as she rattled the ice in her drink with her practiced hand.

"Well, Millie, run try it on for me. I'll want to see where it hits you. I'll get ideas from there," Julian said.

I slid the dress on in the powder room under the entrance hall stairs, well aware I wouldn't fill it out as well as my mother must have done in her day. I returned to the card room with its seed buttons undone in back, holding the skirt high from my waist, and still it swept the floor. Julian scrutinized me through his round-rimmed glasses as I stood with my back to the four-foot portrait he'd done of me. It held pride of place in the card room and was mounted over the sofa, between the two doors out to the gazebo.

"The neck will have to be lowered, we need to remove that net and expose those divine collar bones. It'll need to be taken in here and then again here," he said, gathering handfuls of material on both sides of my waist.

"Julian, just tell us what to do," Mom said just as the colonel clipped into the room.

Julian's manners were so refined that in lieu of genuine interest, he straightened and fixed a smile on his face. "Colonel, what do you think of Millie's pending nuptials?" he prompted.

"Well, I hope it takes. I swear, Aiden McNair's the dumbest white boy I ever heard of." The colonel walked to the bar to fix himself a drink. "When the good Lord was handing out brains, that boy was standing behind the door. He had to drive halfway to New York City with his bags packed, before he turned around and proposed. Never heard of such a slow study in my life."

The colonel's was the same concern as Finley's.

"Wait a minute, hold the phone," Finley had said when I'd called him in Charlottesville. "I thought Aiden was going to NYU to study photography."

"He was. He changed his mind," I said.

"Millie, this is a warning sign. The guy doesn't know what he's doing. Don't get all swept up in the romantic gesture of him canceling his life's plan to stay in Memphis and marry you. Nobody who isn't confused does this. This shows a complete lack of commitment."

In spite of his reservations, Finley came home to Memphis on Christmas Eve and stayed on for the early January wedding. I wanted him to give me away during the ceremony, but Mom vetoed it by saying not only would it look bad, it would offend the colonel. But Finley and Eddie were my escorts at the rehearsal dinner, which was a black-tie affair held in a Victorian mansion that had been converted into Memphis' finest restaurant, Justine's, so named for its flamboyant proprietress, who honored her patrons each night by making a sweeping grand appearance, down the carpeted entrance hall stairs, decked in jewels and a full-length gown.

As it is customary for the bride's family to host the rehearsal dinner, Mom's guest list included ninety-six people: her friends from Minnesota, everyone in the colonel's family, Julian Enzo, Aiden's extended family, our combined friends from high school, and Uncle Wick in his Highland attire. We stayed five hours, which began with cocktails in Justine's wine cellar, then moved upstairs to a cluster of twelve decorous tables, all set for dinner and a series of speeches.

Later that night, in the brisk January air, my age group went down to the bluffs of the Mississippi, to the grassy area of Tom Lee Park. Hoolighan took the hard top off his Jeep and tipped the seats back to use as a dance floor. He pulled the stereo speakers through the windows and blasted songs by UB-40, then reached out with his hand to lift Cissy into his dancing embrace, while Eddie passed around multiple bottles of Veuve Clicquot, which he'd pilfered from Justine's cellar.

We were fifteen assembled beneath connect-the-dot stars, secure in the camaraderie of each other on the night before my wedding. Together, we'd carved out a distinct milieu in Memphis that straddled the line between the staid expectations of what we'd been born into and the seductive possibilities of the changing times. We were a group in the throes of actualizing ourselves beyond the scope of our inherited privilege. We knew our niche in the world because of those who stood beside us, and as I looked at Aiden, in the midst of our friends, with his brotherly arm draped around Finley's shoulders, I thought I'd never been happier or felt more secure in all my life.

Aiden and I settled into an East Memphis duplex on Walnut Grove Road, not far from the shady oak-lined grounds of Galloway Golf Course. I switched radio stations in a move I considered upwardly mobile, while Aiden took photography courses at Memphis State University. And we got a dog. And we named him Bouncer. And were it not for our mutual immaturity as we went through the motions of marriage, Aiden and I might have been better equipped for what lay ahead.

25

What is the fire of inspiration that resides within, if not something to follow along a path? What happens when a person thinks they've discovered their purpose in life, only to see it come to a disillusioning end? How does a dream die? Does the death of a dream one has nurtured with heart and soul mean a person's been on the wrong path all along? If we can't choose our life's purpose, then what mysterious force bestows us with our path to destiny? If we can't see and hear the mysterious force, then how are we to decipher its guiding clues? What are we to do with our good intentions once their application comes to naught? Are we to concede a lack of understanding, dust ourselves off, and embark upon another path, hoping to get it right the next time?

I never considered these questions, until the course of Finley's life brought them to the fore.

It was a long bleeding out, on the way to The Facts disbandment. I heard about the twists and turns whenever I talked to Finley on the phone. It seemed Finley and Luke fielded one bad break after another during the year after their split with Warner Brothers Records. When Linda Horowitz excused herself from the fold, the boys released the record themselves, with Finley acting as manager. They continued to play the Southeast college circuit, while singles from their record were played in local radio rotation.

But the band had an enormous debt after the label released them. They'd been paid an advance, which they had to repay, without the promotional support they'd anticipated. And, they had borrowed money from a handful of sources, and the stress of repayment caused constant inner-band strife. Eric's father wanted him to prepare for a "real job," so it was with great shame that Eric left the band to enter law school. Then their drummer quit when he fell in love and moved to Atlanta, and although Finley and Luke continued to reach out to other labels, without a full band in place, they were running out of hope.

I might have been spared seeing Finley's disillusionment had it not been for the peculiar dynamic of what it means to grow up in Memphis. Because our group of friends stood by each other like extended family, we appeared in person to celebrate the highlights of each other's lives. And so it was when Hoolighan graduated from UVA the June after Aiden and I were married, we took Bouncer to stay with Aiden's parents and drove to Charlottesville, where we stayed at the Boar's Head Inn, not far from UVA's campus.

A lively crew gathered around Hoolighan. Most of the friends he'd acquired while attending the university were scions of the landed gentry of Albemarle County. They were a different breed of cat altogether from my friends in Memphis. They exuded an air of privilege of the agrarian variety. One of Hoolighan's friends was a red-headed direct descendant of Thomas Jefferson. Others had ties to one founding father or another.

They were proud Virginians with assured financial security. They'd inherit estates at the end of rambling driveways, on acres of land settled by their forebears. At the center of this group was a man-child everyone called T-Bone. He drove a flaming red Saab with "Yo-Taxi" on the license plate, and careened through town with its canvas top down. Six-foot-three, blue-eyed, and blessed with a full head of wavy hair, T-Bone was an instigator. His devil-may-care sense of humor caught me off guard the first time we met when he'd picked me up in a bear hug the moment he learned I was Finley's sister. "Oh no, not another Crossan," T-Bone exclaimed, "I thought lightning didn't strike twice. For Pete's sake, let's go get a drink."

We were six piled into T-Bone's Saab on the day before Hoolighan's graduation. Aiden rode on the hood, his back against the windshield and his feet grounded beneath his bent knees. Had we been in Memphis, the police would have pulled us over in an instant, but T-Bone owned Charlottesville, and, had we been stopped, was the kind of guy who could talk his way out of anything. He parked his car by angling it with the right tires tipped up on the sidewalk. Spilling out, we single-filed into a dark, windowless bar. T-Bone scratched a bar stool back and sat with a thud. It was then that I looked up to discover Finley.

"Hey, bartender," T-Bone called out, "I bring you good tidings and the safe delivery of your sister. This calls for a round on the house, although two would more adequately express your gratitude."

Finley stood behind the bar and shot me an arresting look. "I thought you were coming tomorrow," he said.

I shrugged. "We were going to, but we drove straight through."

"You want to come over to my place after the ceremony tomorrow?"

"Yeah, after the reception I can do that. What are you doing here? You didn't tell me you were working anywhere," I said.

"I'll tell you about everything tomorrow," Finley said, and I knew he was silencing me, that he didn't want to go into it in front of my friends.

I was anxious to hear about what seemed like a reversal of Finley's fortune, and worry flitted across my mind about whether I should bring Aiden. But I needn't have worried; the events of that night took away the option.

The whole thing was all Hoolighan's fault. He took offense over what I saw as a minor infraction when he just as easily could have walked away. As we left a local bar at the end of the night, two collegiately dressed black boys walked behind us. One made a comment about the hair of Hoolighan's girlfriend— some snide remark about whether her carpet matched her drapes. In a flash, Hoolighan turned in midstride and got into fighting stance—chin up, knees bent, dukes ready. The crying shame of it all was that Aiden's stance mirrored Hoolighan's. I'd only seen boys fight once, the night Finley and Eddie fought that guitar player outside The Well. But this fight was different in its comical, testosterone-fueled lack of necessity.

The boys circled in a wary dance, throwing and landing strategic punches, while Hoolighan's girlfriend, Trisha, and I stood helplessly on the sidelines. Trisha was a no-nonsense kind of girl, with an auburn shoulder-length haircut dramatically streaked with blonde highlights, and a devastating smile that went on forever. She pointed a finger at the chaos and said, "You'd never see women involved in something like this."

"Hoolighan's defending your honor," I said. "I think it's a matter of principle."

"Yeah, well, I could end this all now by telling them my carpet *doesn't* match my drapes. What do I care?" she said, and I thought she was kidding, yet she walked into the middle of the fight with her hands on her hips and glared at Hoolighan. "Hoolighan, that's enough out of you. Shame on everyone here. When are y'all gonna grow up? T-Bone, stop standing over there laughing. Get the boys in the car."

I didn't have to worry the next day about whether to bring Aiden to Finley's cottage. Both of us missed Hoolighan's graduation ceremony because Aiden wasn't in any shape to go anywhere. His purple right eye was swollen shut, his lower lip was split, and he was in agonizing pain. Since my attempts at ministering aid only irritated him, I cleared out of the way and left him in the shades-drawn hotel room with an icepack and a scowl on his pitiful face.

I navigated the country roads to Finley's cottage, through wooded winding stretches, thick and verdant beneath canopies of pine, red cedar, and poplar that dappled the road in diamonds of sunlight. Thick brambles of black raspberry tangled with kudzu on the side of the road, and every so often I'd catch the beginning of a beckoning path and feel my heart long to walk down it.

A subdued Finley stood in the doorway as I pulled in the driveway. "Now before you ask, I have to tell you about Tramp," he said the moment I got out of the car.

"What?" I stood still, waiting.

"I had to put her to sleep five days ago. I wanted to tell you in person."

I felt like someone had just punched me in the stomach. "What happened?" I managed to whisper.

Finley sighed. I saw him look over my shoulder into the field across his driveway, to that certain spot where he used to take Tramp. I turned to look afield, too, willing Tramp to be where she was not, as the weight of loss descended.

"I don't know, Millie. It's probably my fault, I never had her spayed. She developed mammary cysts. When I took her in to have a cyst removed, the vet found a tumor on her spleen. She had internal bleeding. That's bad news for an eleven-year-old dog. In essence, it was inoperable. I had to make the decision right there to put her to sleep. I didn't want her to suffer."

"I can't believe there was no way to operate," I said.

"Millie, you don't want to put a dog that age through major surgery. If it didn't kill her, she'd never be the same. The thing was, without surgery, her bleeding may have stopped, but it could have started again at any time. She could have been anywhere and just keeled over. When you're talking cancer in a dog's spleen, there's a good chance they've got it in other places as well. I had to do it."

I walked in and sat on Finley's bed. "God, why does bad news always come out of nowhere?"

"I don't know. You're probably not going to want to hear what else is going on either," Finley said. "There've been a few changes in my life."

"No, wait. I didn't mean it that way. I want to hear what's going on with you," I said.

Finley took a few paces outside, then turned to look at me. "Come on, let's go out to the garden."

A wrought-iron bench sat deep in soft grass, enclosed by a green-painted fence at the side of the cottage. Wildflowers spread beneath a birdbath made of tumbled stone at the garden's edge. I could just picture Finley tending to it with ceremonious administrations, driven by a nostalgia strong enough to keep him forever rooted in the woods of Minnesota where Dad stood with his blue eyes cast skyward, waiting for Finley to name the next bird.

Finley lowered himself to the grass as I took the bench. "The first thing to tell you is that the band is over. Luke doesn't want to pursue it anymore. That's it."

"Forever?"

"Yeah, Millie, forever."

I knew I should just listen, let Finley tell me everything in his own way without my interruption. He sounded exhausted. He said he was going to start over again, get some sort of plan for the rest of his life. In the meantime, he was tending bar to generate income. The crestfallen tenor of his voice worried me, but I deflected the discomfort due to my inability to assign Finley any emotion I found uncharacteristic of him. I'd been so long looking up to my brother that I thought surely he'd find a new course.

As I listened, his concerns surfaced. He said it terrified him to think he had gambled and lost. It rang too many of the sad, dark overtones of our father's unfulfilled life, and I knew just what he meant when he said, "When someone in your family comes to a tragic end, you'll always be saddled with a shameful connection. There's no shaking the thought that a similar fate lies somewhere in your defenseless genes. It's like you have to fight the probability for the rest of your life that something like that will happen to you."

And it was apparent to me that the restless scholar in Finley continued to examine our family dynamic. He was convinced it was the source of a pain in his soul that remained unhealed. A menacing, obstructing wound that, if left unattended, would relegate any future pursuit to a position just short of working. He said he'd been feeling as if something was lurking beneath the layers of his damaged personal narrative, and he'd taken to meditating, trying to find its source. He told me he'd gone out to this same garden and prayed to God, and without looking for my reaction, said His answer had come symbolically, in the form of a praying mantis.

"A what?" I interrupted.

"A praying mantis."

"Are you sure, Finley? I wouldn't know a praying mantis if I saw one. How do you know it was a praying mantis?"

"Millie, I know," Finley said, looking straight into my eyes. "It was a sign."

I had a hard time being married. I felt like I was wearing blinders on a fool's errand, and didn't have a clue what was expected of me. It was one thing to grow up with Aiden, and quite another to step into a partnership with any semblance of maturity. With the dynamic of my parents' marriage now faded to a general impression of smoke and mirrors, the only marital guidelines I had were surreptitiously culled from watching my mother's marriage to the colonel and drawing my own conclusions, especially since my mother was not in the habit of pontificating on anything of a personal nature. She issued no morals, axioms, caveats, or aphorisms, and never mentioned the obvious—that her marriage to my father was comprised of unpredictable fits and starts.

And because she never held forth, I had no way of discerning the disposition my mother had by nature, no way of knowing what was authentic and what was an act. Because she was so adept at saying and doing the right thing under any circumstance, I'd been wondering ever since Gaga died whether there was a price she paid for her composure. If she suffered injuries from slights to her self-esteem when she went against her feelings in favor of doing the right thing. But I gathered from watching her that marriage necessitated mastery of the art of manipulation, and that a sunny disposition was required in order to keep the peace. I would have asked her for clarification, but the realization that we were fundamentally two different kinds of women kept me mute. My mother was the kind to lead by wordless example, and I needed two stabilizing hands on my shoulders and eye-to-eye contact without ambiguity.

So I extemporized in the first year of my marriage, and Aiden and I cohabitated like passing ships in the night that docked every once in a while in an effort at playing house. I rose each weekday morning at five thirty to rush to the radio station, and when I returned, Aiden would be at school until well after six that evening. On the weekends, our house was a group crash pad, since Aiden and I were the first of our friends to get married. Our East Memphis home was the setting for every barbecue and televised football game, and quickly became the designated after-hours destination when all of us were still in full swing.

In the first whisper of November's comforting stasis, as the sky settled to molten gray over the tenth month of my marriage, the phone rang in the middle of a Saturday afternoon. I picked it up to the low, saturnine tones of Adelaide's Delta drawl.

"Millie? Oh, good, y'all are there. Listen, I just had lunch at The Half-Shell and I'm on my way home. I didn't eat my entire sandwich, so I'm coming over to give the rest of it to Aiden. Is the dog loose outside?"

"Bouncer's in his pen," I said, looking at Aiden. I covered the phone with my hand and mouthed, "Your mother's coming over."

Adelaide clipped into the kitchen in her Ferragamos and wool blazer. She opened the refrigerator door to insert the Saran-wrapped sandwich, then hovered with her bony hand on the handle to assess the interior with her cold wolf eyes. "I see y'all don't have any mayonnaise. I'll have Trudy bring some on Tuesday." She closed the door and walked over to the burgundy-and-navy area rug I'd put on the floor before the dining room. Bending over, she picked it up and rolled its edge against her middle. "Somebody's going to trip on this rug and hurt themselves," she said, leaning the cylinder in the corner.

"Aiden, are y'all going to paint in here? It should be ecru instead of this white. I'll send paint samples over to help you decide. Millie, if you want the wicker étagères from my house, you can have them. We never go down in the basement anymore, so you might as well. I think they'd be divine in the living room between the two windows."

I looked at Aiden too dumbfounded to ask if he cared about the étagères. Then I pushed down my mounting resentment and smiled sweetly. "Thank you, Adelaide," I said, watching her step into the living room.

"And draperies on the windows to cover these blinds," she continued, pulling out a cigarette from the silver case in her hand. She tapped the cigarette's filter on the case three times and turned to face me. "How are your thank-you notes coming along? Are you finished? Do you need help?" She put the cigarette to her lips and lit it with a monogrammed lighter.

"No, thank you. I'm almost done. I've been writing them on the weekends."

Adelaide scrutinized me with disbelieving eyes. "Well, people say you've got a year, but I've never been a believer in that. You need to rush them off as soon as you possibly can, so people know you're grateful. My sister keeps asking me if y'all like the English soup tureen she sent. She hasn't received her note."

She took a quick draw from her cigarette, then shot the smoke straight up in the air. "The sooner you write her, the better. Don't make me hang my head in shame. And the matching plates and bowls people sent, you really should write everyone all at once. People wait for their thank-you notes, you know." Another draw. Another line of silvery-gray smoke. "Go on and write them. You want to let people know that you know how you do." She turned to her son. "Aiden, it's not appropriate for you to write anyone, but please push Millie along, she's perilously close to a year."

Adelaide swept her glance through the living room, then walked to the sofa, where a rectangular mirror hung centered above at eye level. With her left hand holding her cigarette, she drew her right hand to her face and placed a delicate finger to her upper lip. "And Millie," she said, leaning toward the mirror, "y'all both need to get some sense and quit smoking. See these fine lines on my upper lip? They're from years of smoking. Nothing I do can help. I slather Nivea oil on my face every night, but these will never go away."

"Mom, I can't quit now. I'm hooked," Aiden said. "Anyway, it's yours and Dad's fault. They say if parents smoke, their kid is going to."

Adelaide pivoted. "Aiden, goats have kids, parents have children, and I don't appreciate your smart remark. I'm your mother. Watch how you address me. Now then, I've got to run. I'll see y'all at dinner Sunday night. Six thirty, and be on time."

When Adelaide left, I asked Aiden what I'd wanted to ask many times. "Are we expected to have dinner with your parents every Sunday night?"

"Yes," he said. "Why?"

"I mean *every* Sunday night? We've been doing this for ten months. Is this supposed to go on for the rest of our lives?"

"Not for the rest of our lives. They'll probably die first. Why do you ask?"

"My mother's not expecting us to do anything of the kind."

"That's because your mother is never on the case. She never was. All through high school, she never even knew where you were. She's always been that kind of mother. Summer would come and she'd just set you free and say, 'See you later.'"

But my mother's tactics were better than being smothered, which was the way I saw Adelaide's hovering behavior. Her supervisory presence was so large in our marriage, I felt I'd married into her jurisdiction instead of marrying her son. But I was full of hope that one day Aiden and I would fulfill the promise of marital bliss ... that one day I'd turn around to see we'd created a place where I truly belonged. Stability, dominion, a place in the world where something permanent secured me and negated the tempest of my wavering past.

Here in the Memphis of my mother's world, I'd slip into the covenant of communion and stake a claim that pierced the very heart of this genteel, provincial society. I'd be a card-carrying member of the confederacy with blue-eyed children that looked like Aiden and were just as smart as Finley. There'd be no escaping this foregone conclusion, for I thought life had a vindicating way of balancing the scales. That if I held on tight enough, hard enough, long enough, what was rightfully due me would come floating from the largesse of sheer force of will.

26

When Finley found God, it was with both fists. God came sailing to him on the wings of a praying mantis, the personal light-filled manifestation of His presence come in salient response to the question of his life's purpose as he sat in his Charlottesville garden. The simplicity of God's revelation dawned so clearly, it altered the range and focus of Finley's personal quandary into the bigger concern of spiritual intelligence, which suggested, if he applied himself to decoding His mystery, more would be revealed. Through the scrim of his spontaneous enlightenment, events had profound meaning and chance became personally appointed serendipity, specifically designed to elevate his consciousness.

In one fell swoop of shattering insight, Finley discarded the exoskeleton of his self-identification, and stood weightless and vulnerable in the absence of his defense mechanisms, which, Finley said, were comprised of vanity, pride, doubt, and fear. Suddenly stripped of the neat grid of logic by which he defined himself and all of life's phenomena, he was knocked to his knees in startling humility, and could think of no other recourse than to stay in the abyss and then painstakingly climb his way out.

Eddie Dean fired the warning flare the moment I walked into my home after work on a Tuesday afternoon. In the early greening of May, I'd raised the sturdy catch to Bouncer's enclosure before the kitchen door and found the area unexpectedly vacant. I opened the kitchen door and set my purse down on the sink's counter and felt rather than saw an unnamed presence. Looking to the hall, I saw Eddie lounging at the dining room table. He lazily smoked a cigarette while Bouncer sat submissively at his knee. "How'd you get in the house?" I asked, blindsided. "Was Aiden here?"

"Y'all need a better lock on your door. It's useless having a dog 'round back if anyone can walk through the front door." It was typical of Eddie to issue a declarative statement instead of just answering my question.

I pulled out a chair at the table and sat across from him. "I didn't see your car. Where is it?"

"It's at Galloway. I've taken up golf. The thing about playing at a public course is people are willing to play for a little chump change. Anyway, I heard you sign off the air when I was in the clubhouse. I figured you'd go straight home, so I walked over." He leaned his forearms against the table. "We need to talk about Finley." He slid his pack of Marlboroughs across the table. "You want one?"

"No, thanks," I said automatically. "Wait. Okay, let me have one. We're trying to quit."

"Hey, look, you don't have to explain it to me. If I weren't smoking, I'd be doing something illegal. Ya gotta have a vice. Unless, of course, you're Finley, which is what I want to talk to you about."

"What about Finley?" I started thinking the last time a friend of Finley's wanted to talk about him, it turned out he was doing cocaine. I lit my cigarette, dismissed the vision of Adelaide's lip lines, and waited.

"What's with all this ego, separation, illusion, Holy Spirit nonsense? Have you talked to him lately? He's off his rocker. He got his hands on *A Course in Miracles*. You ever tried reading that book? I'm telling you, Finley's the only one on the planet who understands what the book says. I know this because I actually went out and bought the book after I talked to him."

"I've never heard of it," I said.

"Ever heard of Marianne Williamson?" Eddie prodded.

"Yes. I've heard of her."

"She wrote that book that's all about interpreting *A Course in Miracles*. Her book is hard enough to read, but in order to read the other book, you have to be standing on your head. It's the most backward psychobabble you've ever seen. The author thinks the words came straight from Jesus. And to Finley, it makes perfect sense. Let's just say its premise is the exact opposite of what the world as we know it operates by."

"So what? So he's reading a book? What's the big deal?"

Eddie sighed and cocked his head. His sideways glance told me I wasn't getting the point, and he lowered his voice as if inviting me to lean in closer. "Millie, come on. You know Finley. He's not capable of getting involved in anything causally. He's not the kinda guy who goes through a little phase, then gets over it. Wait for it, man, here we go. He already sounds like a different guy. He's talking about God and Jesus and whatever else, like I want to hear about it. He knows I'm a nonbeliever. It's like he's trying to convert me or something." Eddie narrowed his eyes. "Is he doing this to you?"

"No, but I haven't talked to him lately." I took a last drag of my cigarette, then put it out on the Herend tray Eddie had lifted from the living room and placed on the table. "Maybe I should give him a call."

"Yeah, maybe you should. He's being weird. Try to figure out what's going on with him, then call me." Eddie ran his hand through his hair in a gesture of subject change. His dancing eyes scanned the living room and his crooked smile lifted in amusement. "Look at you. Y'all are living like grown-ups. What'd y'all do, have Posey come over and decorate? Nobody your age lives like this." He pointed to Adelaide's pair of étagères that now stood between the living room windows, on whose fawn-colored rattan shelves pairs of single candlesticks were arranged beside fragile plates on stands, and decorative ceramic bowls centered just so. "You gotta be kidding."

"They're all wedding presents, Eddie. I've got to put them somewhere."

"Absolutely useless. Y'all swells are too much. Kids are set up for life just like their parents, aren't they? One good turn by Bouncer 'round this house and y'all will be living on broken glass."

Later that afternoon, I called Mom. I had no intention of repeating anything Eddie told me, but I figured if I went on a fishing expedition of sorts, she might volunteer something about Finley. She answered the phone on its first ring.

"Mom, are you busy?" I tested.

"Millie, I can't talk right now. I just heard Julian Enzo's going to prison."

"For what?" I asked, completely derailed.

"Tax evasion. The dear thing. There have been better handlers of worldly affairs, but such is the mentality of an artist. I cannot for the life of me picture him incarcerated, but it's a done deal. He leaves in three months. You know, the IRS contacted me last November, but I never mentioned it to Julian. It wouldn't have made any difference if I had, and why be the bearer of bad news?" She sighed heavily. "I guess I should throw him a party before they lock him up."

The night my mother threw a going away party for Julian Enzo, seventy-six guests came to Kensington Park in the seven o'clock hour. Mid-September's cool breeze swirled russet and eerie through the double cathedral doors to the entrance hall, which remained ajar and monitored by Rosa Mae and Tito, so they could ferry the coats of Mom's friends up the front stairs to the sitting room's sofa.

Julian Enzo remained flanked by Mom and the colonel for the majority of the evening, which was Mom's way of publicly displaying her nonjudgment toward Julian's enforced withdrawal from society, a predicament in which she elected to assume leadership by example, in her pursuit of directing the fickle sway of general opinion. But my mother's friends were less animated that night. There was something decanted and funereal to the proceedings, and it seemed to me they chose to tamp down the tone of their attire. There was not a woman in the house in loud-colored frivolity. Not a ruffle, a boa, or a stripe to be had. And although there was little mention of the reason behind the assembly, Aiden and I overheard one of Mom's friends whisper to another in a moment of indiscretion.

"Well, of course Posey's worried about Julian. Just look at her sitting over there in the card room, when we all know she's never had any use for people who sit at parties. The colonel will be driving Julian to Montgomery the day after tomorrow. I can't imagine how Posey talked the colonel into that one, except to say that she insisted on taking him, and the colonel doesn't let Posey cross the street without him. And Maxwell Penitentiary is on an air force base, which is something the colonel knows his way around. He made a few calls and told Posey that Maxwell's thrilled Julian's coming. They're going to put him to work in art restorations, which is what they say is a type of public relations, but that's ridiculous."

Aiden and I widened our eyes conspiratorially at each other as the woman continued on. "They'll have Julian restoring artwork all right, but you know they'll have him painting portraits of government officials, you mark my words. They live large on Maxwell's base down there in Alabama. They have fabulous horse stables and houses in Normandy architecture that the air force people live in. I'm not saying Julian's going off to dance the Charleston at a country club, but if you're going to spend time in prison, let it be Maxwell. I predict two years from now, when Julian gets out, Posey will throw another party like it was all one big skip-to-my-lou-my-darling, and nobody will think otherwise."

Later, having left a bored and impatient Aiden by the front door, I threaded my way to the card room to tell Mom we were leaving the party. Julian got to his feet when he saw me coming. He took my hand in his and looked at me with skittish eyes. There was something delicate and fragile about his willow stature and gentle nature. Something innocent and hesitant, like a shy child uncertain of its standing.

"We're going to leave," I said, looking from Mom to Julian. Somehow, I couldn't bring myself to smile.

"Oh, for God's sake, Millie," Mom quipped. "Don't look so dour. He's not going to the gallows. Let's not turn this into a long, dramatic farewell. Just give Julian a kiss and go tend to your husband." Mom rested a gentle hand on Julian's arm. "Give me a minute, Julian. I'm going to tell Aiden goodbye." Mom sashayed out of the card room with purpose and deliberation, while I remained with Julian, hoping a string of perfectly appointed words would descend upon me.

"We'll miss you, Julian. I know Mom really will," I said.

"Well, your mother is my staunchest supporter, as I am hers. I can't tell you how grateful I am for her friendship. For her to orchestrate this sendoff is exemplary." His eyes roamed around the room. "I'm just so grateful to be here. I've always thought this house is the perfect backdrop for your mother. She's just so theatrical and superior."

"She adores you, Julian," I said, weighing the value of his words. There was something illuminating about hearing my mother's contemporary so effortlessly expound upon her character. It came up smartly against the vantage point of my experience with her parental role, or of that which I thought it should be. The irony was it wasn't my impression that my mother even aspired to a parental role. She was much better suited in the spotlight of a starring one.

"I know you'll take care of your mother while I'm away, not that she needs looking after, but it does seem to me she's perplexed over your brother's—what shall I call it—religious interests?"

"Oh, Finley's all right," I said. "He and Mom don't always speak the same language, that's all."

Which was the biggest understatement I could have possibly made.

Where Finley went wrong was in trying to explain himself to Mom. Oh, he explained himself to me many times over the phone, and he had my attention because he was such a compelling talker, but he should have held back with Mom. He should have kept his religious fever contained within the aggregation of those he called his "disciples" in Charlottesville, who began gathering en masse to listen to him interpret *A Course in Miracles*.

At least Finley's influence started there, before it evolved into a type of group counseling based on the book, which led them all to believe my brother was a holy prelate who served as the mouthpiece of God. To hear Finley tell it, he was chosen, and responsible for this particular sect that clung to his teachings through the miasma of life's complexities. If it was a given they were lost, then Finley was their way-shower, the one with the keys to the kingdom, though I can't say much more because I hadn't met any of them. But Luke Piedmont did, and he didn't like the scene one bit, though he took his sweet time in telling me. Finley's messianic influence over this group had been going on for an entire year before Luke decided to pick up the phone.

"It's a cult around Finley. I'm telling you, Millie," Luke said. "They treat Finley like he's Jesus Christ. I'm not kidding. It scares the bejesus out of me. He doesn't do anything else. Doesn't work, doesn't play music. Nothing. And these people financially support him. I'm not exaggerating ... it's one weird scene. All of Charlottesville is talking about what's going on around Finley."

But because I was geographically removed, I was never confronted with the opportunity to witness anything for myself. Besides, I had my own fish to fry after Aiden caught me off guard when he said he wanted a divorce, just eight days after I suffered a miscarriage.

27

If one knew with certainty that life's defining moments came wrapped in a bow in the arms of good fortune, one would fundamentally trust the life process and go skipping out to greet each day in the blind faith that no matter what, all things work together for good. There would be no struggle with baser characteristics within the multidimensional crucible of the human psyche. There'd be a lightness of being, with freedom from insecurity and liberation from fear. But the powers that be do not explain themselves as they hammer and shape our lives on the anvil of fate, if indeed it is fate rather than the cause and effect to which we are subject.

Whether we are victims or culprits, there's no way of telling. If the creation of our lives comes from within or without, there is no way of measuring our power or powerlessness to influence our destiny and no way of knowing if the dynamic of our lives is as axiomatic as we reap what we sow. What baffles me most are the people who think they know the formula to life's equilibrium. There's a part of me now that can't go beyond being shell-shocked and gun-shy, even though Finley once said the whole meaning of life is to learn how to master ambiguity.

It's life's choices that scare me the most, those crucial crossroads that direct or redirect the course of a life. And what unsettles me to no end is the recognition that the choices that shape our lives are not always of our making.

Sometimes we're on the bitter end of somebody else's.

I considered my mother's habits. I knew if I arrived before ten in the morning on a weekday, she'd be on the phone in her bedroom, probably still in her nightgown and robe. I knew if I timed it right, the colonel would be gone, and I could knock on her door unencumbered.

But it was on a Sunday, in the high heat of July, that Aiden unceremoniously ended our marriage. I didn't believe him at first, but the reality sank in when Van Houghton dropped by and I heard Aiden elaborating through our bedroom window. I watched the aqua-blue draperies billow in puffs as they gasped for air in the electrical charge foretelling a summer storm. I lay on our marital bed in a fetal position, my arms wrapped around my recently dilated and aspirated womb, trying to comfort my broken heart. I couldn't tell where the void began and ended, but it felt like somewhere in my defeated soul.

When I had rushed with the news of my pregnancy, Aiden said he wasn't ready for kids. It took my impressionable womb four soul-crushed days to register the information and spontaneously cramp and dispel, as if conducting itself accordingly, knowing the baby was unwanted. The emergency room visit had left me so traumatized I couldn't bring myself to tell anyone. As I lay on the bed eight days later, the room swallowed me whole, until I became one with a weightless, vacuous inertia so black and complete, I heard Aiden's voice from the driveway as it seeped in from another dimension. In the purple, surreal twilight, lightning bolted the air, punctuating and underscoring in flashes words that sounded queer together ... *can't handle ... too much responsibility ... wasn't ready.*

I thought time would never move forward from the moment; its vise-grip was intractable and there could be no tomorrow now that I'd been stripped of all promise. But the sun rose the following morning, and I awoke to a house so silent and inhospitable, it blinded me with its glare. In my altered state, I got dressed and located my car keys in rote movements that propelled me perfunctorily straight to the safety of my mother, even as I rehearsed my limits. I would tell her that Aiden wanted a divorce, but I would never tell her about my pregnancy.

I knew all too well how tragedy defines a life.

Up the back stairs, having thrown a deceivingly cheery greeting to Ella who stood on a chair adjusting the kitchen's ceiling fan, I knocked on Mom's door. As expected, she was draped in two layers of flowing monogrammed peach. Her matching night ensemble swayed at her ankles as she took barefoot steps to her vanity table after letting me into her sun-spilled room.

"I've got to get dressed and get a move on," she said as she faced the mirror. "God knows what I'm going to wear. In this heat, I should just go naked."

"Where you going?" I asked as my heart sank. I was hoping to unburden myself with my heartbreak, and for this I needed time.

"I'm going to run into Gift and Art before the Junior League luncheon. I have to figure out what to send to Cornelia's daughter for a wedding present. I've never been one to send from the bride's registry, so I'm going to just pick something else out and have it sent over there." Picking up the glass bottle of the custom-blended foundation that matched her skin tone, Mom cast her eyes at me from her mirror. "Didn't you work this morning?"

"No, I'm on tomorrow," I said. "I don't work on Mondays anymore. They put me on Saturdays instead."

"Well, while I'm at Gift and Art, I can see about your registry. Have y'all switched everything out so you have your complete set of everyday china?"

"Yeah, we have it," I said, noticing an opportunistic segue when I heard one. "But it turns out we're not going to need it. Aiden wants a divorce."

Time came to a screeching halt in the room as my mother quit shaking her makeup bottle. She set it down on her vanity table and froze for a beat, then rose slowly from her vanity table and crossed the room with all the theatricality of an actress crossing from stage right to stage left. Her nylon robe swished behind her deliberate steps as she walked to the mirror over the mahogany chest of drawers on the opposite wall, where she turned with arms crossed to face me. Up to this moment, I had never heard my mother lower herself to swearing, but swear she did.

"He's so stupid," she said in the center of a long list of other words. But then, she righted herself, returning to who she was at the core of her being. "Now, then. I want you to go pack your bags and come home right now."

"You're out of harmony," Finley said to me eight months later from over the phone and for what seemed like the hundredth time. I sat on the love seat in the upstairs sitting room in Kensington Park, the phone cradled against my bowed head, resting on my bent knees. Presently I straightened up to accommodate my flaring temper because Finley was making me feel worse than I already did.

"I'm out of harmony? Why do you keep implying this is my fault? You're worse than Adelaide. After all this time, she called me yesterday and told me I needed to change."

"You do need to change. God wants you to change," Finley said. "Stop railing against everything like you're a victim. You need to just be still."

"I am a victim, Finley. I didn't create this. This is my life we're talking about. I can't just be still and do nothing, I have to get a plan. I can't live here with Mom and the colonel forever. I've already been here months. Believe me, I've heard what you've been saying about God and everything for about two years, but I don't agree with you. I have to make a decision about where to go from here and make a move on it."

"No, you don't," Finley said. "I keep telling you to resist the temptation to self-direct. God wants you to renew your humility, sit still, and turn everything over to Him. You're confused."

"Finley, I'm not confused in the least. I'm powerless," I countered.

"No, you're not. That's your ego at work. Your true power lies in simplicity and acceptance. Quit trying to make things happen through the adornment of intellect, title, rights, or other forms of self-assertion. You're dependent on God, so just let go." I heard Finley take a breath and exhale with a sigh, as if searching for patience. "Look, Millie, if you turn the matter over to God, you'll activate the higher power to correct everything according to God's plan, but not if you don't truly let go. Do you think you can do this? This seeming obstacle of being catapulted by fate into a drastic new set of circumstances is only your perception. Your ego is at work, suggesting you have control, but it's an illusion. It's the ego's attempt at maintaining control. You have to relinquish all the ways in which your ego defends itself, and allow things to happen without interference or manipulation. You have to place your faith in He who is the light. In your darkest hour, when all seems lost, He'll send a miracle."

"It's been my darkest hour for close to a year, Finley. I am now without a husband, a house, and a dog. I'm interfering and manipulating? Are you kidding? I don't have a choice. And what about free will? You ever think of that? I'm not a puppet who's going to sit around waiting on God to tell me what to do from here. My life is up in the air because Aiden changed the rules of the game." I shook my head against the enormity of everything I knew. "Get this. Two days ago, he called me over to my ex-house and said he was suicidal and couldn't live without me, like this was just another high school breakup."

"Predictable," Finley said. He paused as if thinking. "Everyone's ego is at work here. For Mom, it's no doubt about pride. What'd you say to Aiden when he begged back?"

"I told him I'm twenty-six now, and if I come back, the next time he'll do this I'll be thirty-six with two children. Finley, he would have done it again. The writing's on the wall."

"Aiden's confusion has been in play. Don't judge him according to his confusion. He's in the dark, but you don't have the right to play God by deciding the future. Just sit still."

"Finley, cut it out. What's wrong with you? Haven't you ever had to make a decision at a crossroads in life? I don't know about you, but God's never once told me what to do. I've just been floating along my whole life at the whim of other people." After I'd said the words, their gravity hit. I hadn't known I'd felt this way until I heard myself say them, but their truth rang so loudly it hurt, even as they brought a peculiar alleviation, as if I'd laid down a heavy burden.

"Exactly," Finley said. "Other people are unqualified to bring you sanity, but God is not. Everything else is an illusion. Your mind is insane. You just think you've been at the mercy of others, but this is completely false. The answer is in the atonement. Atonement brings re-evaluation of everything that's false, and aligns you with the Holy Spirit. You need to remain detached and reticent. You need to acquire an aerial view. There's a bigger picture beyond your illusions. Your illusions are insane, Millie. Seek for atonement first. Try to meet your circumstances without judgment, with the equanimity of an unstructured mind. None of this is real. This world is an illusion and is the opposite of heaven. Everything in this world is the opposite of what is true. Atonement will release you from your falsehoods. Don't try to hedge against what might or might not happen. Turn your life over and wait."

"For God's sake, Finley. It's already happened. I'll be officially divorced in three months. Don't you get it? It's too late to turn this over to God. I have to make a move, I have to basically start my life over. I already can't take it. There's nothing like being in Hucy's and in walks Aiden with his cousins, and not a one of them will acknowledge my presence. They no longer even talk to me. Nobody knows what to say. I'm not just divorcing Aiden, I'm divorcing life as I've known it since I was sixteen." I reached for the bottom line and presented it. "I'm beginning to think I don't have a prayer if I stay in Memphis. Even the friends in Charlottesville that Aiden and I had together have sided with him. Everyone knows me as Aiden's girl, or at the least, the one he threw away. It'll probably always be like this, I don't know, but I've got to figure something out." My free hand formed a fist. "Why don't you get this?"

"Millie, you're not listening to me. You ask for my counsel and you're rejecting it."

"You're confusing me with everyone around you in Charlottesville. I'm not looking for your counsel. I don't want you to be my guru. I want you to be my brother. Come on, Finley, help me figure this out."

Dead air vibrated over the telephone. I was getting ready to ask Finley if he was still there when his voice returned, sounding labored. "If you're not going to follow my counsel, then I don't have time to keep beating my head against the wall with you. God only wants me to fraternize with those who are willing to follow my counsel. I'm overwhelmed enough as it is."

I forgot to count the numbers. I forgot that things happen in threes. And I didn't, for a minute, take my brother seriously when he said he didn't have time for me. But I did think he might have a point in saying I was living under an illusion. But if this was so, it was fine by me.

After Aiden and I divorced, I kept thinking about Dad telling Finley and me that we had to find our own way to God. I didn't have the intellectual acumen necessary to fully comprehend Finley's version of Him, and the more I considered the subject, the more I realized I'd been influenced by my father's interpretation of God, which was simply a sense of His mystery and an understanding that He was perpetually balancing the scales in the interest of life's inherent goodness.

My understanding was almost pagan compared to Finley's. God, to me, seemed best interpreted as a sense of karmic justice played out in many forms as I toed the line between right and wrong. All I was aiming for was resiliency and perseverance in the face of adversity. A positive attitude and my own apartment down by the river, along with a steady schedule at the radio station kept my days on an even keel, and I had plenty of friends who rallied around me as I recalibrated my life without Aiden. For a time, Aiden's absence felt like losing a brother, but that was only because I had yet to learn the difference.

I often marveled at my mother's attachment to decorum. It blessed her with the convenience of adhering to a safe pattern of predictable sameness throughout any given year, as if the execution of compulsory protocol within a twelve-month cycle would anchor her to normalcy and take the glare off the intrinsic variables, now altered and misaligned. She was the queen of acting as if. The employer of denial. And no matter the circumstantial inappropriateness of her gestures, she had a way of lifting her hand to the holiday's rituals and making everything appear status quo. It was the third Christmas season wherein Finley had not come home. There'd been no anxious waiting for him to light up the room as he came swinging into the festively decorated card room in his gray three-quarter coat, and for me the entire season felt flat and anticlimactic.

I still hadn't spoken to him, although I'd written and called repeatedly to no avail. I had little choice but to succumb to joining Mom and the colonel's family for Christmas Day without Finley, and I planned to appear at the party for Julian Enzo three nights later.

"Oh good, you're home," Mom said when I answered my phone. "I need a big favor. Could you run over to Julian's daughter's apartment, pick up his wool suit, and bring it over here? Julian's in a hotel right now, and his clothes are scattered across Memphis. You know, he no longer has his house. He sold it before he went to prison. We have to outfit him in something for Saturday night. Since he doesn't have a car, the colonel will pick him up Saturday afternoon. He'll get dressed over here."

"Sure, I can do that. But I should call before I go over. Do you have his daughter's phone number?"

"Yes, let me see where I put it. I had it right here before I talked to Finley."

"When did you talk to Finley?" I asked as a sense of betrayal fell over me. I knew it wasn't Mom's fault that Finley wasn't talking to me, but irrational feelings made me feel excluded, and I was jealous.

"Listen, it's not like I talk to him anymore. He's too busy preaching. It's always the Holy Spirit this and Jesus that. He's now claiming he hears Jesus. He told me that he himself is Christlike. Did you know that?"

"No, Mom. I told you I haven't talked to Finley. Does he ever mention me?"

"No, except for that one time he told me Jesus doesn't want him talking to you," she said.

I was too hurt at hearing that Finley wouldn't talk to me for it to register that Finley was hearing voices. I blocked the red-flagged warning and planted myself in my defense mechanism of myopic, self-oriented injustice. "Oh, for heaven's sake, Mom. Can't you say something to him?" I implored.

"No, I can't and I wouldn't if I could. I never could tell either of you what to do. Anyway, I'm too dumb to follow along with what Finley's saying—oh wait, here's her number. Do you have a pen?"

28

I used the side door of the house out of habit, even though the lights shining through the front door's glass panes heralded an inviting translucency that highlighted two pine wreaths decorated in Christmas bows. The double doors were slightly parted, and through their glass I saw wall-to-wall guests milling around in jewel tones, with drinks in hand, as a chorus of voices ebbed and flowed in a laughing echo out into the front yard. I'd had to park at the entrance to Kensington Park and thread my way along the sidewalk to avoid the parked cars on either side of the street where valet attendants in white shirts and black vests ran swiftly on the pavement.

Bitter cold had cloaked Memphis in the eight o'clock hour, and I'd left my coat in the car, not wanting the burden of fishing for it later amidst the mound of furs and heavy velvet jumbled haphazardly in the upstairs sitting room.

Ella took one look at me when I entered the kitchen and shook her head. "Ain't you got the sense to wrap up in this cold? What's wrong with you? Sit down here till your face gets back. Don't you go in there to Miz Posey's with your face all froze up."

"Okay, fine, I will," I said, pulling out a chair at the table. I heard movement behind me and turned to see Eddie Dean gliding into the kitchen from the butler's pantry.

"Hey, Eddie," I said completely surprised. "What are you doing here?"

"Your mom didn't tell you? I offered to be one of the bartenders. She's got me stationed in the parlor. Ella, I need lemons and limes," he said, opening up the refrigerator. "Millie, y'all have a nice Christmas?"

"Yeah, pretty much the standard scene. You know, the colonel's family and all that. How about you? Did you go to your mother's?"

Eddie reached into his black blazer and produced a pack of Marlboroughs. "Yeah, I did. Gonna slide out back for a minute. You want one?"

"Well"—I hesitated—"I'm trying to quit ..."

"Run fetch my coat in the cupboard if y'all gonna step out back," Ella said in a tone that told me she wasn't buying a second of my refusal.

I followed Eddie through the back porch and slid into Ella's wool coat, pushing the sleeves up past my wrists and accepting the cigarette Eddie extended. He lit mine first, then stepped back to light his own with a deep inhale. "I came here Christmas night and had a drink with Posey after you'd gone home." He exhaled with his head tilted skyward, then looked at me.

"You did? She didn't tell me you were coming."

"She wanted me earlier, but I couldn't make it until after nine. She was cool with it though. You know how your mom is."

"I guess so. I wish I would have known."

"I should have called you, but when she called me, it sounded like she wanted to see me alone. She knew I was in Charlottesville last week."

"You were? Doing what?" I asked.

"Hanging with Finley. I'm not going to be mobile after the first of the year, so I went on up." He took another drag and looked at me sideways. "I'm gainfully employed. Yes, ma'am, got me a respectable position."

"You're kidding. You?" I smiled and flicked my ashes.

"Shut up, Millie," he said, the corner of his mouth rising up in amusement. "What'd you think? I'm gonna be a lowlife forever?"

"Yeah, kind of."

"Thanks for that. I've got a real estate license. I'll be selling houses," he said.

"Cool," I said. "I can see that. You'll take your professional con-man abilities and put them to good use."

"At least I'm in touch with my talents." He grinned. "But seriously, I'm looking forward. Your mom got me the job through one of her friends. She's been nothing but good to me for as long as I can remember."

"She's always gotten a kick out of you. But then again, you're the world's best flatterer. She loves that kind of thing," I said.

"Funny you'd say that. Finley pretty much said the same thing. He said I flatter her ego."

I almost laughed, then realized Eddie wasn't trying to be being funny. "Everything's about the ego with Finley," I said. "He drives me crazy. He's beat it into my head so much, he's got me thinking there are subpersonalities inside of me I have no control over. He gets into his explanation of the superior man versus the inferior man like there's a crowd living inside me. It's more than I can comprehend. But that's all right. He's not talking to me anyway."

"All that stuff comes from the I Ching, Millie. My mom's into that. She uses it like an oracle pretty much every day. I think Finley does too. He thinks it's the voice of God. You ought to hear him explain how it works. Between that and *A Course in Miracles*, you'd think none of us is qualified to be on earth. You know, like humanity's got it all wrong. But Finley's convinced he's got the truth, and he's up there in Charlottesville straightening everyone out. You seen those people up there around him?"

"No. I haven't been there in years. Last time I was there was right after the band broke up."

"Yeah, well." Eddie threw his cigarette to the ground and twisted it out with his boot. "It's a weird scene, I'll tell you that. I mean, like, man, where's it all gonna go? Those people up there don't even know Finley. None of them knew him when he was in the band or any of that. They just think he's Jesus, or talks to Jesus or whatever." Eddie paused. "Look, I better go back inside. I don't want to keep ragging on Finley. He's my brother. All y'all are family."

He opened the screen door of the porch and stepped in then stopped, as if reconsidering. "Did you know Finley's writing a book? He read some of it to me. Sounds like a manual on how to think. Totally over my head. But he's passionate, I'll give him that. If you're gonna be fanatic and overzealous about something, let it be that. He's either completely screwed up, or he's completely right. Who's to say?"

Public opinion can be swayed if you throw it a party and hand it a drink. I followed Eddie into the parlor from the butler's pantry, and stood at the bar as he poured wine from a crystal decanter and handed me a glass. I could feel the aura of gaiety in the party's collective consciousness. It was a group assembled at the behest of my mother, who had the kind of clout in Memphis society to waltz Julian Enzo around the room, and it was enough said. She still had the Christmas tree up. It rose nine feet high before the fireplace, and its dainty white lights sparkled beneath silver and gold tinsel and peach taffeta bows.

I looked to my right and saw a flush-faced woman I didn't know hanging on the arm of Julian Enzo, who wore the suit I'd brought over the day before. The tailored suit hung loose, no longer fitting him the way it should have. But on Julian it had an elegant drape. He seemed to be listening intently to the woman as she gestured demonstratively with her hands, and there was a look on his angular face of marked humility, but to me, Julian had always been rather subtle and circumspect. He must have felt my eyes upon him. He took the glass in the woman's hand and made his way to the bar just as Mom appeared from the card room.

"There you are, Millie." Julian bowed and kissed my left cheek, then stepped back and scanned me with his brown eyes. They were liquid and soft, innocent and searching, and I thought he must have seen a thing or two in prison that deepened him somehow, something more than he wanted to know about humanity, which now made him skittish, as if he'd seen too much of this world.

"Millie. Oh good. You're here." Mom came sweeping to my side. She wore a maroon-and-silver-patterned cocktail dress evident of her personality—light, frivolous, dancing, showy. "When did you arrive?"

"About fifteen minutes ago. I was running a little late."

Mom turned to Julian. "Julian, I told you about Millie and Aiden." Her tone was factual in its indiscretion and made me feel ashamed with its resonance.

I felt my face flush in my personal failure. It wasn't so much my awareness of everyone knowing I was divorced, as it was the perception that I'd been cast aside.

"Yes, you did make mention, Posey. Millie I'm so sorry," Julian said. He followed with a pregnant pause I thought would go on forever. "But you're young. Life will move on."

"I'd like a word or two with that fool who let Millie get away," Eddie inserted from behind the bar. "What an idiot. He stood up in front of God and everybody and made a vow. I know, I was there. What was he thinking?"

"He wasn't," Mom snapped. "Just as well she's out of the marriage. God alone knows what'll happen from here."

God. God was suddenly everywhere. I tossed and turned in my bed that night, trying to get comfortable, trying to find the sweet spot on my pillow where I could sink into oblivion, but I couldn't find a place for my shoulders. God kept ringing through my head, and I was sick of it. I flopped over on my back and stared at the ceiling. I was tired of everyone invoking God's name. I'd spent my entire life without anybody referring to God, now suddenly Finley was over-the-top, Eddie had made mention, and Mom had invoked His name. Glibly, of course, but her comment about God only knowing what'll happen to me made me feel powerless. I felt hoodwinked, uninformed, a couple of shots short of sinking the eight ball. If everybody was going to keep bringing God into everyday parlance, why wasn't I up to speed?

I couldn't relax thinking about the undercurrent of Finley's tone the last time I spoke to him. It carried a suggestion of reprimand, although I could tell he tried to hide it in his newly acquired piousness. His veiled exasperation with me made me feel stupid, and I'd tried to get the better of him by lashing back. And now he wasn't speaking to me because I didn't understand what he was saying.

Apparently, I wasn't entitled to my own opinion. Apparently, my opinion justified his abandonment. I would have called Finley that instant if I thought for one second he'd pick up the phone. I wanted to yell at him. I wanted to tell him he was being unjust. I wanted to remind him of that time in Minnesota when he shot that bird with his BB gun. We had both heard Dad say he wouldn't tell us how to arrive at an understanding of God. He said he wanted us to arrive at our own understanding when we were older.

I wanted to call Finley and remind him of Dad's directive. I wanted to tell him that, in my mind, Dad still hung the moon. I finally started to relax as I pulled a vision of the woods in Minnesota around me, sensing Dad there, leaning against that tree, while we buried that little bird. In soundness and safety, and with a stronger sense of Dad's presence than I'd felt in years, I drifted off to sleep and crept back from the realm of the netherworld hours later, as a familiar sound floated through my open window in a coo-ah-coo-coo-coo. For a moment, time folded into itself, and I came to consciousness on the wings of a mourning dove.

Then the phone shrilled.

I looked at the six o'clock hour on my clock as I picked up the receiver and managed to say hello.

"Millie?"

"What? Mom?" I said, in that way that rings with selfish irritation.

"Millie?" Mom said again.

"What?"

"Honey, there's been an accident," she said.

"Where?"

"It's Finley."

"Finley? Is he okay?" My heart leaped to that part of my soul so entwined with my brother's that it forgot all hurt and offense, even as my mind tried to reckon why Mom was calling me at this hour.

The mind, when experiencing shock, has a defense mechanism that switches to immediate catatonia. It keeps you in a stronghold until the moment you are ready to comprehend the next level of trauma. All rules and assumptions regarding the order of reasoning no longer apply in this other dimension. The mind registers trauma in step-by-step increments, lest you become overwhelmed. It is the unadulterated meaning of saving grace, a mechanism within each of us that is far too intelligent to make use of the basic instincts of fight or flight, because it is beyond it. The mind freezes in the critical moment, and waits until you are strong enough to take the next step.

"Millie," Mom whispered, her voice choking. "Finley is dead."

29

The colonel scowled as he paced the black-and-white tiled foyer in his black suit. He had the wherewithal to dress quickly, then leave Mom alone in the bedroom to pull herself together for Finley's funeral. He must have had second thoughts about the way he'd told Mom about Finley, because four days later she still gave him the cold shoulder.

She'd been in the midst of her nightly bath, after Julian Enzo's party, when the telephone rang during the midnight hour. In Mom's indisposition, the colonel had picked up the phone in their bedroom and listened as a ranking officer of the Charlottesville police department delivered the news. He put the phone in its cradle by Mom's nightstand and walked toward the master bathroom, then turned the crystal doorknob and entered, standing for a moment on the white tile floor, looking down at her as she reclined in the tub.

"Posey," he blurted. "I don't know how to tell you except to just say it. Finley's dead."

I must have heard Mom's rendition of this moment a dozen times, as if the way the colonel told her about Finley somehow deflected the charge of the news. But I knew there were places my mother wouldn't let herself go. Things she couldn't admit to herself, and the thought of her own culpability in ignoring any warning signs was too painful for her to carry. Somewhere, in the following days, my phone rang, and I picked it up to realize how deeply my mother's denial ran.

"Millie?" Mom said in her quivering, heartbroken voice. "Is Finley making some point? Is he coming back?"

"I don't know, Mom," I said. And I didn't. That Finley had been found with a gunshot wound to his head in what was described as a suicide was antithetical to everything I knew about my brother. I had no idea how to answer. I had no way of knowing what Finley's life had become in Charlottesville during the last year of his life. For all I knew, his claims about being Christlike were true and he'd rise on the third day. I was clouded by my personal feelings of betrayal, and my unreasoning mind couldn't believe Finley hadn't told me what he'd planned to do. Regardless of the coroner's report, up until the day of Finley's funeral, I thought there had to be some egregious mistake.

They missed Finley's standing-room-only service at Independent Presbyterian Church. It seemed everyone who'd ever crossed paths with Finley came to his funeral—the boys from Memphis University School, my friends from Hutchison, and all of Memphis society, because Memphis society suits up and turns out when one of its own is put to rest, no matter the circumstances.

They missed the arrival of the boys from The Facts, Luke Piedmont's eulogy followed by Eddie's, Percy's, and Allen's. They missed the Reverend McAlister reading from the Bible, and Luke singing a song that he and Finley had cowritten when they were in the band.

But they were there on time for Finley's burial at Elmwood. They appeared graveside on that bleak January day, in a five-car caravan from Charlottesville that parked end to end on the grass. Car doors opened and slammed in disruptive staccato the very moment Reverend McAlister began reading aloud.

I stood beside Mom and saw the exact moment her knees buckled to send her collapsing like a marionette to the ground. The colonel angled beneath her arms in awkward haste to hoist her to her unstable feet, and I turned in that instant to look behind me. Fourteen strangers from Charlottesville swarmed to the grassy knoll like locusts, swelling like a wave in unified stride. In that surreal, celluloid moment, it was as if the air had left Mom's body. It took every ounce of her listless energy to lift her hand and point toward two of the women who walked toward us carrying swaddled infants. The look on Mom's face told me she intuited way more than I did. She reached an arm out and pulled me into her shoulder, and I suddenly knew she needed more than my physical support. Of the two hundred people at Finley's burial site, many caught the gist of what was happening. I felt the women in the crowd sway telepathically toward Mom like a protective flock of birds. But not until the funeral procession descended on Kensington Park did I realize what had happened.

Ella had gone to the attic and found a black canvas panel, which she draped over the grandfather clock in the entrance hall. The clock loomed in eerie sentry, and I lifted the panel from its side and peered beneath to see the clock's brass hands stopped at twelve thirty-five. I walked up the back stairs because the upstairs was tacitly off-limits. There were people all over the downstairs, some spilling outside in the biting winter air.

There was no sunshine on the day of Finley's funeral.

The sky was a blanket of immobile gray that seemed too close to the ground, and somebody had turned on Kensington Park's street lights. They cast diffused coronas on the median's grass in circles that glowed hauntingly upon lingering icy dew. I stood at the window in the upstairs sitting room, looking out onto Kensington Park. People streamed in incessant droves toward the house. Everyone seemed to flow in; nobody seemed to flow out.

I wasn't surprised to see Aiden walking up the driveway between his mother and Julian Enzo. Death strips and humbles to a meaningless perspective, and in the face of tragedy, all bets are off. I fought the impulse to jump out of my skin, and was thinking if Finley were here, we'd escape all this. Sneak out the back porch and jump the wall to East Parkway in our own procession of healing, because neither of us were the kind to take to Mom's gestures of formality. Finley and I had our own private universe, where nothing else mattered and everything rhymed. I turned and looked across the hall to Finley's room. It was dark and disturbingly silent, even as voices drifted up from downstairs. But they were not part of my private moment, and they couldn't touch me.

The voices wafted from people who couldn't hear what I heard or feel what I felt. Finley pushed in my blood, and there was no way in the world he would ever get out. I narrowed my eyes in the dark trying to find him, certain he'd have the sense to morph into a presence and haunt this house, like the ghost who knocked William Porter off the wall.

Finley told me these things happen, and I always listened to what he said. And I believed—oh, I believed—because he told me, and Finley never lied. I crossed the hall to his bedroom. I took off my heels and sat on the floor with my legs crossed Indian-style, looking up at his bed, waiting. Notes from his guitar descended like mist upon my vacant heart in thick, resonant, echoing warmth. I couldn't stop my hand from reaching out to touch him. I was sure he was there, he would never leave me.

Not in this house. Not in this way.

I would have sat on that floor for the rest of my life if Eddie Dean hadn't come to find me. He stood in Finley's doorway for a second, then bent down to put a hand on my shoulder, saying, "Millie, come on now. This is no good."

From the front stairs landing, I saw Mom in the entrance hall motioning for me to hurry down. "I don't know why y'all always do this," she said when I reached her. "Neither of you can be counted on to do anything but disappear." I started to state the obvious, but she leaned in and whispered in my ear, "Caroline just walked through the front door."

I met Caroline's eyes as she came toward me with her arms extended. After we embraced, I stepped back and took a good look. She was beautiful, radiant, coiffed, and slender. Her chestnut hair was cut short and parted on the side. She wore a black suit with the skirt cut just above the knee and looked statuesque and elegant in her black leather heels.

Within the next few moments she told me that she was living in Minneapolis, where she worked as a nurse. She'd married a doctor and had recently had a baby. Luke Piedmont had called her to tell her about Finley, she said, and she'd dropped everything immediately to fly down to Memphis.

As we stood in the entrance hall, Luke came rushing to greet her. He seemed relieved to have found a Charlottesville intimate among the throngs in this Memphis crowd, and as I stood between them, it dawned on me how many different lives Finley had led.

The different phases of Finley's life were represented that day by varying groups that stood separated throughout the downstairs. There were those who had known Finley since childhood, who knew his history, his family, his foundation in the world, and all that it meant to come from this particular walk of Memphis, where everybody knew more about a person than they should. In the parlor, Mom's friends gathered amongst themselves, none of them smiling, while my friends, who had always looked up to Finley, congregated in the card room.

And then there was the group from Charlottesville. Nobody I knew acknowledged any of them, including Luke. I could see them in the dining room by the buffet, huddled together. They seemed nice enough from a distance, but Finley had never mentioned any of them to Mom or me. One look at the way they were dressed, and anyone would have known they were not from Memphis. They lacked the refinement of subtle attire, and not one of them displayed the quiet dignity typically appropriated for such an occasion. In undyed fibers of cotton and hemp, they wore socks with their sandals, long skirts, and striped scarves, and kept their coats on in their seeming disinterest of fraternizing outside of their circle.

Eddie Dean cut a bull-in-a-china-shop beeline straight to their center, and because I sensed danger, I excused myself from Caroline and Luke to follow just as Lucy Northrup came out of the card room. She reached her hand out and stopped me just short of entering the dining room. "Wait," she said in an abrupt warning tone. "These are the people who have been around Finley. We don't know anything about them. Stay back and let Eddie take care of it."

"I will," I said. "But you can see he's mad. Just look at his face. He's going to get confrontational."

"He's trying to protect y'all," Lucy said.

"Were y'all raised by wolves?" Eddie seethed. He stood in front of one of the women who cradled a baby in her arms, and he reared back when she said, "This is Finley's son."

"You show up at his mother's house on the day she buries her son? Posey doesn't know who y'all are, you know that, right? She asked me if I knew, since I met some of y'all in Charlottesville, but I don't know the full story." He looked at the tiny bundle. "Finley's son, yeah? And his Mom doesn't know anything about it?"

"Finley has two sons," she said.

I followed Eddie's gaze as he turned and zeroed in on the other baby cradled in the arms of a young woman with hazel eyes. Watching Eddie, it seemed he decided in that moment to change his tactics. He ran a hand through his long hair and stepped into the alcove at the end of the dining room, where he lowered himself onto the settee and gestured for the woman to sit beside him.

I looked at Lucy and said, "I'm going over there. I can't hear anything from here." Lucy walked behind me, and we positioned ourselves on either side of the alcove.

"All right," Eddie said to the woman. "Tell me the deal. What do y'all know about Finley? So he picked up a gun and shot himself. You got any idea why?"

"Finley was on a fast-track to spiritual enlightenment," she said easily. "He no longer fit into this world. I think he was ready to see what was on the other side."

"Why do you think that?' Eddie said, cutting his eyes toward me, then back to her. "Did he tell you?"

"Not the day he did it, but another time. He hinted at it."

"You mean to tell me Finley talked about killing himself, and you didn't do anything about it?"

"I never questioned Finley. He was our teacher. I lived with him as his wife and supported his path."

"His wife? What about the other woman over there holding his kid? Is she his wife too?"

"Neither of us is really Finley's wife. But Finley and I lived together."

"And this was okay with ..." He flipped a hand toward her. "What's her name?"

"Susan," she said.

"This was okay with Susan? Did she live with y'all too?"

"No. But Jesus told Finley to sleep with both of us. At first Finley said there was no way we'd get pregnant, but Jesus had other plans."

"Well, He sure did," Eddie said as he turned fully toward me. He didn't say anything else, he just gave me a bottomless, hollow-eyed look and stood slowly, as if he'd suddenly grown too weary to speak.

"I done heard it all," Ella said a moment later when Eddie and I walked into the kitchen. Rosa Mae and Murl were there, wearing their black uniforms and seated on matching three-legged stools in the corner. "Y'all don't go to Miz Posey with this today, hear?" Ella directed. "Leave Miz Posey be. It more than enough she done buried her son today. Good Lord knows how she gone get beyond this."

But I wondered the same about myself, and there was no way to articulate this to my mother in her prostrate grief. I felt selfish for even considering it. When a child dies before a parent, the world focuses on the parent's loss. I knew this and understood it. I also knew there was no way to explain to my mother, who had been an only child, what it feels like to lose a sibling. To me, it felt like losing a twin, a better part of myself, the ally of and witness to my very existence. And I had no idea how I'd live with the void. I knew I'd be forever tainted.

People are uncomfortable with suicide. It casts a certain pall on a family, as if there is something aberrant in the bloodline. And public opinion is never creative when it comes to death by one's own hand. People jump to desperate conclusions: the poor soul was depressed, despondent in self-loathing, overwhelmed, and hopeless. When, of course, none of this applied to Finley. The truth is, I don't know what does, but then again, he always was a mystery to me.

As for the fallout, time has eked its way onward, and I'm not any closer today to understanding what happened to Finley any more than I was the day my mother called with the fatal news. But it's something I've tried repeatedly to wrestle to the ground so that I can put it in a manageable place. Perhaps incorporate it into the story of my life, as if the act of doing so will leave me with a philosophical understanding instead of this hole in my heart.

The problem is, there's a part of me that will be ten years old and dependent on Finley forever. When the going gets too much in my life, I still struggle with the realization he's gone. He left me alone with a God I don't understand. A God who spoke to him yet doesn't speak loudly to me, although I keep listening.

And sometimes, when I least expect it, I'll think I see Finley in a crowd. There'll be somebody who moves like him, stands like him, has a similar color of russet hair or blue beaming eyes, and for that one fleeting moment, I'll be safe in this world, until reality comes slamming back. And though I try not to, I can call upon the loss of Finley at any given moment and it'll come springing forth anew. For every time I summon Finley, it feels as if my identity is being excavated. It's an excruciating unearthing that affects me physically, and because it's only human nature to run from pain, it remains festering in the resources of my soul.

There are those in Charlottesville who, to this day, believe that Finley was an enlightened leader who wanted to fast-track his way to the other side, and more still who thought there was a cult around Finley that would only have culminated in a bad end. I don't think I'm ever going to know, and even if I did, it wouldn't heal me. All I know is I've lost my brother, and I'm thinking one day we'll meet, wherever the other side is, and we'll examine this together. Perhaps we'll discover great meaning as we look back and realize we handled the same history in two different ways. Perhaps somehow, somewhere, for some reason, on some level, the lesson acquired will have been worth it.

"Mastering the ambiguities of life is the hardest task any of us will ever be called to do," Finley said to me one time. And it is, and Finley was right.

More often than not, Finley was right.

Epilogue

June 2018

I stood looking up the sloping hill to the top of the driveway as if I'd seen a ghost. The magnolia tree I'd shimmied up a thousand times was heavy with blossoms, but I resisted the temptation to select the perfect one and bring it inside to sweeten a room.

Up the driveway, past the jonquils my mother loved so much, I stood before the front door, ringing it for what was probably the first time in my life. Only the uninitiated rang the front doorbell, everybody knew that. If my brother could look down from heaven and see me now, he'd laugh that booming laugh of his.

Who was this stranger walking across the entrance hall to answer the door? I was suspicious of his welcoming smile and easy manner, even though he'd seemed nice enough on the phone. It's not everybody who'd say yes to a request out of nowhere asking for admittance, but I still considered him the interloper standing there in his Southerner's uniform of khaki pants and a pressed button-down shirt.

The new occupants of the house I grew up in didn't have the exquisite taste of my mother, who knew every entrance hall requires a table with a cut flower arrangement in a porcelain vase. My eyes reviewed the breadth of the black-and-white tiled foyer straight to the beveled glass cathedral doors that partitioned the back hall. If Ida Ella Morgan were here, she'd know how to do—she'd have the doors to the back hall open to let the breeze in from the side of the portico. Any fool knows that's the only way to cool the house from the sweltering heat of a Memphis summer.

I had been told the custodians of my childhood home were in the antique business, which many would consider perfectly appropriate for a house with the constitution of 79 Kensington Park. Built in 1911, it has the kind of features calling for antiquity, but theirs had been selected for effect, whereas mine had been handed down gently through a generational line.

I followed the man through the parlor like a spectator on a *Better Homes and Gardens* tour, even though it had the same massive Oriental rug on its floor that was there when I was coming of age. Walking into the adjoining room—the room my grandparents christened "the card room" back when my mother grew up here—I stood wondering why on earth anybody would carpet the gray granite floor. My mother would have had Murl roll up the Wedgwood-blue rug to expose the cool 12-by-12-inch tile in preparation for the summer. It seemed a shame these people didn't know any better.

The wrought-iron cathedral doors leading out to the gazebo were open. If my mother were here, she'd be seated elegantly across from the colonel, drinking a Scotch and soda, discussing the events of the day. She'd have one feminine leg tucked beneath her and the other crossed at the knee left to dangle as she held court in the card room. She'd be entertaining my stepfather after a hard day's work, with news of the latest gossip in a plantation accent lilting lighter than air.

Up the serpentine stairs that swept from the entrance hall, I walked into my brother's room and thought I heard the strings of a guitar. Finley always said sound has a funny way of traveling, and I stood there thinking it also seeps into the walls where it lingers forever. The countless times he sat Indian-style on the floor perfecting some tune nobody else could play made me think the ten-year-old son who lived here must hear it every once in a while. Maybe it resonated in the dark of night, haunting him in his dreams like music from another realm. Maybe it resonated further. And, when I saw them again, this is what I planned to tell Finley's sons. Every chord their father ever played in this room went out into the universe to ring forever, because music never dies, and they were born with it inside them.

I walked through the bathroom Finley and I shared, then entered my room where that old familiar feeling descended, reminding me of my place in the world. Here within these walls it was safe for an inchoate girl to ease her way into womanhood. I wondered if the twins residing in my stead had a clue. If they were here, I'd ask if the mourning dove in the oak against their window woke them with its lamenting coo-ah-coo-coo-coo, the way it had every day of my youth. Then I'd tell them their room would look so much better if it only had an upholstered chaise lounge beside the organza-draped window.

Cordially, I followed the man across the hall, even though I feared my heart would fall through the floor and never return. I walked to the center of the room, fighting back tears, wondering if this longing for my mother would grip me indefinitely. If she were here, she'd be seated before her vanity table in a Lilly Pulitzer dress and Pappagallo shoes, putting on her signature pink lipstick. My mother always dressed to the nines, and she'd turn to me just so, smiling the moment I entered the room.

Back outside the room, I put my hand on the banister, winding down the twisting back stairs where a gallery of family photos used to hover between two servants' buttons built into the wall. Active yet purposeless for three generations. I remembered the game of call and recall Finley and I had invented. My hand reached out perfunctorily, aching to press one more time for a response that would never come.

Downstairs in the butler's pantry, the glass cabinets on the way to the kitchen were filled with odds and ends instead of sets of china. If Ella were here, she'd be taking complete jurisdiction. She'd stand before the double porcelain sinks in a white uniform polishing Francis I, while a chicken casserole baked in the oven.

I wanted to search the entire house until I found her. I wanted to tell her I'd be stepping out for a spell, like I always did when I left the house because I knew exactly what she'd say. "Don't pick up any strangers." Then she'd point a warning finger and add, "Remember the devil. He wear a suit."

Walking out of the stone-floor kitchen and circling back to the entrance hall, my host started for the front door saying it was a pleasure to meet me and that I'd be welcome any time. I smiled, saying I certainly was obliged, but if it were all the same to him, I'd rather see myself out the back. That way I could hear the sound of my feet hitting the iron grate my grandfather commissioned for the landing.

And, that way, I could pretend this wouldn't be the last time I'd ever close the door of the place I'll always call home.

Made in the USA
San Bernardino, CA
30 January 2019